DECEIVING THE HIGHLANDER

Books by Emma Prince

Highland Bodyguards Series:

The Lady's Protector (Book 1)

Heart's Thief (Book 2)

A Warrior's Pledge (Book 3)

Claimed by the Bounty Hunter (Book 4)

A Highland Betrothal (Novella, Book 4.5)

The Promise of a Highlander (Book 5)

The Bastard Laird's Bride (Book 6)

Surrender to the Scot (Book 7)

Her Wild Highlander (Book 8)

His Lass to Protect (Book 9)

The Laird's Yuletide Bride (Novella, Book 9.5)

Deceiving the Highlander (Book 10)

The Sinclair Brothers Trilogy:

Highlander's Ransom (Book 1)

Highlander's Redemption (Book 2)

Highlander's Return (Bonus Novella, Book 2.5)

Highlander's Reckoning (Book 3)

Viking Lore Series:

Enthralled (Viking Lore, Book 1)

Shieldmaiden's Revenge (Viking Lore, Book 2)

The Bride Prize (Viking Lore, Book 2.5)

Desire's Hostage (Viking Lore, Book 3)

Thor's Wolf (Viking Lore, Book 3.5)

Other Books:

Wish upon a Winter Solstice (A Highland Holiday Novella)

To Kiss a Governess (A Highland Christmas Novella)

Falling for the Highlander: A Time Travel Romance
(Enchanted Falls, Book 1)

DECEIVING THE HIGHLANDER

Highland Bodyguards, Book 10

EMMA PRINCE

For Scott. Always.

Chapter One

Late March, 1323
Scottish Highlands

Will Sinclair urged his horse faster. Curse the darkness and the muddy, uneven ground. He risked laming the animal—or breaking his own neck—but he refused to slow down. Not after receiving those seven words scrawled hastily on a scrap of parchment.

Come to the camp with all haste.

His stomach had dropped to the floor of Dundale Keep's great hall, along with the missive, which fluttered to the rushes even as Will had sprinted for the stables, bellowing for Fearghus to be saddled.

With all haste.

Something terrible had happened. Otherwise he

wouldn't have been summoned to the secret camp of King Robert the Bruce's Bodyguard Corps. Will hadn't been to the camp in over a year—not since his father had died and left him in charge of Dundale. He could have returned by now, but the others understood his reasons for staying away. So whatever had warranted the urgent missive, it couldn't be good.

Will leaned over Fearghus's neck, muttering encouragement to the exhausted animal. For the hundredth time that night, he tried and failed to banish the terrible premonition looming like a black shadow.

The Bruce. If aught had befallen the King…

Will was saved from the grim thought when a glimmer of firelight pierced through the trees in the distance. The camp. He was almost there.

He dug his heels into Fearghus's flanks, drawing one final surge from him. They shot through the trees like a fired arrow, the horse's grunting breaths breaking the silence of the night-dark woods.

Without slowing, they careened past the semicircle of huts that housed the other members of the Corps who resided at the camp. Will guided the horse directly toward the bonfire blazing in the middle of the field they used for training. He could see several shadowy figures gathered around the glowing fire, their shoulders hunched and their heads held tensely.

He reined Fearghus in hard as he reached the

edge of the bonfire. The animal scrambled over the soft, wet grass. Will flung himself from the saddle even before the horse had gotten his footing.

"What has happened?" he demanded, charging into the circle of light cast by the fire. "The King. Is he—"

"I am well."

Robert the Bruce himself rose from a chair drawn up to the fire.

Will hastily looked him over. Aye, the King was in one piece, upright, and as sturdy and strong as ever.

He released a hard breath. Yet now that the worst of his fears were quelled, Will noticed that the Bruce's weathered features were set in a hard mask behind his russet and gray beard.

Scanning the others gathered around the bonfire, Will was met with similarly grim looks. Ansel Sutherland, who served as the leader of the Corps, sat to the King's right, a deep frown etched on his face. Niall Beaumore and a very pregnant Mairin Mackenzie—or rather, Mairin Mackenzie Beaumore, as of last summer—both wore tight expressions.

Will's gaze snagged on the man seated on the other side of Niall.

Kirk MacLeod.

Cold fury settled in the pit of Will's stomach. He narrowed his one good eye on the man who had taken the other. Kirk met Will's hard stare briefly before dropping his eyes to the dancing flames.

Will fought to shove down his anger—at Kirk, at the loss of his eye, and at what that loss had done to him. He could resume his wallowing later, once he returned to Dundale.

He started as he turned to the last of the somber faces—Sabine MacKay. Colin, Sabine's husband and one of the founding members of the Bodyguard Corps, passed through the training camp from time to time, but as far as Will knew, Sabine had never visited.

"Ye made good time," Ansel commented, rising and extending his hand to Will. "We didnae expect ye for several hours yet."

Will clasped forearms with him. "The missive said 'with all haste.'"

"Come. Sit." The Bruce indicated a vacant chair between Kirk and Sabine. Will froze, torn between doing his King's bidding and sitting next to the man who'd ruined his life.

Sensing the tension, Sabine slid over so that Will could sit between her and the Bruce. An uncomfortable silence, broken only by the crackle of the enormous fire, settled over the group.

The Bruce cleared his throat. "I appreciate yer speed in getting here, and apologies for causing ye undue worry. But the fact is…something *has* happened." The Bruce's mouth tightened. "Andrew Harclay is dead."

Shite. "How?"

"He was declared a traitor to England and executed," the Bruce said.

Dread crystalized like ice in the pit of Will's stomach.

Andrew Harclay, recently made Earl of Carlisle by King Edward II of England, had secretly been under the Bruce's thumb. The Bruce had leveraged information about Harclay's dubious loyalty to Edward in order to secure the man for his own purposes—blackmailed him with the threat of exposing his lack of faith in his own King, really.

But Harclay hadn't been merely a pliant weakling for the Bruce to use as he saw fit. The man recognized that Edward, who had failed time and again to quash the Scottish rebellion, would never succeed in securing the volatile Borderlands, where Harclay's holdings lay.

Edward's most recent attempt to tame the Borderlands had ended in utter disaster at the Battle of Old Byland last October. He and his army had marched all the way to Edinburgh, but thanks to the English King's mismanagement, they'd run out of food and had been compelled to retreat.

The Scots had pursued Edward all the way to York like greyhounds after a hare. They'd very nearly captured him, too. Edward had been forced to flee so quickly that he'd abandoned his personal belongings, including his royal seal. It was likely the greatest embarrassment of his reign, even more ruinous than his defeat at Bannockburn.

"I dinnae ken how, but Edward learned of Harclay and my treaty," the Bruce murmured into the taut silence.

A slow breath escaped through Will's teeth. Christ, it was as bad as it could possibly be.

After Old Byland, Edward had all but ceded the Borderlands and much of northern England to the Scots, leaving his own subjects to fend for themselves. Harclay had been determined to create peace along the border for his people's sake—even if that meant circumventing his King to do so.

Only a few months ago, Harclay had formed a treaty directly with the Bruce to protect Carlisle. Of course, Scotland and the rest of England were still locked in a bitter war, and entering into negotiations with the enemy amounted to treason.

It seemed Edward, whose efforts against the Scots had been utterly futile thus far, had decided to bring the hammer down on one of his own instead. Which meant a key peace along the border had been shattered, and the Bruce was out a vital ally.

"Harclay's spurs of knighthood were hewn off," Ansel said quietly, tossing a twig into the fire. "And they broke his sword over his head before drawing and quartering him. One of his arms was sent to Carlisle to ensure his people kenned their lord was a traitor."

"Bloody hell." Will leaned back in his chair, drawing a hand over his face. His mind raced, seeking every possible implication of this turn of events.

The Bruce had lost not only an ally, but a point of leverage over Edward. Only a year ago, Harclay had won Edward's trust and praise for aiding in the defeat of the rebellious Earl of Lancaster. Through Harclay, the Bruce had tried to steer Edward toward an end to his war on Scotland.

But now Harclay's body parts were spread across England, and Edward had no one to check his determination to drag out this war indefinitely.

The Bruce must have sensed the direction of Will's thoughts. "Edward is more unpredictable than ever. Between Old Byland and Harclay's treason, he likely feels backed into a corner. Who kens what he'll do next?"

Will frowned as he considered that possibility. Mayhap things weren't as dire as he'd initially thought. "Aye, he may lash out, but it would be an act of desperation. Old Byland proved he cannae launch and sustain an attack against us anymore. He cannae control his own country, let alone ours."

"Ah, but matters are more complicated than that."

Of course—they always were when it came to the Bruce.

Will knew it wasn't vanity to consider himself in possession of a sharp and nimble mind—he'd been raised to be a leader, to hold Dundale Keep for his family line. In the Highlands, that meant not only being able to fend off attacks, but to maneuver between feuding clans, manage trade negotiations, and occasionally plot a raid that would catch even the most seasoned warrior off-guard.

But from the few chess matches he'd shared with the Bruce, he knew he was no match for the King when it came to strategy. The Bruce thought in moves and countermoves dozens of steps ahead, and always seemed to be playing more than one game at a time.

Will lowered his brows, waiting for the King to explain further.

"There are…others involved," the Bruce said, steepling his fingers before his mouth. "Others who count on us for protection, those who may be in danger if England remains volatile."

"Or those who are the *source* of the danger," Ansel murmured, giving the Bruce a pointed look.

Will studied Ansel for a moment, absorbing his words. "Ye are speaking of spies? In Edward's court?"

"We have had eyes and ears around Edward for some time," the Bruce confirmed. "One in particular has gone silent."

"And ye fear he is either in grave danger—or has turned traitor and joined the English," Will surmised.

"*She*."

Will blinked at Sabine's correction. The Bruce's spy in Edward's court was…a *woman*?

He shouldn't be shocked. After all, Sabine oversaw the Bruce's network of spies and messengers. In fact, Sabine herself had once been a spy and missive thief.

Still, the thought of a woman thrown into the viper's den of English court made Will uneasy. The Bruce avoided involving innocent women and children in warfare whenever possible.

Mayhap this woman wasn't so innocent.

"This spy…what is her name?"

"Lady Eleanor de Monteney," Sabine replied.

Christ, the spy was a *noblewoman*? And English, from the sound of it. But of course, she'd have to blend in at court amongst the other English nobles.

"How did she come to work in secret for the Scottish cause?"

The Bruce waved a hand. "The details arenae important at the moment. What matters is that she has failed to send word in quite some time."

"She normally sends a missive once every sennight," Sabine said. "She notes in code Edward's movements, tidbits she overhears—whatever she thinks might be useful to us."

9

"And how long has it been since she last communicated?" Will asked.

Sabine's hazel eyes pinched. "Nearly two months." *way too long to not do Something*

Bloody hell.

"There is, of course, the possibility that she is… dead." The Bruce's jaw clenched for a moment before he went on. "Mayhap there was an accident or illness. Or she may have been found out. Edward clearly has little patience for traitors in his midst at the moment."

The prospect of this Englishwoman's death clearly pained the Bruce. He had made himself personally responsible for every single person—Scot or nay—who'd put his or her life in his hands. This quest for freedom had come at great cost, and the Bruce bore it more than any other.

"She also may have willingly broken her allegiance with us," Mairin offered evenly.

"That is far more likely, is it no'?" Will asked. "She is English, after all."

Sabine's dark head snapped up and she fixed him with a direct stare. Belatedly, he remembered that *she* was English, as was Niall, along with Kirk and Ansel's wives, Lillian and Isolda.

But her umbrage apparently rose from a different source. "I would trust every spy in my network with my life. Aye, there is always the risk of a spy being compromised, or turning willingly, but most would rather die first. Still…" Sabine's gaze shifted back to the flickering flames. She let a long breath go. "It is a possibility."

Kirk spoke then. "I ken something of the position the lass is in," he said cautiously. "Lying, playing a part, making difficult decisions…" His pale blue eyes flashed to Will for an instant before jerking away. "It is hell. We ought to give the lass the benefit of the doubt at least."

Will felt his innards harden with familiar anger. "And *I* ken from experience that trusting blindly can have dire consequences. That those who claim to be on yer side can actually be the most dangerous."

Kirk locked gazes with Will again, but this time he didn't back down. Will gripped the arms of his chair so that he could push to his feet in a split second.

"Enough," the King snapped, dousing the crackling tension between Will and Kirk. Will glowered at Kirk for another heartbeat before pulling his gaze back to the Bruce.

"We dinnae ken if the lass is still loyal, or even still alive," the Bruce said. "She may be in grave danger and hasnae been able to get word to us. That is why I'm here. I need someone I trust to find Eleanor de Montency and get to the bottom of this. If she still lives, she is either in some degree of jeopardy, or has turned against us. If she is in danger, she'll need protection."

"And if she has turned?" Ansel asked, tossing another stick into the flames.

Will knew the answer—they all did—but they needed to hear it from the Bruce.

The King stared into the fire for a long moment, his eyes distant. "The cause must come first," he replied quietly at last. "We have given too much to put it all at risk now."

The implication was clear—eliminate the threat. But what remained unspoken was who exactly the King had in mind for this mission.

Even before the Bruce's gaze began sliding from the fire toward him, some instinctive sense of foreboding swept through Will like a cold breeze.

"Nay," he blurted, uncaring that he'd just flatly denied his King.

The Bruce lifted a russet brow. "Och, aye."

"I cannae—"

"I want ye for this, Will," the Bruce interrupted. "Ye'll go to England, find the lass, and suss out—"

"I *cannae*." The word was forced through Will's clenched teeth. Heat that had naught to do with the blazing bonfire rose up in him. Embarrassment. Anger. *Shame.*

The Bruce pinned Will with keen, dark eyes. Though Will hardened himself to the piercing look, he knew the Bruce could see past his armor and into the heart of his resistance.

"I'd like a moment with Will. Alone." The Bruce spoke to the others, but his gaze remained steady on Will.

Sabine, Kirk, and Ansel rose instantly and hurried out of the fire's warm glow. Mairin, who was nigh bursting with child, was slower to get to her feet. Niall helped her up with a muffled grunt, which earned him a glower from her.

"Just as well," Mairin muttered. "I have to relieve my bladder anyway—*again*."

Niall shot the Bruce and Will an apologetic look before taking Mairin's arm and guiding her slowly toward their hut.

Will would have chuckled under any other circumstances. Mairin, the youngest member of the Corps and the only woman, would apparently rather face open battle than the final month of pregnancy. And Niall, God love him, would never speak against his wee, fierce wife, no matter how ornery she grew.

But given the Bruce's request—nay, *order*—Will's mirth was nowhere to be found.

"Ye'll have to assign someone else," he said once Niall and Mairin were swallowed by the surrounding shadows. "I have Dundale to look after, and—"

"We both ken this isnae about yer keep. Yer staff managed it on their own for years while ye were training here and yer father was unwell."

Despite the mild spring air and expansive night

sky overhead, Will felt as though invisible stone walls were moving in on him, penning him in.

"Send Kirk," he said flatly. "Or Ansel. Or better yet, Niall. As an Englishman, he would have no trouble—"

"After all Kirk's service to the cause, I willnae ask so much of him again," the Bruce murmured. "Besides, he and Lillian have a new babe to look after. Ansel has his family as well. And would ye truly send Niall on what could be a dangerous mission when his own bairn will arrive at any moment?"

"Nay," Will muttered, silently cursing himself. "But if this mission truly is dangerous, ye cannae send me either." His hands squeezed into tight knots. "Ye ken I am no' the warrior I was before…"

His teeth locked, refusing to let the rest of the words out. All he managed was to vaguely wave toward the patch over his right eye.

The Bruce rose slowly and set about adding more logs to the fire. The silence stretched as he poked at the fire with a stick until he seemed satisfied with the blaze.

"Ye have been hiding at Dundale," he said softly as he settled into his seat once more, his eyes on the kindling logs. "Hiding from the camp, the Corps. And hiding from yer duty to the cause. To me."

Pain slashed into Will's chest as sure as a knife. He couldn't deny it.

While Dundale was his responsibility now, he wasn't truly needed there. As the Bruce had so astutely pointed out, his seneschal and chatelaine had things well under control. They'd managed the keep after Will's father had been permanently debilitated from a horseback riding accident.

Will had been too young to handle things on his own then. His cousin, Daniel Sinclair, had helped run Dundale and train Will to be its eventual leader, yet Daniel had been called away on a mission for the Bruce when Will had been just fifteen. And when Will had come of age, he'd dedicated himself to the Bruce's cause. He'd moved to the camp to train with the other members of the Bodyguard Corps, leaving Dundale in the hands of his seneschal and chatelaine once again.

There was a time he'd felt needed here at the camp, honing his skills with the others so that they would be ready at a moment's notice if the Bruce called upon them.

But ever since he'd lost the vision in his right eye —or rather, ever since it had been *taken*—Will hadn't been the same. Without the ability to perceive depth or judge distances, he'd lost his aim with bow and arrow, and with throwing daggers.

And he was ashamed to admit that he failed to notice some things now—things that made him a liability as a warrior. Once while training with swords,

Ansel had approached from behind Will's right shoulder. Because of a strong wind in the trees overhead, Will hadn't heard him, nor had he seen him moving in his blind spot. If it had been a truly dangerous situation, Will would've been dead, as would anyone he might have been protecting.

"I dinnae belong here anymore," Will said, his voice like gravel.

"Ye are still a member of my Corps," the Bruce replied firmly.

"The Corps is for yer most _elite_ warriors, Robert. I am no' that. I dinnae ken what I am anymore." Will swallowed hard. "I am a liability to ye and the others. To the entire cause. At least at Dundale, no one will die because of my eye."

"Damn it all, Will." The Bruce scrubbed a hand over his beard, shaking his head. "Ye think all ye are to me is a sword and shield? Ye have _always_ been more than just a warrior. Aye, the Corps represents my most skilled fighting men, but it also contains my best men of any sort. Ye belong in that lot. But ye seem to have forgotten that."

The Bruce leaned forward on his elbows, his dark eyes intent. "Yer mind has always been as sharp as yer sword—which is exactly why I need ye for this mission. Aye, ye may need to fight, for I dinnae ken what dangers await ye in England. But I also need someone who is clever and cunning to determine exactly what is afoot within Edward's court."

Though Will's pride stirred to life at his King's praise, his misgivings still surged far stronger. It was futile to argue, he knew, for the Bruce had clearly already made up his mind. And when he was determined, the King was as immovable as a Highland mountain.

Still, Will grasped at what few straws remained.

"How the hell would I even pass myself off within Edward's court? I am a Highlander, for God's sake. I am exactly the kind of barbarian Edward is so hellbent on bringing to heel."

The Bruce's lips quirked behind his beard. He knew he'd won, damn it.

"Play the part of a Lowlander, then. God kens there are plenty of Lowlanders who loathe me. Quite a few have sided with Edward in the hopes of securing more lands and riches. And I doubt those peacocks at court will ken the difference as long as ye are convincing."

"And what about the lass?" Will demanded. "How am I supposed to determine the loyalties and motives of some English chit?"

Now the King's face split into a full grin. "I suppose ye'll just have to get close to her somehow. Ye're a clever lad—I'm sure ye can come up with some way or other to accomplish that."

Bloody hell.

It was bad enough that the Bruce wanted Will to go to England, find this spying noblewoman, and suss out her true allegiance. But now he was suggesting that Will…*seduce* the lass? He wasn't some chivalric knight or courtly fop to gently woo some well-bred English lady. But damn it all, he had no other option if he meant to see this mission through.

And he did. His King—and what little was left of his pride—depended upon it.

"Where ought I begin looking for her?"

The Bruce sobered. "She has been serving as one of Queen Isabella's ladies-in-waiting for some time now. Her last several missives came from Langley Palace, north of London. If she is still alive, she's likely there. Determine what ye can of her loyalties. She may be in danger, in which case, she'll need yer protection. And if she has turned…"

"I'll ken what to do."

The Bruce gave him a single nod. "Ye leave for England at first light."

Chapter Two

Eleanor lifted her voluminous riding skirts as she exited the great hall and crossed the outer courtyard. Aware of the eyes of the guards waiting before the stables, she kept her head modestly slanted down and carefully maintained her position a pace behind Queen Isabella's trailing skirts.

In her usual fashion, the Queen had a smile and a kindly spoken word for everyone.

"We shall go through the woods today, John," she said to one of the guards.

He bowed. "Very good, Highness." John turned to the others who would serve on the Queen's retinue for this outing and began giving orders.

Eleanor followed as the Queen swept through the men. Once she was past, they hurried to secure their mounts in the modest barn on the other side of the yard. Isabella went straight into the royal stables, where only the steeds of the highest quality were kept.

The stable lads snapped instantly to attention as the Queen entered.

"What sort of mood is Milly in today, Tom?" the Queen asked one of the older lads.

He yanked his cap from his head and bowed. "She is still favoring that hoof, Highness, but she's progressing nicely."

"Thank you, Tom. I'll take Scarlett out today then. And Nutmeg for Eleanor, if you please."

Eleanor's heart hitched with excitement. It was to be a lively ride, then. The Queen had selected two of the most spirited horses in the stable. Isabella would likely wish to let the horses run at full tilt across the grassy expanse between the palace and the royal woodland beyond. It was one of the few moments of true freedom Eleanor ever experienced.

The Queen turned warm, knowing blue eyes on Eleanor. "We mustn't waste this fine weather. We shall make it a long ride today."

Eleanor smiled. "Aye, Highness." It seemed they both craved a taste of freedom this morn.

With a swish of her skirts, the Queen turned and glided out of the stables. Eleanor followed her into the yard to wait for their mounts to be brought out.

The sun was buttery yellow and held the sweet, mild warmth of spring to it. Eleanor lifted her face up to it, letting the heat soak through the green velvet of her riding gown. Beside her, Isabella hummed a soft tune and smiled gently at the entire courtyard, despite the fact that it was mostly empty.

The tranquil scene was shattered as harsh voices rose not far away. The shouting was coming from the guard tower above the palace wall's main gate.

"What on earth is that?" Isabella said, frowning in the direction of the ruckus.

"I'll find out, if you wish," Eleanor replied.

Isabella nodded, but before Eleanor could take more than three steps, a guard came rushing down from the gatehouse, his face contorted in confusion.

"What's going on?" Eleanor demanded in a lowered voice.

"It's the strangest thing, milady. There is a man…"

"What is it, Harold?" the Queen asked from a few paces away.

"A man, Highness," Harold replied, raising his voice. "A Lowlander—a *Scot*."

The Queen drew back her chin. "Here?"

"Aye, and he is demanding to see *you*, Lady Eleanor."

Eleanor's breath froze in her lungs. Her stomach cinched tight and did a strange tilt to one side.

Nay. It couldn't be… Of course it wasn't David.

Yet even four years later, her mind flew straight to him at the mention of a Scot.

Eleanor fought to bring herself under control. She could not give even the slightest indication that something was amiss.

"...in heaven's name could a Scot want with Eleanor?" the Queen was saying.

"I cannot imagine," she said, willing her voice to remain neutral.

"He claims to be a...close consort of yours, milady," Harold said, his face flushing red.

What in...

Eleanor's thoughts spun, searching for purchase. Her heart filled her ears. If not David, then... Could it be her contact? Nay, James MacGregor would never risk coming to her in the open like this, endangering both her life and his own if their true roles were revealed.

She lifted her gaze to find Isabella's brow creased. "Let him in, Harold. We shall reach the bottom of this."

Reluctantly, Harold called out the order. The main gate began to creak open. Simultaneously, the heavy portcullis was ratcheted up by the guards in the gatehouse.

As the gate swung out of the way, Eleanor's gaze landed on a solitary man sitting astride a large chestnut stallion. The portcullis lifted clear, and he nudged his horse into a walk. Silence descended on the courtyard as he rode in.

He certainly looked like a Scot. The horse he rode was massive, but as he approached, she realized that the animal matched the proportions of its rider. The man was in his prime, his large frame lean yet stacked with impressive muscle.

He wore breeches and a tunic in the style of the English, but a sash of red woolen plaid lay draped over one broad shoulder. His golden-brown hair was long enough to be tethered in a queue at the base of his neck. Stubble a few shades darker than his hair covered his angular jaw.

A black patch covered his right eye. He swiveled his head slowly so that his other eye, alert and sharp, could scan the courtyard. He reminded her fleetingly of one of King Edward's hunting falcons—and she, standing frozen in the middle of the yard, a startled rabbit.

She felt the exact moment his singular eye landed on her. It was blue-green like a mountain lake, keen and intelligent. Despite the thick velvet sleeves on her gown, the fine hairs on her forearms prickled.

He reined his horse to a halt and fluidly dismounted, approaching on long, muscular legs. His gaze shifted to the Queen, who stood silently beside Eleanor.

"I cannae mistake ye for anyone other than

Queen Isabella," the man said. His lilting accent stirred a memory of the past. Yet he sounded… different than David and the other Lowlanders she'd known.

He dipped into a deep bow before the Queen. "Legend of yer beauty comes verra short indeed, now that I see the reality for myself, *ma belle Reine*."

Isabella put on a practiced smile, one she used when surrounded by flattering courtiers, yet Eleanor didn't miss the cautious assessment in her eyes.

"You are most kind, sir. And you impress me with your command of my native tongue. But while I was born in France, I am England's Queen now, and so have adopted English ways."

"Verra good, Highness," the man amended, rising out of his bow.

He turned to Eleanor then. "And could this bonny lady be Eleanor de Monteney?"

"You know my lady-in-waiting, sir?" the Queen asked evenly.

"Ken her? Aye, indeed." He dropped his dark-gold head in another bow, this time directing it at Eleanor. As he dipped before her, he snagged her hand in his much larger one and pressed a kiss to it. His lips were shockingly soft, a stark contrast to the rough scrape of his stubble.

He lifted his head, fixing her with that piercing eye. "She is my fiancée."

Chapter Three

W ill watched Lady Eleanor's face keenly for her reaction.

She was skilled, he'd give her that. The only indication of shock at his declaration was a brief flickering of her dark eyelashes. Yet despite her unreadable countenance, he found he could not stop staring at her.

She had the heart-shaped face of a cherub, but Will doubted she was an angel given her surprisingly unflappable composure even after his bold announcement. Her lustrous chestnut hair was swept back from her face and woven into an elaborate plait, the thick, glossy tail of which rested over one slim shoulder. A faint pink tinge sat on her creamy cheeks. Dark eyes watched him guardedly.

She was petite in stature, yet shapely curves filled

out her frame. She wore a tight-fitted gown of green velvet which flared at her hips, the skirts made fuller for riding. Had she been going somewhere? Judging from the lads gawping at him from the open stable doors behind Eleanor and the Queen, the two women had been preparing to go for a ride.

The prospect of doing aught other than sitting and preening in such lavish clothing struck Will as ridiculous. He glanced down at her hand, which was still enfolded in his. A linen sleeve of the finest weave poked out from the wrist of the velvet gown. It was embroidered meticulously with minute leaves and flowers.

The purpose of not only the embellished linen undergown but also the sumptuous velvet outer gown was to display wealth—extravagant fabrics, rich details, and an excessive use of cloth.

Aye, her bodice was not pearl-studded like the Queen's midnight-blue velvet riding gown, yet the decadence stirred suspicion in him. Mayhap the lass had grown too comfortable in her post here, coming to favor the easy life afforded to one of the Queen's ladies-in-waiting rather than the far less glamorous work of a spy for the Scottish rebellion.

"You must be mistaken, sir," the Queen said, interrupting Will's musings. He dragged his attention from Lady Eleanor to find the Queen frowning. "My Eleanor is not engaged. I would know if she was."

Her Eleanor? Aye, mayhap the lass had lost her way, believing the English Queen was a true companion rather than one of her enemies.

"I assure ye, she is." Will gestured vaguely. "All the arrangements have already been made."

If Eleanor and the Queen had grown close, he risked saying something that was demonstrably false, since he knew next to naught about the lass himself.

He'd already made the bold claim of being acquainted with her once the guards at the gatehouse had confirmed that she was inside.

When he'd laid eyes on her, he'd made the last-minute decision, which he'd concocted and mulled over on his fortnight-long journey from the Highlands, to declare that they were engaged. It would provide the cover he needed to remain close enough to determine her loyalties.

He remained at the ready in case she sounded the alarm and called him out for the liar he was. The true work began now. This would be Eleanor's first test.

"Ye were sent a missive, Lady Eleanor," he continued, his gaze sliding once more to her. "About the arrangement—yer new…Scottish union, as it were. But ye never responded." He spoke evenly, yet he subtly emphasized a few of the words to make clear what he was getting at.

I ken ye are a spy. I ken ye work for Scotland. And I ken ye've gone silent.

Comprehension glimmered in her eyes for an instant, then was gone.

"Ah. That." She ducked her head as if in contrition. "Please forgive my silence. I did indeed receive the missive from my parents informing me of the engagement they'd made over Yule."

Interesting. She was playing along. What was more, she was tossing Will a rope, offering information so that they could build this lie together.

"What? And you didn't tell me?" The Queen seemed to have forgotten Will for the moment as she stared at Eleanor in confusion.

"I-I did not wish to acknowledge that it was true," Eleanor replied. "I thought if I ignored their missive —didn't respond, didn't speak of it or even think of it —they might drop the matter."

She lifted her gaze to the Queen's and took her hand. "You must know the news wasn't welcome. I have made it clear to them that I wish to stay on here as your lady-in-waiting, Highness."

Damn, but she was good. She spoke with such earnestness that Will wasn't sure if she was telling the truth or not.

"Yet they seem to have flouted my wishes and ignored my pleas to remain here undisturbed," she continued, her eyes flashing to Will before returning to the Queen.

Will narrowed his good eye on her. It seemed the

wee hellion didn't intend to fall in line. Och, he didn't mind a challenge.

"As ye can see, ignoring the matter didnae make it disappear," he said. "In fact, yer silence had yer family worried. I am relieved to see ye alive, milady. They sent me to check on yer wellbeing—and introduce myself, of course."

"And who exactly are you, sir?" the Queen asked, annoyance edging into her otherwise cool voice.

Will gave another of his best impressions of an English courtier's overdone bow.

"I am William Stewart, Highness, a loyal servant and subject of yer husband the King."

"Yet you are clearly a Scot, Sir William," the Queen probed.

"Please, call me Will—William was my father, and neither of us can rightly be called 'sir' any longer, thanks to that son of a bitch Robert the Bruce. Pardon my tongue, Highness."

The Queen blinked in surprise, but some of the wariness seemed to leave her features. He had her attention now, and an opening to gain her trust.

"My family hails from the Lowlands," he continued, launching into his invented history. "We pledged our loyalty to King Edward, and his father before him, God keep him. English rule over Scotland could have brought peace and prosperity to our country— especially those unruly Highlands."

The words galled, but he forced himself to continue, feigning disgust. "Of course, as soon as that bastard the Bruce gained power, he stripped those of us who wouldnae lick his boots of our lands and titles. My family has lost much, but we havenae faltered in our loyalty." He pinned Eleanor with a look. "And we are hopeful for the future, especially for a union with the de Monteneys."

Eleanor's mouth tightened ever so slightly. "My parents no doubt hope to gain an ally on the other side of the border."

"After all that has happened, I am surprised they would consider such a thing again," the Queen murmured.

Again? Will's suspicion blazed at that. Had the lass already been engaged—or married? And to a Scot? She looked to be in her early twenties—plenty old to have more than a few secrets in her past. She was a spy, after all.

He was forced to tuck the string of questions rising in his mind away for later, however, for the Queen continued. She plastered on a smile and turned to Will.

"But let us not dwell on the past. You must forgive my initial confusion, Sir Willia—Will. I did not realize when you first arrived that you ought to be treated as a most honored guest—for anyone who is to marry my dearest Eleanor must indeed be honored."

The Queen waved over a guard who'd been standing before what appeared to be an enormous barn. The man instantly snapped to the Queen's side.

"John, I'm afraid we'll have to delay our ride. Lady Eleanor's fiancé must be given a proper welcome. Would you care for a tour of the palace, Will?"

Will glanced at Eleanor. Her dark lashes flickered again, the only indication of her distress. He felt a smile tug at the corners of his mouth. *He was in.*

"Aye, Highness, I would like naught more."

Chapter Four

B last the Queen's hospitality.

From the four years she'd spent as Isabella's lady-in-waiting, Eleanor should have known the Queen couldn't refuse the role of hostess. Isabella prided herself on charming even the most reticent nobles and cantankerous diplomats. Of course she would give this Will Stewart—if that was even his name—the same treatment.

But all Eleanor wanted at the moment was to be alone with the interloping Scot. She needed answers —now.

For starters, who was he really? He most certainly wasn't her fiancé. Her parents would never arrange for her to marry another Scot—not after David. '

And if he was part of the Scottish rebellion, as he'd hinted, what the hell was he doing here? She'd made it clear in her last missive that she needed time —and space—to work alone in England. Now this giant of a man came barreling into her carefully constructed life, threatening to destroy everything.

Starting with the Queen's trust in her.

Eleanor hadn't missed the hurt that had flashed in Isabella's eyes when she'd been forced to play along with Will's claim that they were engaged. Another mistake like that and all Eleanor had been working toward might be ruined.

"You've already seen the moat and the curtain wall upon your approach to Langley," the Queen was saying to Will.

"Aye, indeed," Will replied in that dancing accent. "Most impressive."

"And here we are in the outer courtyard," Isabella said, smiling and gesturing open-palmed at their surroundings. "The royal stables—Edward keeps many of his finest coursers here for hunting. Tom, please see to our guest's horse," she said to the stable lad, who stood wide-eyed in the open doorway.

"Much obliged, Highness."

The Queen turned back toward the keep and began gliding toward it. She pointed out the barn, storehouses, mills, and chapel that ringed the yard as she went. Eleanor was forced to hurry after them, clenching her jaw to keep from speaking out of turn.

"The kitchens are just there," the Queen said,

nodding toward the leftmost wing of the massive, sprawling keep. "We recently added a wine cellar belowground, and there is an attached bakery around the other side. Please do feel free to ask anything you like of the cooks—lemons from Spain, dates from the Holy Land, ginger and cinnamon from the East— anything at all."

Will chuckled. "I am a man of simple tastes, Highness, but thank ye."

The Queen flashed him a radiant smile. "Perchance you have not had the opportunity to sample such wonders. Fear not—we will remedy that."

She continued on toward the massive double-doors leading to the great hall. The guards stationed outside deftly hauled them open so that the Queen didn't have to slow her pace.

Eleanor nearly bumped into Will's wide back just inside the doors. He'd halted abruptly to absorb the sight that met him.

She tried to think back to the first time she'd laid eyes on Langley Palace. She'd been a girl of just ten or eleven. Her family had been invited, along with several other noble families, to celebrate Easter with Edward and Isabella the year after they'd been wed. Isabella, the beautiful new Queen from France, had only been a few years older than Eleanor. Though Eleanor had grown up in a respectable and moderately powerful estate in the north, the wealth and splendor of Langley had been like naught she'd ever seen before.

The great hall's vaulted ceilings were easily forty feet high. From the rafters hung pennants from England's various earldoms, along with Edward's coat of arms. Several massive gilded chandeliers with dozens of beeswax candles were also suspended from above.

One entire long wall was covered in an enormous painted image of four knights engaged in a tournament. Edward's favorite colors, gold and vermilion, had been used heavily to highlight the image. Fifty-four shields, polished to gleaming, served as the frame to the mural. The other walls displayed rich woven tapestries with scenes of hunting and battles.

Because it was after the morning meal, the floor had been cleared except for the fresh, sweet-smelling rushes softening the stones underfoot. The tables and benches had been moved to the walls. Only a few large, upholstered chairs sat behind the table on the raised dais centered on the back wall. Still, even empty and quiet, the scale and lavishness of the hall was stunning.

Queen Isabella smiled at the space. "Fit for a King, is it not?"

Will cleared his throat. "I havenae seen its equal."

"I think you will enjoy the gardens then." Isabella crossed the hall and headed toward the system of corridors to the left. Most of those passageways led between the kitchens and the great hall, but one forked off and opened to the inner courtyard, where the King and Queen's private gardens lay.

The gardens were filled with cheery sunlight. Scents of spring blossoms and rich soil hung in the air. Isabella strolled across the grass toward her roses, her smile more genuine now.

This was her favorite place in the entire palace, Eleanor knew. When the weather was fair, they would spend hours here together, tending the flowers, reading, embroidering, or simply enjoying the songs of the birds.

"My rose garden is my pride and joy. And notice the fruit trees there." The Queen indicated the orchard lining the back of the garden. "Pears, apples, plums—I even brought several of my favorite cherry trees with me from France."

"What is that there, Highness?" Will was looking off to the right, at the deep pit cut along the inside of the curtain wall.

"That is my husband's menagerie." The Queen approached, but with a markedly more restrained pace than earlier.

Will moved to the edge of the pit. Fifteen feet

below was a series of iron fences that segmented the space into ten cages, plus a walkway for the servants in charge of the exotic beasts.

"That strange-looking animal is called a camel," the Queen commented. "And of course my husband owns a lion, his favorite."

The lion lay sprawled in its hay-strewn cage. It gave its shaggy, sand-colored head a shake and yawned, its massive white teeth flashing. The other animals were equally subdued, except for one peacock, which had managed to escape its confines and now strutted around the cages along the servants' path.

Eleanor looked away. The menagerie made her uncomfortable, as it did Isabella. The animals made strange noises of protest at their confinement from time to time, and the lion had already mauled two servants, killing one. But Edward insisted on keeping the beasts caged at Langley, even though he was hardly ever here.

Somehow, Will seemed to pick up on the direction of Eleanor's thoughts.

"I dinnae suppose the King is available to regale me with tales of how these magnificent creatures came into his possession," he ventured, watching the Queen with that keen greenish-blue eye.

"Edward is away," Isabella replied shortly. Placing

a deliberate smile on her face, she brightened her tone. "You must be tired from your travels. Come, I'll show you to a chamber. Besides, only the east wing remains for your tour."

The Queen turned back to the keep once more, this time angling toward the private chambers attached to the other side of the great hall. She led them through a series of corridors past her own chambers, the King's quarters, and their respective solars. But to Eleanor's shock, the Queen halted just one door down from Eleanor's own bedchamber.

"I'll have one of the lads bring your saddlebags," the Queen said. "He won't disturb you, though." She arched a brow at them both.

Eleanor couldn't stop from speaking then.

"Highness, I do not think—"

"This will do nicely," the Queen said, completely ignoring Eleanor and speaking to Will. "You see, Eleanor's chamber is just there. In fact, there is a connecting door between the two rooms. That will allow you two to...become acquainted with each other before you marry."

Unease filled the pit of Eleanor's stomach. The Queen was playing the part of a cheerful, knowing hostess perfectly. No one else would notice, but Eleanor didn't miss Isabella's sudden coolness toward her.

"Surely it isn't prop—"

The Queen cut her off once again. She leaned conspiratorially toward Will. "Eleanor must protest in the name of her virtue, of course, for she is a lady. But I understand the way of things when one must wed a stranger. It can do a great deal of good to spend some time *alone* together. After all, I may have adopted English ways, but I am still French."

The Queen gave Will another smile, then smoothed her skirts. "Well, I'll leave you to it, then."

Panic seized Eleanor's throat. Though she'd been eager to question Will in private, the Queen's subtle displeasure was a far more urgent matter.

"But what of our ride, Highness?" Eleanor asked, grasping for a reason to stay in the Queen's company so that she might smooth things over. "The day is still fine, and no doubt Scarlett and Nutmeg will give the grooms trouble if they are not worn down."

"Do not fret, Lady Eleanor," the Queen said in a rather formal tone. "I'll give the horses plenty of exercise. Mayhap Marietta can go riding with me. Besides, I suppose I will have to get used to going without your company if you are to be married." She glanced significantly at Will before returning her gaze to Eleanor for a moment before gliding away.

Damnation. It was as Eleanor had feared when Will had first proclaimed that they were engaged. He'd forced her into a dangerous lie, but what was more, he'd given the Queen reason to doubt her.

Isabella was clearly hurt, not only because she would lose Eleanor as a companion, but because she believed Eleanor had lied and hid such important information from her. And Eleanor's entire mission hung on keeping the Queen's trust.

She watched the Queen's rigid back disappear around a corner. When the soft rustle of Isabella's velvet skirts no longer echoed down the corridor, Eleanor rounded on Will.

He loomed over her, studying her with that too-intelligent stare.

"Inside," she said through clenched teeth. "Now."

He lifted a sandy-brown eyebrow at her, but did as she bid, holding the door open for her. Clinging to the last threads of her composure, she stalked inside and waited for him to close the door behind them.

Only after the door was tightly shut against the servants' eyes and ears did she let herself speak.

"Who are you? The truth."

He remained placid except for a faint tightening around his one good eye. "I thought we already established this," he said coolly. "I am yer fiancé."

"Like hell you are."

He moved a step closer so that she was forced to tilt her head back. "The Queen seems to think I am."

He might not fully understand what a tangled mess Eleanor was now in with the Queen, but he'd clearly noticed the simmering tension between them thanks to his arrival. Damn him. Her control was slipping, but she didn't care.

"You are a liar," she hissed through clenched teeth. "I have only ever had one fiancé." ◈

"Oh?"

"Aye. And he is dead."

Chapter Five

Will fought to remain composed at that particular revelation, but the damned lass kept surprising him at every turn.

While she was the picture of serenity beside the Queen, now that they were alone she had transformed into a wee virago, her dark eyes blazing and her refined voice drawn taut. Her entire body seemed to hum with barely-pent energy.

"Ye were engaged?"

Will frowned. He'd opened his mouth to demand to know what the hell she was about, befriending the English Queen and throwing her loyalty to the Scottish cause into question, but instead he found himself asking about her fiancé. The thought of this hellion becoming some other poor fool's wife was strangely jarring.

"Aye, and not to you, last I checked," she shot back. "I ask again—who are you? I know you're not a Lowlander, so we can start there."

He narrowed his gaze on her. Och, he'd told himself he didn't mind a challenge, and damn if this lass wasn't one. "Is that so? Ye seem awfully sure of yerself, despite the fact that ye are an *English* noblewoman."

Instead of backing down, she swept him slowly with those deep brown eyes. "You wish to do this, then? Very well. You dress like a Lowlander, but in all my years growing up mere miles from the Scottish border, I've never seen that particular pattern of plaid associated with a Lowland clan."

She jabbed a finger at the length of wool draped over his shoulder.

"Aye, the Stewart plaid is red checked with green, like the one you wear," she continued. "But their pattern bears an additional blue thread woven into it —which yours lacks."

Will felt his face darken. He'd chosen the Stewarts for his false identity because they were a large and dispersed clan. Some in their Lowland branches had surely sided with Edward over the Bruce. But he'd used his own Sinclair plaid, assuming none of the fops in the English court would know the difference.

Eleanor lifted a brow at him. "Shall I continue?"

"By all means," he replied tightly.

"Then there is the matter of your accent. It is unlike any Lowlander's I've ever heard. And now that you are growing frustrated, it is deepening further."

Will opened his mouth, but he knew anything that came out would only confirm what she'd just said. He clamped his jaws together instead.

"Between that barely-tempered burr and those clan colors, I'd guess you are a Highlander. Which would make sense if you were sent here by the order of a mutual...*associate* of ours. He tends to trust his loyal Highlanders more than any others."

Finally, he'd reached the limit of that bold tongue of hers. She eyed him warily, clearly unwilling to come out and name Robert the Bruce as their shared link. Or mayhap she wouldn't name him as her ally because she had already betrayed him.

There was no point in continuing to dance around the matter.

"Yer assessment is impressive," he commented.

He broke their gridlocked stare at last, glancing around the chamber. It was just as lavishly appointed as the rest of the palace.

Thick tapestries interwoven with gold thread softened the stone walls. A massive four-poster bed draped with crimson velvet curtains took up the back third of the space. The rest of the wooden furniture —an armoire, a dressing table and chair, a trunk at the foot of the bed—were all inlaid with gold and silver metalwork. A washbasin and pitcher of solid silver sat on the table.

"Then again, mayhap I shouldnae be surprised. Yer powers of observation and deduction should be well honed," he continued. He strolled toward the hearth, where a tidy fire lay ready to be lit, and pretended to examine it. "Ye are a spy, after all."

Silence filled the room. He turned to find her face smooth and unreadable, yet her hands had tightened on her green velvet skirts.

Will dropped his feigned interest in his surroundings and pinned her with his gaze. "Let us speak plainly."

"Fine. Start with your name."

"Will Sinclair. And yers?"

"Eleanor de Monteny is my real name. The Bruce sent you?"

"Aye."

"Why?"

"What do ye mean, why? Ye ceased yer communications."

Her dark brows lowered. "I made it clear in my last missive that I have been working on something of a most delicate nature and wished to be given the freedom to pursue it."

Will considered her for a moment. Neither the Bruce nor Sabine had mentioned aught about her request to be left alone. Of course, it was possible

Eleanor was lying. Aye, from what he'd seen so far, she did so readily and without compunction.

Regardless, he was less interested in the contents of her last missive than in why she'd gone silent in the first place.

"Mayhap the Bruce doesnae believe ye should be given free rein in deciding how to wile away yer time here at the palace."

Her slim shoulders stiffened, but she did not refute his jab at her apparent life of ease as the Queen's lady-in-waiting.

"So that's why he sent you? To spy on his spy?"

"Nay, I'm no' here to spy, lass," he said, flashing her a lazy grin. "If I were, I wouldnae be speaking to ye now. Unlike ye, I dinnae mind being forthcoming with ye about my aims and intentions."

Again, she didn't rise to his bait. Instead she only narrowed her eyes and waited for him to continue.

"The Bruce's first concern was that ye might be dead. That clearly isnae the case, which I'm sure he'll be relieved to hear."

"Is that all, then?" She cocked her head, as if she grew weary of this conversation.

"No' even close."

He stalked toward her, halting only when he was a hair's breadth from brushing the edge of her skirts. She lifted her chin, holding his stare defiantly.

"Ye see, now that I've found ye alive, I am to

determine if ye are still loyal to the Bruce and his cause. If ye are in some sort of danger, then I am here to protect ye. And if ye've betrayed him…"

For the first time, fear scuttled behind her dark eyes before she quickly regained her composure.

"I am still loyal," she said simply.

But of course, that could easily be a lie.

"And I am supposed to merely accept yer word? Nay, I think no'."

"I have done naught to warrant suspicion," she shot back.

"Other than falling silent for the last two months, ye mean."

"I told you, I wrote in my last missive that—"

"Aye, but ye would have the Bruce—and me—believe that naught could change since ye sent that missive? Christ, lass, I have kenned ye for a mere hour and already I find yer behavior suspect."

She drew back her chin indignantly. "What could I have possibly done in so little time to merit your distrust?"

Will crossed his arms over his chest, glaring down at her. "For starters, where is the bloody King of England—ye ken, the one ye were sent here to spy on? Why arenae ye with him?"

Eleanor clucked her tongue in annoyance. "The King is never in one place for more than three or four days. He travels with nigh five hundred members of his court from one palace to another, all over the country."

"Then why arenae ye one among the five hundred?"

"You understand so little," she muttered. "Almost the entire royal retinue is men. Unless the Bruce thinks I can overhear and observe important strategic information amongst the washer women, it would be utterly useless—not to mention dangerously obvious —for me to attempt to follow Edward across England."

"And what of his mistress?" Will demanded, frustration now warming him. "If ye had insinuated yerself more...*intimately* into Edward's company, ye would likely learn far more than ye do sitting on yer duff here with the Queen."

Eleanor jerked back a step as if he'd struck her. Her eyes went wide and a flush of color rose to her cheeks.

"You...you are suggesting that I should become a *whore* to remain close to Edward?"

Will ground his molars. Damn it all, he was being an arse, but the lass seemed to make a brute out of him with her quick, sharp tongue and those imperious eyes. Where were the blade-like wits that the Bruce had praised him for a fortnight earlier?

Eleanor had recovered somewhat. She glared at him, clutching her skirts in white-knuckled fists.

"Once again you've proven how poorly you understand the situation you've barreled into. Even if I were to stoop to the level of a mistress, I doubt the King would be interested."

"I'm sure ye would tempt any man." Will instantly wished to have the words back, for he feared they revealed more about the heat simmering in his own veins at the moment than he cared to admit.

Her lashes flickered in surprise, but fortunately she chose not to address his comment. "You misunderstand yet again. Edward doesn't have a mistress at all. He doesn't...favor women in that way." *oh*

Will frowned in surprise. "What?"

"It is complicated," she said, shifting her gaze to the shuttered window. Mayhap she was considering ways to escape this conversation.

"Try me."

She let a long breath go. "Edward and Isabella once shared an affection—mayhap even love. And they have both done their duty to England. They have produced four heirs to the throne. But the King has always had...favorites. Noblemen. First Piers Gaveston, and now Hugh Despenser." *omg*

While the information was certainly surprising, Will cared little about what Edward did behind closed doors. Yet he sensed this revelation bore some greater weight in relation to Eleanor's recent evasiveness.

He watched her closely. "Does this have aught to do with yer silence these last few months?"

Her gaze lingered on the window. "I cannot say."

Will's hackles rose once more. His instincts had been correct. She was up to something, but damn if he knew what. "Cannae, or willnae?"

At that, her dark eyes snapped back to him. "You do not comprehend just how precarious my position here is, do you? Nor the danger you have put me in with your arrival."

"Lass, I am a member of the Bruce's Bodyguard Corps. Do ye ken what that means?"

She hesitated. "I have heard rumors of such a group, but little more."

"We are the Bruce's best warriors, hand selected to defend those most vulnerable in Scotland's fight for freedom."

She started to look away again, but he caught her chin in a gentle grasp, holding her gaze.

"That means if ye are truly in danger here, I can protect ye."

She tried to shake her head, but he held fast. A jolt of awareness went through him—her skin was warm and unbelievably soft against his callused fingers.

"Aye, I can," he continued, his voice darkening. "Unless this danger ye are in is of yer own making."

"I already told you, I am working on something...

a plan that is years in the making. One which your presence now threatens."

He released her chin and crossed his arms once more to keep from touching her. Blast him, but he couldn't think clearly all of a sudden. "Aye? Then I ask ye again—what is this plan of yers?"

"I can handle this myself."

"That isnae an answer."

She huffed a breath and matched his stance, her arms lacing together under her breasts. "I will not tell you, Will Sinclair."

Will barely resisted the urge to growl in frustration. "Why the bloody hell no'?"

"As you say, you have known me for a mere hour, and you've already managed to insult my virtue, question my loyalty, and prove with your ignorance of this situation that you have no right to be here, let alone interfere with my efforts."

As she continued, her jaw grew tighter and tighter until she was speaking through clenched teeth. "I would be mad to confide in you. You accuse *me* of being untrustworthy, yet I have no reason to trust *you* with all I know and all I'm working toward."

"Ye speak in circles, lass."

She gave a vexed sigh. "All I can do is assure you that I am working toward the greater good for the Scottish cause."

"I will be the judge of that."

Her lips thinned. "Is that so? And just how do you plan on determining my allegiances?"

He leaned over her, lifting one side of his mouth in a cold smile. "Och, dinnae fash about that. I'll be watching yer every move. If ye so much as sneeze, I'll ken it. And I plan on staying for as long as it takes." He held his arms wide to take in the chamber. "Besides, it will be no great hardship to remain, given the luxuries of King Edward's palace—as I'm sure ye ken."

She muttered something about idiotic, rock-headed Highland men, but the fact was, there was naught she could do about his plans to stay close.

Naught, that was, except expose him for the liar he was.

"I trust I can count on ye no' to do something foolish like tell the Queen—or anyone else—that I am no' a Stewart and our engagement is a sham. If ye do, ye ken it will be *both* our necks on the chopping block, aye?"

That was true enough, but given the close companionship Eleanor seemed to share with the Queen, the wee hellion just might find a way to spin matters such that she came away free and clear while he swung from the end of a rope.

With a ripple of unease, Will realized that his life was in this enigmatic lass's hands.

She must have realized that he, too, could end her

with a single word—*spy*—for she pressed her lips together and gave him a single, curt nod.

With that, she spun on her heels and stalked away. But instead of heading for the door leading to the corridor, she moved to one of the tapestries. She yanked aside the wall-hanging, revealing a wooden door inlaid into the stones. With a hard shove, the door came open on loud hinges.

Eleanor slipped through the door, the tapestry ruffling back into place behind her. A heartbeat after the door slammed, he heard the heavy thunk of a wooden bar being lowered across it on her side.

It seemed there would be no more "acquainting" himself with his mock fiancée this day.

Chapter Six

Eleanor rapped softly on the Queen's solar door before slipping inside.

The shutters on the glazed windows along one wall were pulled back, letting in the overcast light. Isabella sat in a silk upholstered chair at the far end of the row of windows, gazing down at the gardens below.

She lifted her head at Eleanor's entrance and waved her in wordlessly. She was already dressed for riding in a purple brocade gown. She looked small tucked within the voluminous folds of the fabric, her skin and hair pale in the gray light.

"Highness, I—"

"We are alone, Eleanor."

The Queen had given Eleanor permission to be far less formal with her when it was just the two of them. It had allowed them to form an easy friendship over the years Eleanor had served as her lady-in-waiting.

A friendship which had never been strained until yesterday.

"Isabella," Eleanor began again, approaching. "I hope you will allow me to explain things better than I did yesterday."

"Help me with my veil?" Isabella motioned toward the length of gold silk lying on a small table next to her chair.

Normally when they went riding together, the Queen didn't bother to cover her hair, for a short gallop would send even the most secure of veils sailing away. It seemed they were in for a sedate ride today.

Uncertain if she should broach the subject of her surprise—and false—engagement a third time, Eleanor picked up the veil and began fastening it with pins into the pale blonde plaits ringing the Queen's head.

Eleanor had managed to slip from her chamber yestereve—after taking a good long time to calm herself and regain her composure after her confrontation with Will. She'd sought the Queen in hopes of smoothing matters between them, but just as she'd arrived at Isabella's private chambers, Marietta and the other ladies-in-waiting were slipping out. They'd told her that the Queen had retired for the evening and didn't wish to be disturbed.

Then this morning Eleanor had received a note from the Queen requesting that she accompany her for a ride. It also informed her that her assistance in readying for the day wasn't necessary.

That wasn't troubling in and of itself. Over the years, Eleanor had gone from a lady-in-waiting to more of a companion to Isabella. The responsibilities of dressing the Queen, preparing her toilette each morning and night, and seeing to small tasks and errands for her had largely fallen to the other ladies-in-waiting. Meanwhile, Eleanor was favored with rides, quiet reflection in the garden, and private moments like this one where they might speak of more personal matters.

But it seemed the Queen did not wish to speak at the moment. When she was finished securing Isabella's veil, Eleanor sat in a nearby chair, staring out at the gardens. It had rained overnight, and looked like it might again later that afternoon. The silence stretched, broken only by the occasional rustle of fabric.

"I am not hurt that you are to marry," Isabella said at last.

Eleanor straightened in her chair, her gaze latching onto the Queen.

"Of course, I knew it must happen someday. You

are young and beautiful, an unmitigated prize for any man, regardless of what happened before."

Eleanor swallowed hard. The shadows from her past still clung to her, no matter what the Queen thought of her beauty or marriageability.

"The prospect makes me sad, of course, for your future husband will want to keep you for himself. He won't want to give you up to the court, and when children come along, it will be even harder for us to enjoy these quiet moments together." The Queen smiled half-heartedly. "I suppose that is what it means to be a woman—to answer to a husband and children ahead of oneself. And what it means to be Queen—to be left alone when all is said and done."

Isabella gave herself a little shake to draw out of her melancholy musings. "Nay, what hurts is that you did not *tell* me." She fixed Eleanor with pained blue eyes. "I thought after all we'd been through—David and Edward and Roger—" Her voice caught on the last name. She swallowed before continuing. "I thought you trusted me, for I trust you, Eleanor. With everything. With my very life."

Eleanor reached for the Queen's hand and squeezed it tightly. Silently, she cursed Will Sinclair for making her lie to this woman, her only friend. Damn him for putting Eleanor in danger, and damn him twice more for hurting Isabella.

"I do trust you, Isabella," she said, her voice low

and strained with emotion. That much was true. Just as Isabella's life depended on Eleanor's trust, so too did Eleanor's life depend on the Queen's.

Yet now she had to reach for the words of deception.

"I...I am sorry I kept news of the engagement from you. I did not wish to burden you in the midst of your own hardships. And I truly hoped I could get out of the arrangement so that I might stay here with you, but—"

Eleanor's words were cut off by a knock at the solar door. Hastily, Isabella yanked her hand away and dashed it across her cheeks, which were damp with tears.

"Enter," she called, her voice slightly croaky.

Just in time for the door to swing open, Isabella plastered on one of her practiced smiles, jerking her spine rigid in her chair. Eleanor's aching heart went out to the woman, who refused to show even the faintest cracks despite all the pain she bore inside.

"Ah, Will," the Queen said brightly. "What a pleasure that you can join us."

Eleanor's head whipped around. Sure enough, Will stood in the solar doorway, his large frame filling it.

He'd shaved and his hair was pulled back into a neat queue. The black eyepatch slashing across his face made his skin and hair seem all the more vibrantly golden. He wore a fresh tunic with the length of red wool plaid over one shoulder. His breeches were tucked into tall riding boots.

Dread swam in the pit of her stomach. The Queen had said he was joining them—she couldn't mean on their ride, could she?

"I was most honored to receive yer note inviting me this morn, Highness," Will said, stepping into the solar with a bow.

His gaze slid to Eleanor. Awareness rippled over her skin.

Curse his imposing presence. She'd been making progress with Isabella, but judging from the tightness lingering around the Queen's blue eyes, Eleanor had more work to do in regaining her trust. She wouldn't be able to finish mending things if Will remained close, making her tongue feel heavy and her wits tangled.

"Come, let us set out," Isabella said, rising gracefully from her chair. "I'd hoped to show you the royal woods, Will, but the clouds to the west threaten rain." She cast Eleanor a meaningful look. "I suppose we will simply have to make the best of the situation."

Eleanor inclined her head, grateful for the indication that she'd made some progress with the Queen.

But the lightening in her heart vanished all too soon, for as the Queen swept through the door, Will lingered. He extended his arm toward her, waiting.

Reluctantly, Eleanor rose and approached him.

"Come, milady," he said, raising his voice for the benefit of the Queen, who stood out of sight but just on the other side of the doorway. "Another opportunity to *acquaint* ourselves with each other awaits."

Shooting him a narrow-eyed glare, she placed her hand atop his forearm. The contact jolted her like a tiny bolt of lightning passing between them. He was warm and hard beneath her palm, his muscles twitching as if he, too, were affected. Yet his stony face revealed naught.

She ratcheted her lips into a smile she normally reserved for the most odious of courtiers.

"I can imagine naught more pleasing."

Chapter Seven

U nbeknownst to Eleanor, it seemed the Queen
had already arranged the whole outing.

John and a retinue of twenty guards awaited them
in the outer courtyard. Lucy and Copper, two rather
staid mares, also stood saddled and ready, their reins
held by Tom. Another stable lad, Toby, struggled to
control Will's enormous steed.

While a groom positioned a mounting block next
to Lucy for the Queen, Eleanor snatched her hand
from Will's forearm and approached Copper. She
discreetly lifted her crimson skirts and fitted her boot
in one of the stirrups. But before she could boost
herself into the saddle, big hands closed around her
waist.

She was lifted into the air as if she weighed

naught more than a leaf and deposited onto the horse's back. Eleanor stared down at Will in shock.

"I am quite capable—"

"Aye."

Yet his hands lingered, giving her a little nudge to adjust her position in the saddle. He fussed for a moment longer before removing his grip on her waist.

Eleanor went warm beneath her gown—from annoyance at Will's constant need to interfere, she told herself. Her gaze trailed after him as he moved to his own horse and vaulted with easy, graceful strength into the saddle.

He glanced at her, lifting a golden-brown eyebrow. With a silent curse, she snapped her eyes away and set about arranging her skirts so that they draped artfully over her legs.

At the Queen's word, the palace gates were opened and their party filed out. Eleanor made sure she followed the Queen closely, but somehow Will managed to wedge himself next to her as they crossed over the drawbridge spanning the moat.

His stallion was so large that she was forced to rein her mare close to the edge, yet she refused to pull back and lose her position behind the Queen. Once they were on solid ground on the other side of the bridge, Eleanor shot Will a glare.

"Ye seem an accomplished rider," Will commented, ignoring her scowl.

"It is my privilege to ride almost daily with the Queen," she replied evenly.

"So many outings must leave ye little time to keep up with yer correspondence." He fixed her with that cold, lake-colored eye.

"Do not be too hard on my Eleanor, Will," the Queen said over her shoulder. "It must have come as a great shock to learn of a new engagement by letter."

But Eleanor knew what the Queen did not—Will wasn't referring to the make-believe missive from her family informing her of a marriage arrangement. He was speaking of her reports to the Scottish—in front of the Queen and twenty of her guards, no less.

She gripped her reins hard enough that Copper shook her head in annoyance.

Will cast her one last piercing look before nudging his horse alongside the Queen's.

"Och, ye are right, Highness. But ye cannae blame a man for being slow to forget a wound to his pride. To be assured that I was to marry the bonniest, most sweet-tempered lass in all of the north, only to be met with silence…it was most unsettling. Of course, being here to put my mind at ease has helped. Especially given all the comforts of yer hospitality."

Eleanor fell back a few paces while Will droned on with his flattery. He affected a charming courtier quite well, though his brogue made him sound rather rough. His voice seemed to rumble right through her, even as she let them pull farther ahead.

Willing herself to remain collected, Eleanor focused her gaze on the landscape surrounding them. They rode down the gently sloping hill atop which the palace sat, then across the grassy expanse toward the royal woods. The sky was leaden, the air hanging heavy with the promise of rain, yet the weather held for them as they walked along toward the trees.

The sound of one of the guards clearing his throat drew Eleanor's attention.

"Milady, the Queen's retinue is spreading rather thin…" The guard looked pointedly ahead.

Blast. Without realizing it, Eleanor had let a fair bit of space form between her and Will and the Queen. They'd already reached the tree line, while she'd been dawdling in the middle of the grassland. The guards who surrounded their little party seemed unsure if they should close ranks around the Queen or continue to keep Eleanor within their circle.

"Forgive me," she said to the guard. She dug her heels into the mare's flanks, urging the animal into a reluctant canter to catch up.

By the time she reined in a few paces from Will and the Queen, they were both watching her.

Will was frowning at her. "That mare's gait is off."

"Is it?" She glanced down at the horse. She hadn't noticed anything.

Without further prompting, Will swung down from his steed and approached. He laid a hand on the mare's right shoulder and slid it along her leg, urging her to lift her front hoof.

He made a very Scottish sound of displeasure in his throat. "She's thrown a shoe."

Damn and blast. Eleanor shouldn't have let her mind—and the mare—wander in the first place, nor should she have made her canter over muddy ground.

At that moment, a smattering of fat raindrops began to fall. Just Eleanor's luck.

"Make haste back to the palace, Highness. I'll follow behind you."

"Ye ought no' ride her now," Will said, looking up at her. "Else she'll strain a muscle with those uneven shoes."

Eleanor fought to keep the annoyance from her voice. "Then I'll walk the mare back myself."

The Queen looked at the sky, which was opening in earnest now, then back at the palace sitting in the distance. "Oh dear. It is too far to go on foot."

"She'll ride with me."

Both Isabella and Eleanor stared for a moment at Will. His voice brooked no argument, despite the fact that he spoke to a Queen.

"We'll walk the horse behind us," he continued. "Ye go ahead without us, Highness, and get out of this rain."

The Queen's brows drew together in distress. "I cannot leave you both without protection. But if I split the retinue…"

Eleanor instantly understood the Queen's hesitation. "Nay, do not bother dividing the guards, Highness. They ought to remain with you."

"If it is Lady Eleanor's wellbeing ye're worried about, Highness, I can assure ye she'll be completely safe in my company."

Eleanor slid her gaze to Will. He still stood beside her horse, his shoulder brushing the skirts over her thigh. *Safe?* From brigands or thieves, aye. But from him? She wasn't so sure.

But she couldn't cause a scene just to alleviate her own discomfort at the bullish Scot's nearness, especially not when the Queen was clearly growing uneasy.

"Go," she said more gently to Isabella. "We will be perfectly safe. Besides, your veil grows wetter by the moment. And that poor brocade will never forgive me if you don't get out of this rain. We will be right behind you, do not fear."

The Queen cast them an uncertain look, but at Eleanor's reassuring nod, she kicked her horse into motion. The guards fell in around the Queen and they thundered off toward the palace.

Leaving her alone with Will.

"It's true," she said, reaching for a casual tone.

"We are in no danger. These are the King's royal woodlands, not the Highland wilds. No interloper would dare step foot here. You can go ahead if you like. Get out of this rain. I'll walk the mare back and—"

Completely ignoring her ramblings, he reached up and wrapped his hands around her waist once more. She made a strangled noise of surprise as he lifted her down from the saddle. But instead of setting her on her feet, he shifted her against his chest, sliding his arms around her so that he could carry her.

"Cannae have this ridiculous getup getting muddy," he muttered.

His arms were like bands of steel under her knees and around her back as he strode toward his own horse. The stallion shifted as he approached, but with a click of his tongue, the beast instantly stilled.

He hoisted her up and set her sideways across the saddle, then turned his back to fetch her mare. In the few seconds she had before he returned, she fought to regain control of her body, but a telltale heat crept up her neck and into her cheeks. She gulped a cold breath, willing away the tingles that raced along her skin where her body had touched his.

When he approached once more with her mare in tow, she jerked her head down and busied herself with the folds of her gown.

While he fastened the mare's reins to the back of

his saddle, she reminded herself of all the ways he had made her life worse in a single day.

The Queen believed Eleanor had broken her trust in not telling her about the pretend engagement. What was more, Will had created a lie that would bring more scrutiny upon her. Who would believe that her parents would be foolish enough to marry her off to another Lowlander after the terrible disaster with David?

She had nearly managed to regain cold clarity about the dangers Will posed to her when he swung up into the saddle behind her. She attempted to lean over the stallion's neck to give him room. But once again he ignored her efforts and simply dragged her across his lap.

Eleanor stiffened, clamping her teeth against a gasp of shock. His thighs were hard as stone beneath her bottom, and even through the thick layers of her skirts, she could feel the heat of him.

He grunted and shifted her until her shoulder rested against his chest and her legs draped over one of his thighs. While he arranged her, she remained rigidly still—all except her heart, which beat wildly against the inside of her ribs.

At last he had her how he wanted her. He took up the reins, creating a cage around her with his muscular arms, and nudged his horse into motion.

He kept them at a walk to accommodate the

trailing mare. The easy gait made them rock together as one in the saddle. The sound of the rain filled her ears, along with the occasional snort of a horse.

"Ye said it was safe."

His low voice vibrated through her, jerking her from the lull of their slow progress.

She blinked up at him in confusion, squinting against the rain.

Muttering something, he dragged the red plaid from his shoulder and draped it over her head. It was surprisingly warm and dry. It smelled of him—of fresh air and wool and man.

"Ye said no one would trespass on the King's lands," he began again. "Yet the Queen seemed… fearful. Afraid to divide her retinue. Why?"

Eleanor hesitated. She hated the idea of betraying the Queen's confidence, but nor did she wish to draw any more of Will's suspicion if she refused to answer.

"Isabella has been through much," she offered after a moment.

He waited, but when she didn't say more, his mouth turned down. "That is all? She's been through much? I may only have one eye, lass, but even I can see that she lives a life of comforts and pleasures most of her subjects couldnae dream of."

Defensive anger flared to life in Eleanor's chest. "Once again, you prove how little you understand of this situation. You have no doubt heard of the Battle of Old Byland?"

He frowned. "Aye, of course. It was Edward's most recent—and mayhap greatest—failure on the battlefield. We halted his advance across the border, then chased him all the way to York until he tucked his tail and fled farther south."

"Were you there?"

He faltered for a heartbeat. "Nay."

"I was." She

When he started in surprise, she amended, "Not on the front—not at first, anyway."

"What the bloody hell happened?"

"Edward was full of vim after he defeated the Earl of Lancaster's uprising last year," she began.

Will nodded. "I ken something of that." At her questioning look, he added. "The Bruce had a stake in the outcome—and the Bodyguard Corps was involved."

Though that was news to her, Eleanor wasn't surprised. She'd never met the Bruce in person, but from her slim experience, his network of influence was vast and his larger schemes far more complex that she would ever fully comprehend.

"Edward believed himself invincible against his enemies, both at home and abroad," she continued. "After quashing his rebellious nobles, he decided to turn to Scotland. He planned to reclaim the Borderlands, all the way to Edinburgh. He was so sure of himself that he requested the Queen and her retinue accompany him part of the way. We went as far as Tynemouth Priory, near Newcastle-upon-Tyne."

Will shook his head in disbelief. "That is damned close to the border."

"Aye, but Edward assured the Queen that we'd be safe there. She was meant to take the sea air and entertain herself until he secured the border for England, after which time he would return and fetch her."

"But he was so ill prepared that his army nigh starved and he retreated," Will said slowly.

"The Queen became nervous about the state of affairs and requested that Edward send her a guard of a hundred soldiers. Edward offered to send Hugh Despenser and a few of his knights instead."

"Despenser—the King's favorite?"

"Aye." Eleanor chewed on her lip for a moment, choosing her words carefully. "Isabella and Hugh… they do not get on well. She and Piers Gaveston, the King's former favorite, had an understanding. They accepted one another's position in relation to the King. They even became amicable. But Hugh…things are different with him." She shook her head. "The Queen refused the offer of Despenser's presence and again asked for the King's aid. But by then, it was too late."

"Edward had already fled," Will surmised.

"Aye. To York. Without the Queen."

"He *left her behind?*" Will growled.

Eleanor knew Will had little sympathy for the English—he was a Highland warrior pledged to the Scottish cause for independence, after all—yet his defensiveness of the Queen sent warmth low into her belly.

"He retreated so quickly—with the Scots close on his heels—that she was cut off from escape," Eleanor murmured. "The Scottish army surrounded her on three sides, and the sea was patrolled by Scottish ships."

Eleanor swallowed against the sudden tightness in her throat. She had not spoken aloud of the incident before. "She only had a handful of squires to hold back the Scots while she sought safe passage on an English ship. Those boys gave their lives for hers."

Silence descended for a long moment before Eleanor could go on.

"Two of her ladies-in-waiting died as well," she whispered. "I was one of the lucky ones."

The memory of that terrible night six months past still haunted the dark corners of her mind.

The shouting. The terror. The desperate scramble to get to the docks as the squires fell beneath the Scots' swords like wheat under a scythe. And the horrible screams of Mary and Alice as they were swallowed by the descending army. Mary had tripped as they'd sprinted for the ship. Alice had slowed to help her. A heartbeat later, they were both gone.

Eleanor shoved the memory away harshly. She dared a glance at him, steeling herself for his cold stare. "Ironic, isn't it? The traitorous spy in the Queen's midst survived, but two innocent women and a dozen lads of less than fourteen died."

"I am sorry." The solemnity in Will's deep voice surprised her. His gaze searched her, gentle for once. "I didnae ken…"

Eleanor tugged her eyes away. "We managed to evade the Scottish ships and land farther south. Isabella returned here to Langley, while the King retreated to London with Despenser. Things have been…different ever since."

"That is why the Queen rides her own lands with a retinue of twenty guards," Will murmured.

Eleanor nodded, not trusting her voice.

Will was quiet for a time, and Eleanor sank into the slow, steady sway of the horse's steps. She found herself leaning against Will's chest, the steady thump of his heart a counterpoint to the rain drumming on her plaid-covered head.

"And mayhap it also explains why ye fell silent," he said after some time.

Her brows compressed. "What?"

"Mayhap ye couldnae stomach the idea of

helping the Scots after what ye'd been through," he continued evenly. "They nearly killed ye, after all. So mayhap ye decided to stop sending yer reports. Throw yer lot in with Isabella instead."

She jerked away from him as if she'd been burned. Her mouth slackened with outraged disbelief as she stared up at him.

"You would accuse me once more of turning against the Bruce after what I just told you? After all I've faced for the sole benefit of the cause? I might have *died*, and I would have taken the secret of my true role to the grave with me."

He leveled her with a hard stare. "Mayhap that's true. But I would be a fool to take yer word at face value. Ye are a professional liar, after all."

That did it. She squirmed out of his lap, shoving against one of his corded arms in an attempt to slip from his horse's back.

"Hold still, ye wee hellion," he snapped. "Else ye'll aggravate my horse—or worse, fall and break yer damn neck."

"I'd rather walk back to the palace in the rain than face your accusations," she shot back.

She writhed in another attempt to break free, but his hands clamped down on her, pinning her against his chest. He must have dropped the reins, for she felt his thighs clench beneath her bottom as he used his knees to guide the horse.

It would be futile to struggle in his hold. He was like a wall of stone, his arms steely around her and his hands like vises. His fingers sank into her hip and along her ribs. Her bottom was wedged against his groin. A strange thrill stole through her at his complete control. All she could do was pant in frustration and glare at him.

Their gazes clashed for several long heartbeats before he spoke again.

"Ye arenae helping matters by withholding this secret plan of yers. Tell me the truth—the whole of it —and I willnae have a reason to be suspicious of ye."

Blast it all, she was good and bound—and not just by Will's powerful arms. She still didn't fully trust Will with the knowledge of just what she was working toward. It was too bold, too delicate. And even if she did, she knew all too well just how dangerous information could be.

"I *can't*," she rasped. "Not given the danger it would put us both in."

"I told ye before, whatever danger ye face, I can protect ye—unless it is caused by yer own treachery."

She shook her head. "You don't know what you're asking. Just speaking of it is a risk. And after what happened to David—"

Eleanor snapped her mouth shut, silently berating herself. She'd already revealed too much.

"Who is David?" Will asked, his voice dropping

warily. When Eleanor didn't answer, he ventured, "Let me guess. He is yer previous fiancé. The one who is dead."

Damn him. He saw through her far too easily.

At her telling silence, Will stiffened. "What does he have to do with this?"

Tears stung Eleanor's eyes. In the four years since David's death, she had never been able to speak the truth aloud—not even to Isabella. But if what had happened to David had taught her aught, it was that she could never truly trust anyone.

She wouldn't make the same mistake again.

Blinking away the tears, Eleanor locked her teeth together and turned her head away, silently refusing to even acknowledge Will's question.

He huffed a vexed breath and loosened his grip on her enough that she could lean forward and put a hair's breadth between them.

"Verra well then," he murmured. "Ye can keep yer secrets. For now. But I vow to ye, Eleanor, I *will* get to the bottom of this."

A shiver that had naught to do with the cold rain rippled over her.

She believed him.

Chapter Eight

✿❀✿

Will plunked down onto one of the benches in the great hall. He hunched over his bowl of porridge and watched the servants surreptitiously.

Of course, it was bloody hard watching surreptitiously with only one eye. He had to keep swiveling his head to catch the tables on his right side.

Not that there was much to observe, even in the bustling midst of the morning meal.

It had been five days since his conversation with Eleanor, and he hadn't learned a damn thing. Playing the part of the perfect hostess, the Queen had invited him to ride with Eleanor and her each morning. Yet he hadn't managed to get a moment alone with Eleanor again.

In the afternoons, the Queen retreated to her solar with Eleanor and the other ladies-in-waiting to embroider or read. Will's presence hadn't been requested at those events. And of course at night, Eleanor kept the door connecting their chambers barred on her side.

Today, instead of taking a tray in his room, as was the Queen and Eleanor's habit before their morning ride, he'd opted to break his fast in the great hall with the servants. He'd hoped they could provide a clue about the mysterious Lady Eleanor.

Thus far, however, they'd given him a wide berth. Following the Queen's lead, they were respectful toward him, accepting his presence in their midst, but they skittered away like leaves in a gust of wind anytime he drew near. Which meant he was left to sit alone at the end of one table with his porridge.

The other ladies-in-waiting were worse. Will had attempted to speak casually with a few of them, aiming to learn how they perceived Eleanor. But they scattered like hens whenever he approached, tittering amongst themselves and casting wide eyes over him.

Despite the dearth of information thus far, his instincts still told him Eleanor wasn't to be trusted. The fact that she'd nearly been killed by Scots a mere six months past may indeed have inspired a change of heart when it came to her allegiance. It was a plausible explanation for her sudden failure to deliver her reports—and her clear loyalty to Queen Isabella.

As she'd been sitting in his lap atop his horse, he'd

felt the way her soft, small body had tensed when he'd suggested as much, and again at the mention of her fiancé. She'd begun to turn pliant and warm against him until he'd confronted her.

The memory stirred an unwelcome heat in him. Damn him for the desire that simmered in his blood. She was strikingly bonny, intelligent, and captivating in a way he couldn't quite discern. Yet he couldn't fall under her spell. Something foul was afoot, he was certain, and he meant to ferret it out.

Even if it meant exposing Eleanor as a traitor.

A commotion outside the great hall drew Will out of his brooding. It sounded as though several people were shouting in the courtyard beyond the doors. And they were drawing closer.

On instinct, he jerked to his feet and reached for his sword. But of course he'd had to surrender his weapons even before entering Langley. And this was the King of England's palace, not a castle in Scotland, where a siege was to be expected at any moment.

The hall doors flew open. A squire of perhaps thirteen, red-faced and panting, skidded to a halt in the doorway.

"The King," the lad squeaked. "The King approaches."

For one heartbeat, everyone froze. Then it was as if all the servants had been lit on fire, for they began scrambling in every direction.

Before Will could reach for his porridge, the bowl was snatched up by a scullery maid. An instant later, the table and bench he'd been sitting at were dragged away along with the rest of the furniture filling the hall. They were all pushed against the walls. Several other servants carried in more ornate chairs, including one that could more accurately be called a throne, from one of the corridors at the back, placing them on the raised dais.

Will twisted out of the way as the servants flew by, frozen in the chaos.

Edward. Will had steeled himself to meet the King of England upon his arrival at Langley, but once it had become clear that Edward wasn't in residence, he'd assumed he'd see neither hide nor hair of him.

Now he was to come face to face with the man who'd made it his mission to crush Will and all his countrymen under his boot. Will had managed to convince the Queen and the others that he was an English-sympathizing Lowlander. Could he do the same with the King?

Women's voices drew his attention to the corridors leading to the wing of private chambers. The Queen hustled into the hall, her ruby-red skirts clutched in her hands, followed by a stream of her ladies-in-waiting.

Will's gaze snagged on Eleanor, who was hastily attempting to pin a cream-colored silk veil over the

Queen's hair even while keeping pace with Isabella's rushed steps. She wore a snug emerald gown with ferns in silver thread dancing across the silk. Her head was uncovered, as was typical for an unmarried woman, yet her normally tidy plait was only half-done.

It seemed that the Queen and her ladies were just as caught off guard as the servants by Edward's unannounced arrival.

Uncertain of what he was meant to do, Will fell in behind the Queen and the ladies as they crossed the hall and exited into the courtyard. Trumpets cut through the air on the other side of the curtain wall. The gates groaned as they were ratcheted open. As the portcullis lifted, Will caught his first glimpse of the royal retinue.

It was *enormous*. Even with his view limited to the size of the open gates, Will caught sight of several hundred mounted men. They covered the sloping hillsides atop which the palace sat like a swarm of finely garbed locusts. Beyond them, the grasslands separating the palace from the woods teemed with hundreds more servants on foot and several dozen supply wagons.

The trumpets blasted again, and a score or so of men rode into the courtyard. Will's gaze instantly fastened on the King. The man was unmistakable.

Tall, lean, and golden-headed, Edward sat his

horse with confident ease. He was swathed in an ermine-trimmed blue velvet cloak that cascaded to his horse's knees. A gold circlet rested on his head.

As one, the servants, guards, ladies-in-waiting, and even the Queen lowered themselves before him. Like the other men, Will dropped to one knee and lowered his head. Eleanor and the other women dipped so deeply into their curtsies that their skirts made jewel-toned pools around them.

Will dared a glance up. The King swung down from his saddle with athletic grace. The courtiers surrounding him, dressed in an array of brightly colored silks and velvets, followed his lead.

The King approached Isabella, extending a hand to her. She placed the very tips of her fingers into his palm and allowed him to bring her up.

"My most honored lady wife," Edward said, dipping his head over her hand.

"My liege husband. A warm welcome back to Langley to you and your companions." She tilted her chin to the courtiers, who bowed crisply as one to her.

The King released the Queen's hand and began striding toward the great hall. "Refreshments," he called to no one in particular. "My men and I are parched."

That set the servants into another flurry of activity. The courtiers began sauntering after the King, but Will's gaze remained on the Queen. One of the courtiers, a tall, well-built man of middling years, lingered before her. He tilted his copper head toward her, but he held her eyes with his.

The Queen wore a polite mask, yet even from several feet away, Will didn't miss the tightness around her mouth.

"Lord Despenser. Welcome."

The man—Hugh Despenser—lifted an arrogant brow at her.

"Isabella," he said simply before sliding past her toward the hall.

Eleanor had said that Despenser and the Queen didn't get along. From the taut exchange Will had just witnessed, that was a vast understatement.

Despite Despenser's clear insolence, the Queen held her head high as she glided after the others into the hall, her ladies falling in behind her. Still uncertain what he ought to do, Will followed.

Edward had already taken up his throne on the raised dais. A few of the other courtiers, including Despenser, sat in the chairs to the King's right. Isabella moved to the seat on the King's left, while her ladies remained standing at the base of the dais. Will edged in beside Eleanor at the back of the group.

As the servants flitted about with silver goblets of ale and wine, more and more of Edward's retinue streamed into the hall. Some appeared to be lower ranking nobles, while others were clearly the King's personal servants. They wore livery in red and gold, with three golden lions rampant, the English King's coat of arms, on their chests.

"Bloody hell. How many of them are there?" Will muttered as the stream of men continued.

"The King travels with a retinue of nearly five hundred," Eleanor whispered.

Will barely managed not to guffaw. He had spent enough time with Robert the Bruce to know that *his* King didn't require the efforts of so many servants, nor did he surround himself with sycophantic courtiers day and night. Nay, the Bruce traveled with little more than a canvas tent for shelter, surrounded himself with warriors, and used his own two hands to fetch himself a drink. *good*

The ridiculous extravagance of it all—the nobles swathed in silks and bedecked with jewels, the red and gold clad servants dashing about, the sheer number of them all—struck Will then. He realized that the quiet life at Langley he'd experienced thus far was a result of the fact that the Queen lived here with a skeleton crew of servants. While she had the enormous privileges that the role of Queen afforded her, she lived simply compared to Edward.

When perhaps two hundred nobles and servants had crammed into the great hall, the King lifted his goblet. Silence instantly fell.

"A toast. To our dearest Queen, who makes Langley the home of my heart."

The courtiers responded to the toast with a robust cheer. While they drank, the King continued.

"Let us feast tonight in honor of our arrival at Langley."

Another cheer went up. Will frowned. Eleanor had mentioned that the King never stayed in any one place more than a few days. Which likely meant the King and his courtiers spent their time traveling from one celebratory feast to another, eating, drinking, and making merry from palace to palace across England.

Aye, it was clearly good to be in the King's favor. But it was no wonder Edward couldn't sustain a military campaign. He and his nobles were too busy enjoying their lives of pleasure and luxury to be bothered with the harsh realities of warfare.

The nobles began milling about and talking amongst themselves, but Will remained rooted behind Eleanor like a sentinel. He wasn't sure if he did so in order to be able to watch her for any indication of her true motives so near to the King, or if he meant to protect her from this glittering, outrageous vipers' den. Either way, he planned to stay close.

"...do not recognize that man there."

The hairs on Will's nape rose as he felt several sets of eyes from the dais shift to him. He turned to find the King, Despenser, and a few of the others studying him.

"Allow me to introduce Will Stewart," the Queen said. "He has recently become engaged to one of my ladies-in-waiting."

She motioned Will forward. Grudgingly, he stepped away from Eleanor and came to stand before the dais. The King's throne was so large that even sitting, Edward was a head higher than Will. The King assessed him with cool blue eyes.

"Stewart? Are you a Scot, then, man?"

"Aye, Highness." Will bowed deeply. His accent drew several more sets of eyes.

"Will hails from the Lowlands, husband," the Queen commented smoothly. "He has been displaced by the Scots because of his loyalty to you."

The King visibly relaxed into his chair. "Ah. There are a few others like you amongst my retinue, Stewart. Good Anglo-Scottish men disenfranchised by that bastard King Robert."

"Indeed, Highness. Would that all my countrymen could be made to see the madness of following the Bruce. Then we would finally ken peace under yer steady hand."

"I couldn't agree more, Stewart," the King said. A shadow crossed his features. "It is long past time for Scotland to fall in line. Yet they insist on resisting me. Just this morn I received word that they are once again assaulting Carlisle Castle in an attempt to claim it for themselves."

Will's mind fired at that tidbit. It seemed the Bruce didn't plan to honor the peace he'd formed with Harclay. Then again, the Earl of Carlisle's body parts were currently strewn across England at Edward's order. Mayhap the Bruce meant to harangue Edward for that particular decision.

"A scheme to sow more purposeless chaos, no doubt," Will commented airily. "The Scots—especially those barbarian Highlanders—shouldnae be left to their own devices, for they dinnae ken aught but savagery and destruction."

Will forced a smile through gritted teeth while the courtiers laughed uproariously at that. The King, too, chuckled.

"It is most entertaining to hear such words from the mouth of a Scot," he said. "You are rather amusing, Will Stewart. Tell me, how did you come to wear that eye patch? Not in a battle against your countryman, I hope—or worse, mine."

"Hunting accident." Though Will aimed for a casual tone, the words came out clipped.

Fortunately, the King didn't seem to notice. "A shame. Hunting is one of my favorite pastimes," he said, smiling fondly. "I keep the woods near Langley well stocked with deer, hares, foxes—aught that can be hunted by man, hound, or hawk."

While Edward waxed eagerly about a favorite excursion in which he'd pursued a particularly ornery wild boar, a new understanding slowly broke inside Will's mind. While Edward had taken up his father's quest to conquer Scotland, his heart wasn't truly in it. Nay, his ambition didn't seem to extend beyond feasts and hunts and other diversions.

Will also realized that he'd apparently passed some critical test with the King. Edward seemed to accept Will's story about himself without question. Will had amused Edward, thus winning his trust and favor.

Relief flooded him. Grave danger could still meet him at any point on this mission, but at least he'd won the acceptance of the King. And he could build on that.

"I was fortunate enough to see yer royal forests a few days past, Highness," Will commented once the King had concluded his story. "The Queen showed them to me. They are by far the most impressive woodlands I've ever beheld."

A pleased grin lifted Edward's mouth. "Mayhap there will be time for a hunt tomorrow or the next day. You'll accompany us, Stewart."

The Queen interjected by rising gracefully. "It seems you two have much to discuss. If you'll excuse me, I must prepare for this evening's feast."

"Aye, of course." The King waved her away, fixing

Will with a keen look. "Did you perchance ride along the western border? Because there is a stream with trout in such numbers you could nigh walk across their backs without getting your boots wet! You won't believe…"

As the King droned on, the Queen and the ladies-in-waiting discreetly slipped away.

Will's gaze caught on Eleanor. Though he had disparaged her for playing her part almost too well amidst the luxuries and frivolities of court life, now that he had to join this flock of self-important peacocks, he was no different than her.

As she disappeared through the passageway, Will remained rooted, an amiable smile plastered on his face while the King and his courtiers drank and laughed at naught.

Chapter Nine

E leanor followed Isabella and the other ladies toward the Queen's private chambers, but once she was in the dimly lit corridor, she fell back. Skirting the wall, she retraced her steps toward the great hall.

Once she reached the arched mouth of the corridor, she lingered just inside the shadows, her gaze settling on Will.

He appeared at his leisure, his feet planted wide and his hands clasped behind his back before the raised dais. His normally hard features had relaxed in an easy smile. But behind the façade, the man was an enigma.

Publicly, he was charismatic, if a fair bit less polished than the Englishmen of court. In private, he let the guise drop and became a rough-edged, hard-hearted Highland warrior with little patience for her obfuscation.

Yet neither version of Will Sinclair was the whole truth.

She hadn't realized it until the King had asked about Will's eye. Will had managed a nonchalant tone, but his comment about a hunting accident was a lie—mayhap not an outright falsehood, but there was clearly far more he didn't say.

The King hadn't noticed, for he cared little for details—one of his greatest failings and the reason his reign had been so ineffectual—but Eleanor didn't miss it. As Will had spoken, his hands had subtly tightened at his sides like knotted ropes pulled snug.

He was hiding something. The realization had knocked the air from Eleanor's lungs. Will, who had baldly called her a traitor for not trusting him with the knowledge of this most fragile and dangerous mission, had secrets of his own. And if anyone could discover them, who better than a trained spy?

Eleanor eased back from the mouth of the passageway, her mind whirling with questions. But just as she turned away, a firm hand caught her elbow.

"There you are, my dove."

When Eleanor lifted her gaze to the man holding her arm, her stomach plummeted. She hastily curved her mouth in a well-mannered smile.

"Lord de Russ."

"Come now, Eleanor," he coaxed in a low murmur. "We are more familiar than that. I've already told you to call me Conrad."

"Indeed, but we see each other so infrequently that it seems wrong to slip into such informalities." She hoped her modestly spoken words would put him in his place.

Judging by Conrad's coy grin, they hadn't.

"Nonsense, sweet lady. Even if I were never permitted to see you again, you would linger in my heart and mind forevermore as the fairest maiden in all of England."

Eleanor just managed to quell the urge to roll her eyes. Such an overwrought sentiment from a man who only wanted her for her family's holdings in the north and the favor she had with the Queen.

She lowered her head as if his words had made her blush. "You are too kind, sir, but I must return to the Queen now."

Conrad's wide, confident grin slipped a fraction. "I have thought of little else beyond this moment, now that the King has returned to Langley and I can lay eyes on you."

But instead of drawing her toward the light spilling from the great hall, he maneuvered her deeper into the corridor by her elbow.

"Won't you greet me?" he continued, blocking her

against the stones with his tall frame. "Or have you turned cold after my long absence?"

A warning bell clanged in the back of her mind. She could not risk causing a scene or alienating Conrad. But nor could she let him grow so bold with her. She still needed him—held at a safe arm's distance.

"Let us not forget ourselves, sir," she said with an attempt at a shy smile. "I have hardly had a moment to catch my breath since your arrival."

"Ah, who needs to breathe when kissing is so much more stimulating?" He dipping his dark head, angling toward her mouth.

Blast and damn. Eleanor's mind raced as she sought an escape, but there was no way out.

A heartbeat before Conrad's lips met Eleanor's, someone loudly cleared his throat in the mouth of the corridor.

Conrad jerked back, his head whipping around, but his body blocked Eleanor's view.

"Och, there ye are, *my bride.*"

Relief surged through her like the breaking of a dam.

Will.

An instant later, however, she cursed her instinctual reaction to him. He was about to tangle yet another carefully woven segment of her life. And from his narrow-eyed glower at Conrad, he wouldn't be subtle about it, either.

Conrad recovered from his surprise with a haughty huff. "How dare you insinuate a connection with Lady Eleanor?"

"I insinuate naught," Will replied flatly.

Taking a step forward, Conrad swept Will with sneering brown eyes. "Will Stewart, wasn't it? What a curiosity you are here at Langley. To turn traitor to your own kind and come slithering on your belly to King Edward's court for his favor—an oddity indeed."

Eleanor stiffened, but to Will's credit, he didn't so much as blink at Conrad's barbed words. "If ye ken my name, then ye were in the hall to hear that I am at Langley because of an engagement." His good eye slid to Eleanor, who was still boxed against the wall behind Conrad.

"You would presume to lie to your betters?" Conrad hissed. "I am an English lord, you Scottish—"

"Ask Eleanor," Will cut in, lifting his chin toward her.

Conrad spun, pinning her with wide eyes.

"It's true," she said apologetically. She lifted her shoulders in a show of helplessness. "I am truly sorry, Lord de Russ, but I cannot go against my parents' wishes. The arrangement has already been settled."

Conrad stared open-mouthed at her for a long moment. Then his teeth clicked shut and his gaze turned cold. He bowed formally before her. "Apologies for my imposition then, Lady Eleanor. Good day."

He spun on his heels and strode toward the great hall, but as he passed, Will caught his arm. Even in the low light, Eleanor could see that Will's fingers were turning white from the force of his grip.

"From here on out, I'll thank ye kindly to keep yer hands off my fiancée, milord," Will said quietly. "Else I'll be forced to remove them from yer wrists. Do we understand each other?"

Conrad's neck stiffened and his nostrils flared, but he gave Will a curt nod. Instantly, Will released him, and Conrad hurried back into the great hall.

Will turned a searing gaze on Eleanor then. "Who the hell was that?"

"I really must return to the Queen. She will be wondering about me, and she'll expect me to help her prepare for tonight's feast."

Will extended his arm to her, his face set in a stubborn frown. "I'll walk ye there, then, and ye can explain on the way."

Eleanor sighed but took his arm and set out with him. "That was Conrad de Russ, one of the King's lesser nobles. He has traveled with Edward's court for a few years now." no job

"He seems to think he has some claim over ye."

Was that an edge of *jealousy* in his gruff voice? Nay, Eleanor corrected herself quickly. Will had made it clear that he had naught but disdain for her thanks to her secretiveness.

Just to annoy him, she waved her hand airily. "Oh yes, that is because I wanted him to."

A muscle in Will's forearm jumped under her palm. "Ye *wanted* that bastard to paw at ye?"

Eleanor dropped her voice. "Nay, but I wanted him to *think* I can be caught in his web. His estate is small and short on coin. He sees a match with me as advantageous, and so has been attempting to woo me for over a year now. And in that time, he has let a number of useful tidbits slip within my earshot."

Will's pace slowed as he absorbed that. "Which ye have used to yer advantage."

"To the *cause's* advantage," she corrected tightly. "If I recall, you accused me of neglecting to find a way into the King's inner circle. While I have not had to resort to using my body for such a purpose, I have found Conrad to be quite valuable. You see, when he travels with the King's court, he sees and hears far more than I ever could. And because he views me as a mere woman to wed and bed, he does not consider his words as carefully as he should in my company."

They reached the outer door to the Queen's private chambers then. Will drew them to a halt, but

96

instead of dropping his arm and returning to the hall, he lingered.

"A shame ye willnae be able to use him for information anymore," he said evenly, his gaze challenging her to contradict him. Again, she sensed a hint of possessiveness in the hard set of his jaw, but she couldn't be sure. His piercing gaze had a way of rattling her, making her second-guess her own intuition.

"Aye, thanks to you," she whispered, glaring at him. "Are you beginning to understand why I don't welcome your presence? In roughly a sennight you have managed to erode the Queen's trust in me and scare away one of my sources of information. At this rate, in another fortnight we'll both have our heads mounted on pikes outside the Tower of London."

That slow, knowing smile curved one side of his mouth. "I'm sure ye could use yer considerable skills to avoid such a fate, milady. In the meantime, I'll endeavor no' to underestimate ye as de Russ has."

He plucked her hand from his arm and bowed over it, brushing his lips against the back in a mock show of respect. Just as before, a jolt of awareness shot from her hand up her arm and into the pit of her stomach. Her skin rippled with tingling warmth that made her want to be rid of her confining gown.

Curse him for attempting to befuddle her.

"Does that mean you'll put more trust in me?" she

asked cautiously. "Give me space to continue my mission unimpeded?"

He straightened to his full height, her hand still enfolded in his. He snorted. "God, nay. It means I'll be even more vigilant than before. Now that I've had a glimpse of how that clever mind of yers works, I'll be more on guard for yer schemes."

He lifted her hand to his lips once more, branding her skin with his mouth for one long heartbeat.

And then he was gone, striding back toward the hall. She was left standing alone before the Queen's door, her heart pounding and her legs trembling unsteadily.

Chapter Ten

Will was staring, but he didn't care.

Nay, that wasn't exactly true. He *did* care, but he couldn't seem to stop himself.

He glowered over the rim of his silver goblet, watching the dancers circling in the middle of the great hall.

One dancer in particular, rather.

Eleanor wore a gown of deep scarlet brocade threaded with a pattern of golden birds in flight. Her hair was pinned up in a series of plaits and gold clasps so that the glossy chestnut locks caught with a shimmer in the light of the chandeliers overhead. It left her long neck and creamy décolletage exposed to all in the hall.

And if the lush swell of her breasts wasn't enough to hold his gaze, the back of her gown certainly was.

The laces trailing down her back were pulled snug to reveal her cinched waist, but they didn't stop at the base of her spine. Nay, the ribbons continued over the upper curve of her backside, highlighting her shapely bottom before the material flared more loosely over her hips and legs.

The courtiers had begun some circle dance where the women wove between the men in an elaborate pattern, eventually ending where they had started. Each time Eleanor took a turn around some grinning English dolt, Will was given a glimpse of that tantalizing view.

He took a long pull of ale, swallowing hard against the memory of that soft, supple bottom wedged between his legs atop his horse. Thank God he was not dancing with the others. He wouldn't be able to stand without revealing his evident desire.

Instead, he'd remained at a table below the raised dais for the entirety of the feast, glaring over his mug at every man who danced with Eleanor.

Despite his victory in winning Edward's trust earlier that day, he'd been in a foul mood all evening. The arrival of Edward and his retinue already nettled him. Their self-involved merrymaking grated like nails on slate.

But that wasn't the real source of Will's annoyance. The truth whispered in his ear. He'd been agitated ever since catching Conrad de Russ looming over Eleanor, about to take her lips in a kiss.

What was this woman doing to him? Aye, she was certainly bonny enough to catch his eye and fire his lust. But it was more than that. She was clever. Capable.

Cunning.

He drove that reminder into his brain like a hammered spike. She was as beautiful and polished as a pearl—and as slippery as one, too. He couldn't trust her, no matter the unwelcome heat she kindled in his veins. But at least in front of the others, he had some claim to her. To them, she was his fiancée.

His.

The possessiveness knotting his gut disturbed him. Blessedly, his dark musings were interrupted by the hushed voices of the King and Queen. They sat behind him on the dais, along with Hugh Despenser and a few other courtiers. Without daring to turn, Will leaned back in his chair, straining to hear their words.

"...don't understand why you can't simply take men from elsewhere," the Queen was saying, her voice low and tight. "The Tower of London, for example. You have hundreds of soldiers stationed—"

"I need men from *everywhere*," the King interjected. "Our defenses are already too thin in the north. And now with this blasted attack on Carlisle…"

The minstrels' music rose as the end of the dance approached, and the King's words were drowned out for a moment. As the women glided to their starting places and the dance concluded, the courtiers cheered and shouted for another song.

Only when the minstrels struck up a new tune and the courtiers repositioned themselves for another dance could Will pick up on the King and Queen's conversation once more.

"…be fine here, Isabella," the King said, annoyance edging his voice. "You have every comfort and plenty of guards to keep you sa—"

"That's what you said about Tynemouth Priory."

At the Queen's whispered hiss, the high table fell silent for several moments.

"This isn't up for discussion." Edward's voice rose with each word. "*I* am the King. *I* shall decide what to do with my own bloody soldiers."

Another man spoke then, his voice too low to discern his words, but Will guessed it was Despenser attempting to soothe Edward's pride.

Will was careful to keep his face blank, yet inside his thoughts roiled like a storm-swept sea.

The rift between Edward and Isabella had been evident upon their tense greeting earlier today. Even if

Will hadn't known about the events of Old Byland, their discord was plain.

But understanding the Queen's fear after nearly being captured, Edward's plan to siphon off some of the guards at Langley seemed cruel. Langley had been operating on a skeleton staff as it was before the King's arrival.

Which meant that Edward's need for soldiers must truly be great.

Mayhap he only meant to strengthen his northern border with more men. Or did he mean to launch a full-blown counterattack against the Scots at Carlisle?

The Bruce would certainly want to hear of any repositioning of soldiers along the border. What was more, if Edward planned to gather forces for a counterattack, the Scots at Carlisle needed to know so that they might be prepared.

A thought struck Will then. This was the sort of information—a casual word about Edward's movements, a squabble that revealed a counterplot—that Eleanor might overhear frequently, buried as she was so deep within the royal court.

It made her silence of late all the more damning. The lass had the Queen's favor, de Russ's loose tongue, and any number of other sources of information. Yet why hadn't she made a single report in over two months? Something didn't add up. What was she playing at?

"I grow weary of Langley already," the King muttered behind Will. "There is so little amusement here, and so many irritations."

The Queen sucked in a short breath at the insult. Edward ignored her, lifting his voice over the musicians. The minstrels' song died and those dancing skidded to a halt.

"This visit lacks entertainment," the King said testily. He paused, pursing his lips for a moment. Then he rose from his throne, his royal blue robes settling in rich waves around him. "What we need is a pursuit. For diversion. A tournament, mayhap."

The courtiers crammed into the hall murmured with excitement.

"Aye," the King continued, building momentum as he spoke. "A friendly tournament of three or four events. The winner of each individual event shall claim a prize of his choosing, and the man who performs best over the entire tourney shall be crowned King for a night at a grand feast."

The courtiers roared at that, stamping their feet and pounding each other on the back in anticipation of their grand tourney.

Will pretended to clap. While these men frittered their days away on amusements and faux competitions, other men's lives hung in the balance—their own countrymen, and his. He had far more important matters to occupy him than a damned fabricated tournament.

He needed to get word to the Bruce that Edward was gathering soldiers. But first, he had to confront Eleanor about her recent reticence. Enough was enough. It was time to have some answers.

Rising from his table, he began scanning the crowd for her. Fortunately, he stood at least a head higher than most of the English courtiers filling the hall. He could look over nearly all those gathered. What was more, her crimson gown should have been easy to spot.

But after his third sweep of the hall, there was no denying it.

She was gone.

Chapter Eleven

The roars of approval at the King's announcement echoing after her, Eleanor slipped from the hot, crowded hall and into the dimness of the passageway leading to the inner yard.

As she stepped out into the night-dark gardens, some of the tension eased from her shoulders. She breathed deeply of the cool, sweet air. It hung heavy with the smells of life—rich soil, budding flowers, verdant greenery. The moon was a silver shard overhead.

Only in these rare moments when no one was near, no eyes watching her, no ears waiting nearby to overhear, did she let herself lower her guard.

And only then did she truly feel the weight of the shield she carried every other moment.

Four years. Four *long* years of this life—lying, sneaking about, spying on everyone around her.

She still had her head, for which she was grateful, but the work had taken its toll. Dead was the innocent, trusting girl she'd been at seventeen, so hopeful for the future and rather moon-eyed over David. She'd lived an easy life before this—that was, until David had died and her whole world was flipped inside out.

She swallowed against the lump of sadness—and burning shame, even all these years later—at the memory of that terrible turning point. She could never forgive herself for what she'd done, nor forget.

But she did not regret what she had become in the years since David's death. Nay, she was proud of devoting her life to Scotland's cause for freedom. Nevertheless, it cut into her, etching away at her core. It had altered her the way a stream carved into a mountainside, the vein of water like a scar in the rock.

She sauntered over the dew-damp grass, suddenly too weary to worry about letting the hem of her fine gown drag. What would it be like to live a simple life, one free from deceit and lies? Mayhap it was too late for her. Mayhap she shouldn't even let herself fantasize about such a thing—a quiet, peaceful existence away from court and all its secrets.

Her thoughts heavy, Eleanor trailed through the tidy rows of the Queen's roses. Their fragrance was as heady as honeyed wine, their blood-red blooms limned in silver moonlight. She wandered toward a vine-covered bower where a bench was positioned to capture the view of the roses. At least here, for one moment, she might find tranquility.

But before she reached the bench, a hard hand clamped around her arm.

"You little tart."

Conrad spun her around and caught her by the shoulders with both hands.

Fear seized her, but she managed to repress the instinct to scream. There was a chance—albeit a small one—that she could find a way out of this situation without drawing attention or suspicion.

"Conrad," she breathed. "You startled me. What are you—"

"Leading me around by my cock all this time," he went on as if she hadn't spoken. "Making a fool of me in front of the King and the others."

He gave her a quick, hard shake that made her teeth clack together.

"And all so that you could trade me for another. A *Scot*, no less," Conrad hissed. "They are little more than slavering animals, Eleanor. Is that what you want? To exchange a nobleman for a barbarian? To *humiliate* me?"

Eleanor's pulse sped to a gallop. She fought to assess the situation calmly. Conrad was dangerous.

His temper was rapidly escalating beyond her control.

Her gaze flicked past him, searching for an excuse to return to the great hall. She'd come to the gardens for solitude, but now that she'd found it, she longed for the arrival of a courtier or servant to give her an opening to escape.

"Conrad, I am sorry," she began, lacing her voice with regret. "It is as I said—my parents made the arrangement. I had no choice in the matter. Believe me when I tell you that if it were up to me, I would never—"

"I find that hard to believe, given what happened before," he cut in.

Eleanor's insides turned to ice.

Conrad continued, seemingly unaware of her sudden panic.

"You couldn't have imagined that I didn't know about your past. Everyone does. And of course before I began courting you, I had to make assurances about your…*quality*. I could overlook your rather unfortunate history given that you are clearly in the Queen's good graces now. It seems you are innocent of all unsavory implications. But you expect me to believe that your family has made *another* Scottish connection for you? Nay, Eleanor, I think *you* want that Scottish mongrel."

"Conrad, I—"

"I suppose you enjoy all the attention." He glowered down at her with cold, dark eyes. "While you were leading me along, you were also busy setting your sights on him in my absence. My little notes of affection, the gifts I sent you—and you'll just walk away from me, free and clear. But you *owe* me for all I've done."

Simmering anger began melting the frozen fear in the pit of her stomach. This cowardly man, who would lay hands on a woman in anger, dared to insinuate that she was indebted to him because he'd scrawled a few notes and given her a few trinkets? His purpose had always been to use *her*, to gain her dowry and her connections with the Queen for his own advancement with the King.

She should have held her tongue, but she couldn't help herself. "But Conrad," she replied, all sweet innocence. "I thought the very definition of a gift was something offered freely and without obligation?"

Though Conrad wasn't particularly clever, he caught the gist of her indirect barb.

"You bitch."

Faster than she could blink, Conrad's hand lashed out and slapped her across the face. The air rushed from her lungs at the shock of the sting.

Conrad took the opportunity to shove her toward the shadows hugging the inside of the curtain wall.

"I'll take what should have been mine," he

muttered, pushing her again. "What *is* mine by rights."

Eleanor's back hit the wall's cold, hard stones. Her mind, which a moment before had raced with schemes and counterschemes, fear, anger, and a dwindling number of options to evade Conrad without causing a scene, suddenly went quiet. The door on alternate methods had closed. It was time to fight for her life.

One of Conrad's hands dropped from her shoulder to the front of his breeches, his other hand holding her in place. This was her opportunity.

With a swift jerk, she drove her knee between his legs.

A strangled sound rose in his throat and he froze, the hand on her shoulder clenching reflexively. She tried to twist out of his grasp, but his fingers dug deep into her flesh. A heartbeat later, he folded partway over with a groan, yet still he clutched her arm.

"You'll…pay…for…" He lifted a wobbling fist and drew back to strike her again.

Eleanor threw up a forearm to absorb the blow at the same instant she thrust her knee upward once more.

But her arm blocked naught and her knee whooshed through empty space, for Conrad no longer loomed over her. He went flying backwards and landed several paces away in a heap of silks.

And Will stood before her.

"Are ye hurt?" His voice was a raw, low rasp.

She exhaled sharply. "Nay."

Will spun on his heels and stalked toward Conrad, who was beginning to pick himself up with a moan. In one smooth motion, Will grasped one of Conrad's hands and twisted it behind his back, forcing Conrad back onto his knees.

"I believe I told ye if ye touched my fiancée again, I'd take yer hands. Mayhap I ought to break them instead." He torqued Conrad's wrist ever so slightly, and Conrad whimpered. "Would that make my intentions clearer?"

"Will."

His head snapped up and he fixed her with a blazing eye.

She shook her head slowly, praying he could read the meaning in her gaze. "Let us not give this matter any more *attention*. I do not wish to cause a scene."

His mouth tightened, but after a heartbeat, he dipped his chin in terse comprehension.

"Have I made myself clear enough, then, de Russ?" Will asked in a deadly calm tone.

Conrad began to nod, but when Will tweaked his wrist again, Conrad yelped and hurriedly said, "Aye, aye, you have."

"And has Lady Eleanor made herself clear as well?" Will dragged Conrad from his knees to his feet, gripping the back of his tunic and turning him to face Eleanor. "She doesnae want yer attentions anymore. Understand?"

"Aye," Conrad muttered, his gaze sliding away from Eleanor. "I understand."

"Then consider yerself a lucky bastard indeed, for the lady sees fit to let ye leave with only a kick to the bollocks. If it were up to me, I would cut them off."

Will gave Conrad a hard shove toward the main keep. Conrad stumbled away as fast as he could while still cupping his battered groin. When he reached the keep's doorway, however, he turned, pinning Will with a hate-filled glare.

ha "I cannot *wait* to beat your arse in the King's tourney tomorrow, you Scottish dog."

Before Will could reply, Conrad darted inside and slammed the door, no doubt fleeing back to the safety of the great hall like the coward he was.

In two strides, Will was before her. "Are ye truly well?"

"Aye, I am fine." Her voice sounded strangely flat and distant to her ears.

Will frowned. He lifted a hand between them slowly, showing her he meant no harm. Then he laid his palm on her shoulder.

"Ye are shaking, lass."

Carefully, he slid his hand around her back and guided her toward the bench beneath the bower.

Once she was seated, he drew the length of plaid from his shoulder and shook it out, then draped it around her.

The wool was surprisingly soft and still warm from Will's body. As before, it carried his scent, of the outdoors and clean male skin.

He sat down on the bench beside her. With a gentle hand, he took her chin, angling her face toward the moonlight. Her cheek must have been red from Conrad's slap, for Will made a displeased noise in his throat.

"He struck ye?"

"Aye."

"And pushed ye against the wall?"

"Aye."

The fingers on her chin remained soft, but Eleanor noticed that Will's other hand was clenched into a white-knuckled fist on his thigh. He must have realized the same, for he flexed the hand, letting a breath slide through his teeth.

"And ye kicked him in the bollocks?"

Eleanor met his gaze. "Aye."

His mouth eased then. "Good lass. I only wish ye would have let me give the bastard a few more injuries to nurse."

"No good would have come of it. We are in enough danger as it is without drawing unwanted attention to ourselves."

His brows lowered and his gaze slid over her face. "Aye, but all the same, I dinnae like him touching ye."

Eleanor's heart stuttered against her ribs. Something hot and possessive in the depths of his river-colored eye held her immobile. His hand lingered on her chin, his thumb tracing her jawline with a feathery stroke, neither pulling her to him nor easing her away.

Of its own accord, her gaze dropped to his mouth. She realized distantly that only a hand-span separated their lips. She could kiss him right now. What would his lips feel like? What would they taste like?

Some small, rational voice screamed in the back of her head that she wasn't thinking straight. Why on earth was she considering kissing this man, who so clearly distrusted her?

Nor did she trust him—not completely. But she could not deny the feeling of safety that enveloped her —like his plaid around her shoulders, warm and soft —whenever he was near.

What a tangled web she was caught in. Aye, Will's presence here was a threat—to her mission, and mayhap to both their lives. But in his blunt way, he had also dealt with Conrad far more effectively than she could have, which was a boon. Mayhap he truly could protect her from the dangers of court, as he'd claimed. Yet then again—

Eleanor closed her eyes. She was so tired of constantly running such assessments through her head. Calculating dangers and advantages, risks and gains every moment of every day.

She didn't want to think anymore. Only feel the warmth and solidity of him. Feel his mouth on hers.

Without further deliberation, she leaned forward and brushed his lips with hers.

Chapter Twelve

The softness of Will's mouth jarred Eleanor, sending tingling reverberations over her skin.

It had been so long.

Will, too, jerked at the grazing contact. He froze, seeming to wait for an indication from her that this wasn't some accident. She lingered, showing him silently that she didn't mean to pull away.

A long heartbeat passed. They both hung motionless, their mouths barely skimming. Then with a groan, Will pressed into her. His hand slid along her jaw to her nape, his fingers tangling in the coiled plaits at the back of her head. Sensation prickled from her lips to her scalp as he clenched his fist in her hair.

He seemed to surround her, his scent, his lips, his hands. She reached for him, laying her palms on his chest. His heart thudded swiftly under her fingers. He was so strong and warm. So steady under her touch, yet his kiss held an edge of urgency that belied his normal control.

He caught her lower lip between his teeth and nipped her, tugging a breath from her lungs. At the parting of her lips, he flicked her tongue with his, all satin heat. She sank into him then, surrendering to the kiss, to the mad desire tangling them together in this moment.

Their tongues delved and caressed, sending need spiraling through her. She was growing dizzy on it. She clung to his tunic, to the hard planes of him underneath. His hands had grown clumsy and rough, sinking into her back, clutching at her hair. She forgot how to breathe. Her lungs burned, her mind spun, but she hardly noticed over the blaze building inside.

Abruptly, he ripped his mouth away and lurched to his feet. She gasped for air, the night shockingly cold against her enflamed lips.

He kept his back to her, his shoulders rising and falling rapidly with his ragged breaths. He stood like that for a long time, revealing naught.

When he turned at last, his face was a mask of neutrality, yet his gaze was piercing and...uncertain.

"What the bloody hell was that?"

For the first time since she'd known him, Eleanor told the complete and unmitigated truth. "I don't know."

He scraped a hand over his face and around the back of his neck, letting his head hang forward. When he lifted his gaze again, his singular eye was narrowed.

"Was that some sort of ploy? Because if ye think ye can win my trust with wiles—"

The accusation stung enough to make her inhale sharply. "*Nay.*"

Will muttered another curse. He shook his head as if attempting to clear it. "I came looking for ye for a reason."

He began pacing in front of the bench, apparently struggling with how much to say to her. At last, he halted. "I overheard the King and Queen fighting. It seems Edward means to siphon soldiers from several locations—including Langley. He mentioned the border. And Carlisle."

That snapped Eleanor's attention back where it belonged—on her mission.

"The Scottish raid on the castle?"

"Aye, that was my first thought as well. Edward likely means to mount a defense, though he may also have grander plans in mind—another all-out attempt at a campaign, mayhap." He leveled her with a hard stare. "I mean to alert the Bruce."

Eleanor's chest compressed like a crumpled piece of parchment as she realized what she must do.

"The Queen was no doubt distressed at the

prospect of losing a portion of her guards," she said carefully.

"Aye," Will replied, frowning. "But her displeasure is of little import. It has no bearing on the need to get word to the Bruce's forces."

She rose slowly from the bench, smoothing her skirts. "Leave it alone."

"What?"

Eleanor met his incredulous stare. "I said leave it alone, Will. Do not send word to the Bruce. Not just yet, anyway."

"What do ye…" He blew out a harsh breath. "What do ye mean, *no' just yet*? Ye'd like me to sit on my thumbs instead, waiting for Edward to launch a counterattack against *my* countrymen?"

"We both know Edward isn't capable of gathering an army and mounting an assault in a matter of weeks. For God's sake, he's had *years* as England's King and hasn't managed to successfully initiate a significant campaign yet."

He took a step toward her. "Ye've accused me of no' understanding yer world here, of spies and secrets and lies. Well, ye dinnae understand a damn thing about open warfare, lass. Aye, Edward's victories have been few and far between, but soldiers have still given their lives and innocents have died along the way."

"I know that," she choked out. "I saw it firsthand

at Old Byland. And I want it to stop more than aught else. That is why I am asking you to wait."

"Why?"

She squeezed her eyes shut for a moment. "I cannot tell you."

"Because ye are no longer loyal?" he demanded, low and tight. "Because yer reasons would reveal yer treachery?"

"Nay."

"Dinnae claim again that ye cannae trust me," he snapped. "Ye have no reason to doubt me, yet ye give me *every* reason to doubt *ye*."

Eleanor swallowed. It was true that when he'd first arrived she was loath to confide in him, a complete stranger. But now it was something more.

"Have you ever heard the saying 'secrets have a way of ending in the grave'?"

He gave her an incredulous look. "So ye are taking yer secrets to the grave, then?"

"That is one meaning, but it also means that shared secrets, secrets spoken aloud, usually end in one or both people dead."

"Ye speak in riddles now," he muttered.

"The safest course is for me to keep the details of my larger play concealed," she continued. "I know I am asking a great deal, but I can assure you that what I am working toward has been months—*years*—in the making. You cannot see it now, but Edward's actions will ultimately help the Scottish cause."

"Is this about ye protecting the Queen? It is obvious ye are bonded to her. But dinnae be fooled, Eleanor. Just because ye havenae thrown yer lot in with Edward doesnae mean ye are still loyal to the Bruce. If ye are choosing her over yer mission—"

"It is quite the opposite," Eleanor snapped. She swallowed, fighting to regain her composure. "I cannot deny that Isabella has become a friend. It pains me to think of her in distress if Edward takes away some of her guards. But that is exactly what must happen in order for—"

"For what?" Will probed.

She stared up at him helplessly. She was so tired. Tired of lying and hiding. Only moments ago, their lips had been fused, his hands branding her body, her skin ablaze under her gown. But when reality came crashing back, they returned to this—squaring off against one another, Will seeking answers and Eleanor withholding them.

Could it ever be different between them? Could it ever be *more*? His kiss still warmed her lips. She had never felt so alive as she had a moment ago in Will's embrace. Not even with—

David.

The memory of him was like a splash of ice water against her face. Her heart twisted. Aye, she needed this. Needed a reminder of just what was at stake if she let her guard down and revealed all. Especially with Conrad sniffing about, calling into question their story about an engagement.

Still, her chest ached standing before Will, asking him to trust her and giving him no reason to.

"Please." The word came out a whisper. She held his gaze, lowering the shield behind her eyes and letting him see the turmoil inside—the fear, the pain, the doubt that gnawed at her.

And the longing—to confide in him. To gain his trust. To feed the fire that kindled between them.

He stared at her for a long moment. At last, he flinched, another curse slipping out under his breath. "Fine. I willnae seek to send a missive to the Bruce." He held up a warning finger. "Yet."

He brought his thumb beside his finger and drew them together until only a hair's breadth separated them. "I am giving ye this much leeway, Eleanor. Understand?"

"Aye."

"And ye should ken," he said darkly. "My trust, once lost, is lost forever. If ye betray that trust, if ye so much as—"

"I won't," she cut in. Relief swelled within her. "You can count on me, I swear it."

Will shook his head slowly. "I cannae believe I am doing this," he muttered.

"Thank you. Truly."

At the earnestness in her voice, his gaze lingered.

"We'd best return to the hall before the gossips take up our names."

"But we are engaged in their eyes," she said, watching him keenly for his reaction. "We are certainly allowed a few liberties."

"Aye," he said, his voice soft and low with promise. "I suppose we are."

Chapter Thirteen

❧❦❧

Will squinted against the brilliant sun. Fifty paces across the grassy field, the row of targets looked like little more than toys. But this was the furthest thing from some lighthearted game to him.

His hand tightened around his bow. *Damn it all to hell.* Why had he ever agreed to participate in this ridiculous mock tournament?

Earlier that morning, quite a few blade-edged jests had filled the great hall as the courtiers participating in Edward's little competition had broken their fast. More than one English nobleman had made a loud comment about being eager to try his abilities against a Scotsman.

It seemed Will was to be these peacocks' measuring stick. And though they believed him to be an English sympathizer, the enthusiastic glowers on their faces revealed that to them, this was some sort of test against all of Scotland.

They'd seemed eager to be shown their place, and Will had been all too eager to oblige.

Once the meal had concluded, the men had made their way through the palace gates and down the hillside to the open expanse below. A makeshift raised platform had already been erected on the grass, with a canopy of red and gold damask strung over it to provide shade from the cheery sun. Several chairs had been positioned on the platform for the King and Queen and their chosen companions.

Edward and Isabella had processed from the palace to the platform not long after the courtiers, with Hugh Despenser and the Queen's ladies, including Eleanor, trailing them. Despenser was to compete with the others, but he'd lingered by the King's side as long as possible.

The King had stood to make a few comments about the friendly nature of this tournament, and expressed the hope that both those watching and those participating would find ample amusement in the events.

But when the King announced that the first event of his tourney would be archery, Will's stomach had plummeted.

Now he stood with the others, bow in hand,

waiting for the first round to begin. There were to be multiple rounds, with each man getting three arrows per turn. Half of the archers would advance to the next round based on their three shots, until only one man with the best cluster remained.

But even without taking a single shot, Will knew that man wouldn't be him. Nay, he was about to prove just how incapable he was. It felt as though a stone sat on his chest. He couldn't do this.

Even as a handful of the other courtiers began taking a few practice aims, Will turned his back on the targets, muttering a curse. His gaze landed on the raised platform. Edward leaned back in his throne, his legs lazily crossed. Despenser's empty chair sat on his right, and the Queen on his left. Eleanor was positioned on the Queen's other side with the rest of the ladies-in-waiting.

She wore a sky-blue silk gown with a cream-colored underdress that poked out along her wrists and at her scooping neckline. Besides two woven strands that were pulled back from her heart-shaped face, her hair fell in a cascade of polished chestnut over her shoulders. Even from several dozen paces away, he could feel the intensity of her gaze on him.

He didn't care what the King of England thought of him. Nor did he give a damn about the others on the platform, nor the nobles who weren't competing who stood clustered around its base. Though he relished the opportunity to best every one of the score of men participating in the event, he didn't truly need to prove aught to them.

But he couldn't say the same about Eleanor. Damn him, he *did* care how she viewed him. Especially after what had happened the night before.

He had nearly lost his mind at the sight of Conrad de Russ pinning her against the shadowy wall. Touching her. Hurting her. They were both lucky he hadn't beaten the bastard until he was unrecognizable. Eleanor was right that they didn't need the added attention. But still, his blood had been running hot, the need to expel some pent energy nigh painful.

And then she'd kissed him.

He'd practically come out of his skin at the desire it had unleashed inside him. If he hadn't put a stop to it in the nick of time, who knew what trouble they would have gotten themselves into?

Aye, and it would have been trouble. *She* was trouble, for despite all reason, he'd granted her a sliver of his trust. It very well might cost him his life. But something in the depths of those velvet-brown eyes bewitched him, worming its way inside his chest.

Making him care.

Mayhap being forced into an archery competition in front of her was fate's cruel jest. Or mayhap it was a reminder of why he should keep his distance. Sometimes those in whom one placed trust were the very ones to betray it.

"Did you sleep well last night, Stewart?"

Will snapped his gaze from Eleanor to find Conrad de Russ sauntering toward him, his bow slung over one shoulder.

"No' particularly," Will grated out, leveling Conrad with a narrow-eyed glare. "Something kept nagging at me—a sense that I'd left something unfinished, I suppose."

Conrad came to a halt before him. "I imagine you had a taste of that tart last eve." He tipped his head in Eleanor's direction. "Mayhap you found it satiating, but in *my* experience, it grows rather bland and unsatisfying after a while."

Will took it back. He *did* wish he'd pounded Conrad's face until he could never smirk again, the consequences to his mission be damned.

"But we Englishmen have a more refined palate than the Scots," Conrad continued, cold arrogance nigh dripping from his dark eyes. "I doubt you would notice the difference between a woman like Eleanor and a common who—"

His words were cut off as Will's hand clamped around his throat. Will moved close enough that he could speak softly into Conrad's ear. "Go on, say another word. Put her name in yer mouth again. Give me an excuse to rip out yer tongue and feed it to the King's pigs."

"Take your spots, men!" a squire called nearby. "The first round is about to begin."

As the courtiers hurried to their shooting lines, Will and Conrad drew several stares. Murmuring an oath, Will released Conrad's throat and turned away as if naught had transpired.

But it seemed Conrad didn't know what was good for him, for he took the open shooting lane directly beside Will.

"You are full of grand threats and rough words, Stewart," Conrad said, nocking his first arrow. "But the truth is, you cannot do aught to me. I am a nobleman, one of King Edward's courtiers. And what are you, other than a landless, titleless Scottish brute with only one eye?"

The horn sounded at the end of the row to initiate the first round. Will yanked an arrow from the quiver on his back, nocked it, and fired without bothering to take aim. Even if he had, it wouldn't have made a difference.

The arrow caught the outermost edge of his target. Without pausing, he drew his second arrow and let it fly. It hit the wooden stand upon which the target was propped. His third flew over the target altogether and skittered across the grass behind it.

Spinning on his heels, he tossed his bow and empty quiver to the ground and strode away.

Conrad's sharp laughter followed him. "Good God. Is this what we can expect from Stewart for the rest of the tourney?" A few other courtiers snickered. "No wonder the Scots don't want him on their side."

Will clenched his fists against the urge to face Conrad's taunts. Aye, he could thrash the man into oblivion, but he was right about Will's abilities, at least when it came to archery.

He stomped toward the palace, leaving the event —which was to last several more hours—behind.

Chapter Fourteen

Eleanor's gaze tracked Will until he disappeared through the palace gates. Something was clearly amiss with him. What was more, he'd drawn a fair deal of attention for storming off after such a disastrous performance.

She attempted to focus on the rest of the first round, but her eyes kept tugging over her shoulder in search of him.

As the courtiers finished firing their arrows and the shots were tallied, the Queen's gaze slid to Eleanor.

"The sun is very bright today."

Eleanor nodded distractedly. "Aye, Highness."

"I believe it has made you weary."

At Eleanor's puzzled look, the Queen continued.

"Mayhap you had better retire to your chamber,

Eleanor," she said, lifting her brows meaningfully. "Give yourself the remainder of the day to rest. The other ladies can attend me."

But as Eleanor rose, the Queen caught her hand, halting her. "Remember, friend, a man's pride is more fragile than the finest glass." She dropped her voice. "I'm sure you can find a way to put the poor dear back together, though. I have so enjoyed seeing the two of you grow fond of one another of late."

Eleanor coughed in surprise. "*Fond*, Highness?"

"Well…" The Queen's mouth lifted into a smile. "Mayhap that isn't the exact word for what a new couple does alone in the gardens. Aye, I saw you return to the great hall together through that passageway last eve. Oh Eleanor, you should have seen the way he was looking at you all night. Like he meant to devour you."

A flush that had naught to do with the warm day climbed up Eleanor's neck and into her face.

"I…"

Isabella squeezed her hand. "Go. Enjoy yourself." Her face clouded for a heartbeat before smoothing once more, but melancholy lingered in her blue eyes. "There is so little joy in the world. Take yours where you can, dear Eleanor."

The Queen released Eleanor's hand with an encouraging smile. Little did she know that Eleanor meant to upbraid Will for attracting so much unwanted attention, not soothe his pride with sweet intimacies. Still, she was grateful for the opportunity to leave the tourney.

She stepped from the platform and strode up the hill toward the palace. Once she was inside, her feet carried her toward their adjoining chambers. She suspected Will would go there to be alone.

As she rounded a corner just before her chamber, she spotted a servant approaching at the other end of the corridor. She had been intending to go straight to Will's door, but she hesitated.

The Queen might think herself quite forward-thinking with her French outlook on relations between unwed men and women, but this was England, and servants spread gossip. So Eleanor slipped into her own chamber, waiting behind her closed door until the servant's footsteps echoed away.

Only then did she move to the door that adjoined her chamber with Will's, lifting the heavy bar. She pushed open the door to find him perched on the edge of his bed, a dagger and a whetstone in his hands and his gaze fixed on her.

"Didnae expect ye to ever use that door," he said gruffly before returning his attention to the dagger.

"Desperate times call for desperate measures." She closed the door behind her and crossed her arms over her chest. "What the hell are you doing?"

He gave her a flat glance. "What does it look like?

I'm sharpening the only bloody weapon I have to my name at the moment. The damned guards may have my sword, but they forgot to check my boot for this."

"Nay, I mean what were you doing out there. In the archery event."

"This is bloody ridiculous," he muttered, dragging the whetstone along the blade. "The entire thing. Those men out there—they are so bored that they resort to playing at warfare. In Scotland, when we fight, we dinnae do it for fun."

"Well, you're in England now," she shot back, "pretending to be a loyal subject serving at the pleasure of King Edward. You aren't supposed to act any different from the other courtiers. Instead you cause a scene and storm off like a petulant child."

"I was going to lose anyway. No point drawing it out for all to see."

Annoyance building in her like a stoked flame, she stalked toward the bed. "You could have at least tried. I watched you shoot. You didn't even bother to aim."

"It wouldnae have made a difference," he replied tightly.

"But why couldn't you—"

"Because of *this*." He jerked the tip of the dagger up, pointing it at his eye patch. His other eye pinned her with a glower. "I cannae gauge distances anymore, nor perceive the depth of things. It makes it bloody hard to hit a target without both of those abilities." He bent, jamming the dagger into the concealed sheath in his boot. "Satisfied now?"

Eleanor's anger drained away like water from a leaky bucket. She remained rooted before him, studying his obvious irritation.

"This isn't just about the archery competition, is it? There is something more."

He gave her a dismissive glance. "What are ye getting at?"

"I watched you when you told the King that you'd lost your eye in a hunting accident. That was a lie."

Will stood, striding past her and toward the window. He drew back the shutters and squinted out at the bright day. "And I suppose ye think ye can always tell when someone is lying."

Eleanor smiled faintly. "As you've pointed out before, it is my job."

He closed the shutters testily and moved to the hearth. Snatching up a poker, he stirred the ashes despite the fact that no fire had burned there since earlier that morning. "Aye, well, ye are supposed to be watching the King, no' me."

"What happened?" she continued, undaunted by his sudden caginess.

Will tossed the poker aside and turned back to the window. When he opened the shutter once more, the sunlight caught on his hair, turning it dark gold. She was reminded of the lion in Edward's menagerie, wary and uneasy, powerful yet trapped.

"Why the hell do ye want to ken?"

"Because whether we like it or not, we have been thrown into each other's lives for the foreseeable future. Because we've been forced to trust each other, but mayhap we could choose to, also."

His gaze snapped to hers.

"Have ye lain with Conrad de Russ?"

Eleanor sputtered at the abrupt swerve in the conversation. "What?"

"Conrad de Russ," he practically growled. "Have ye shared intimacies with him?"

"I don't see how that relates to…"

"He claimed to have…*sampled* yer charms."

"Damn him," she hissed. "That pompous, lard-headed, lying—"

"I take it he misled me, then?" Will was watching her cautiously, his shoulders rigid.

Through the thick fog of anger blanketing her mind, a realization cut through her like a shaft of light.

Will was indeed jealous. And at least part of his brooding frustration was because of it. Aye, he was clearly prickly about his eye, but he was also furious over the thought that Eleanor had let Conrad take liberties with her.

"Whatever that horse's arse told you, it was a lie,"

137

she said, taking a step toward him. "He has not so much as earned a kiss from me. The only man I have…given myself to was David."

Will released a breath. He raked a hand through his hair, clearly struggling with something that Eleanor couldn't quite grasp. Silence fell over the chamber for several moments.

"The truth about David bothers you more than the lies Conrad told you?" she ventured.

"Nay, for I cannae be angry with a dead man. Besides, if ye gave yerself to David willingly, he must have been one hundred times the man de Russ is."

Some of the tension eased from her neck at that, but another question rose to her tongue.

"Does it offend you to know that I am not an innocent, then?" she asked evenly. She didn't care what he thought of her, she told herself firmly. Her choices were her own. Yet she held her breath as she waited for his answer.

"Nay," he replied without hesitation. He shook his head, one corner of his mouth tugging up. "The fact is, Eleanor, regardless of whether ye are a virgin or no', ye are far from innocent."

Though the same words spoken a few days earlier might have been an insult, a curious respect glinted in Will's gaze. A moment later, though, it was gone, replaced once more with uncertainty.

At last, he spoke quietly. "Will ye…will ye tell me of him?"

Eleanor froze. "David?"

"Aye."

She opened her mouth to offer an instant denial. The memories were painful enough inside her head. She didn't need to make them worse by speaking them aloud.

But as she met his searching gaze, the rebuff died on her tongue. She had asked him to open up to her, to tell her the truth about what had happened to his eye when clearly the topic grated on him.

And he had accepted her plea to leave the matter of Edward's plans untouched for the time being. He'd extended a thin thread of trust to her, despite the fact that she had been cagey and at times downright hostile since his arrival.

After David, it had become instinctual for Eleanor to conceal, evade, lie. She'd done what was necessary to protect herself. But she wasn't alone in this world anymore. Will knew who she was—or at least, he knew she was a spy. She could reveal so much more to him. Mayhap everything someday.

It could start with this moment.

On stiff legs, she turned and walked back to the bed. She rested her palm on one of the bed's oak posters, taking strength from its solidity.

Then she began to speak.

Chapter Fifteen

"He was Scottish."

Will's brows shot up in surprise. Some part of him hadn't truly expected her to agree to open up to him.

She glanced over her shoulder at him. "A Lowlander—a true Lowlander," she continued with a wobbling smile. "Not like you."

"How did ye come to be engaged?"

"His clan—the Maxwells—claimed the lands directly across the border from my family's estate. We were engaged practically from birth. The Maxwells had remained neutral in the early years of the Scottish fight for freedom. So close to the border, they understood that they needed to remain on good terms with both their Scottish and English neighbors."

Will nodded slowly. "The politics of distant Kings

often has little to do with how people must live each day."

"Precisely. Many along the border found the wars at odds with the practicalities of living side by side with each other. The Maxwells and the de Monteneys proved that. They saw the potential for a powerful marriage alliance. David and I were to wed when we came of age. Knowing that from the first, our families allowed us to spend time together, get to know one another. We grew fond of each other, which developed into a youthful love. He was…kind."

She visibly swallowed, her slim throat tightening. Then she sank down on the edge of the bed, mindlessly arranging her skirts.

Will saved her from having to speak while she fumbled for composure. He pursed his lips in thought. "Kindness isnae often a trait ye find in these times of war. Especially no' along the border." He met her gaze. "He must have been a good man."

Sudden tears filled her eyes—tears of sorrow for David's memory, no doubt. But Will also saw a shimmer of gratitude at his understanding in the depths of her chestnut gaze. "He was," she whispered. She blinked until the tears abated. "But as you say, it was a tumultuous time. We who lived through the turmoil along the border were changed by it. Including David."

"How so?"

"David wasn't exactly loyal to England, but nor did he overtly support the Bruce's cause—at least at first. But as the war stretched on and the Bruce kept fighting, many Scots along the border who had intentionally remained neutral could no longer ignore matters. There was honor in the Bruce's cause—he fought *for* something. And what could be a more valiant cause than freedom? The more the English tried to take it away from them, the harder the Scots fought. David was moved by that."

"David's allegiance shifted?"

"Aye. As did mine."

Will approached, assessing her. "What do ye mean?"

"I grew up in an English household. My family was in the King's good graces. We were even invited to Isabella and Edward's wedding. Without ever considering why, I thought myself a staunch supporter of England—until David began discussing his doubts with me."

Eleanor's gaze drifted to the still-open window behind him, clearly losing herself in the memory of that time and place.

"We would often meet at the border and ride together, speaking of everything in our hearts. David began to tell me of the battles that raged elsewhere alone the border. Sheltered girl that I was, I had no idea the English were killing whole villages of innocents, women and children, and burning everything to the ground—crops, homes—all in an attempt to subdue the Scots, to deny them the freedom to rule themselves."

She gave her head a little shake before continuing.

"After a few years of such news, David could not accept it any longer. He resolved to join the Bruce's cause, but the Maxwells as a whole, fearful of facing retaliation no matter whom they sided with, were still intentionally neutral. So he decided to keep his allegiance a secret."

"Any ye?" Will asked cautiously. "Where did ye fall in all of this?"

"I was but seventeen then. Yet David had opened my eyes. I could no longer turn away from the atrocities committed by my own countrymen. I vowed that once we were married, I would join him in doing aught in our combined power to help the Bruce's cause."

A stone of foreboding sank in the pit of Will's stomach. "But I gather things didnae go according to plan."

Eleanor's jaw clenched. "Not long before our wedding, a Scot approached David in secret. He said he'd heard of David's loyalty and hoped to find a purpose for it, a way for David to help the cause. He knew of David's impending marriage to me and saw an opportunity. Because he was marrying into the favored de Monteney family, David would be invited to court. The man suggested that David might see and hear all manner of useful things as a guest of King Edward's."

Understanding dawned. "He recruited David to be a spy."

"Aye. David was uncertain, for he didn't like the idea of using my family, nor potentially involving me in something dangerous. On one of our rides, he told me everything and asked what he ought to do. I, too, was unsure. Isabella, especially, had been kind to me in the few times I had met her. I didn't want to betray her. But the prospect of saving innocent lives with only a few overheard tidbits of information was powerful. So I…"

Her throat closed on the words then. Whatever was coming next clearly hurt her greatly to say aloud.

Will crouched on his haunches before her so that his gaze was level with hers. He kept his voice soft.

"Go on, lass. It's all right."

"I was so foolish," she whispered. "I was still not yet eighteen, but that is no excuse. I was too naïve to the reality of things, too trusting."

As fresh tears gathered in her eyes, Will longed to reach for her, to pull her against his chest and make her pain stop. But there was more to tell.

"I…I went to my mother and father," she said. "I told them what David was considering and asked their advice. I thought that after all they'd seen with their own eyes, they would be sympathetic, as David had been, to Scotland's strife, and open to the possibility of aiding them. But I was so, so wrong."

Damn it all. "What did they do?" Will asked, his voice like granite.

"They were horrified. Called David a traitor and me a thoughtless child. But they also asked for time to consider all I'd said. Fool that I was, I believed they might still come around. Unbeknownst to me, they sent word to an English garrison nearby, naming David a Scot-sympathizing conspirator with plans to spy on the King himself. That night, a hundred soldiers were sent to Maxwell lands. They...they trampled crops, burned crofts, and stormed the Maxwell stronghold. And they t-took David. I n-never saw him again."

Her delicate features crumpled and her voice broke on a whimper.

Will reached for her then, enclosing her shaking shoulders in his arms, silently willing her to take strength from him.

"Shh," he murmured into her hair. "Easy, lass."

She gulped several breaths against his chest, fighting to regain control.

When she spoke, her voice was flat and hollow. "I learned later that he was named a traitor and beheaded. It was a small mercy, but he was dead before they quartered and disemboweled him back at the garrison. They mounted his head on a pike and left his entrails in the mud for the ravens." *omg*

She shook her head as if to be rid of the dark images inside. "At least I didn't see him like that. At least my last memory of him is of his smiling face. But I know clinging to that minuscule blessing is selfish of me. He is dead and it is my fault."

"Nay, Eleanor, ye cannae—"

She rocked out of his embrace, dashing the tears from her eyes with her palms. When she lowered her hands, her eyes had gone hard.

"I vowed after that to serve David's memory by giving my life to the cause that we both believed in so completely. David was supposed to meet with the man who'd approached him a sennight later. Thank God I did not tell my parents that, else he, and likely I, would be dead right now as well. I went to the meeting in David's place."

So this was how an English noblewoman became a spy for the Scots. "Who was this man?" Will asked gently.

"His name is James MacGregor."

Will frowned but nodded. He recognized the name, though he hadn't met the man. "He works in Sabine MacKay's network of messengers and spies, correct?"

"Aye, he told me as much—after I explained what

had happened to David and insisted that I wanted to take his place."

"And he agreed?"

Despite the sadness in her eyes, Eleanor half-smiled. "Well, nay, not at first. But I was insistent. And persuasive."

Will snorted. "Aye, I can imagine."

"I told him that I was already familiar with a few of the King's palaces, having visited them with my family, and that I had a rapport with the Queen. I also pointed out that people were far less suspicious of women, especially young women. For all that men like Conrad de Russ think to take advantage of us, we are also disregarded as feather-headed and insignificant. When I explained all this, MacGregor agreed to be my point of contact within the Bruce's cause."

"Is that how ye ended up here at Langley, then?"

"Nearly. My parents also played a part, though they didn't realize it. They feared David's death would tarnish their reputation, so they requested that I be given a position as one of the Queen's ladies-in-waiting. They imagined that if I—and by extension, they—were welcomed into court, it would prove our innocence and loyalty. Unknowingly, they put me in the perfect position to spy."

Will considered that for a moment. "How much does the Queen ken of all this?"

"She knows that I was engaged to a Lowlander,

and that he turned against England. She also knows that I loved him, for I was a bit of a mess the first few months in her service, grieving as I was for David. But she accepted me as an innocent in the matter, and she's never given any indication that she suspects my true purpose here. That was why she was surprised at your arrival. She likely found it hard to believe my parents would arrange for me to marry another Scot."

"And why ye said my presence endangered ye," Will concluded. "Yer second Scottish fiancé undoubtedly reminds people of the circumstances surrounding the first."

She nodded solemnly. "It raises questions that are difficult to answer. Conrad has already voiced his suspicion. I can only imagine what others are thinking and saying behind my back."

"And if yer parents discovered our lie about being engaged—"

"They won't," she cut in. "They were all too happy to send me to court and be rid of me four years past—as I was them. Privately, I believe they no longer think of me as their daughter, which is just as well. They put their fealty to a distant King above their future son-in-law's life. They are naught but strangers now."

Eleanor fell silent then, her story apparently concluded.

Will absorbed all she'd said, tumbling it over in his mind.

She was a strong lass, that was for damn sure. After the man she'd loved had been given a traitor's death, she still had the courage to go into the heart of this vipers' den and risk her own life to help the Scottish cause.

Guilt pinched his stomach. He'd called her loyalties into question many a time, not knowing how much she'd lost, how much she'd sacrificed to be here.

Then again, she still hid whatever larger plan she had concocted.

Secrets have a way of ending in the grave, she'd said.

Though she had entrusted him with the knowledge of her past, she still meant to protect herself— and mayhap him, he realized with a start—by keeping some of her secrets.

At least now he understood her reasons for withholding information. She felt responsible for David's death. She blamed herself for sharing the information that had led to his demise. And now she seemed determined never to make the same mistake again.

"I appreciate ye telling me all that," he murmured. "I ken it is an act of trust for ye."

Eleanor stood abruptly, smoothing her skirts. "Aye, well. Now you know about David."

He rose, too, studying her in confusion. She

looked at the floor, then at the walls behind him— anywhere but directly at him.

With a softening heart, he realized she was scared —scared to have just opened up to him so deeply. She likely felt vulnerable, exposed. She had probably rarely—or mayhap never—spoken of the events surrounding David's death and her decision to become a spy. And who would she tell? Even the Queen, with whom she shared a close companionship, couldn't know the truth about David, nor Eleanor's dedication to Scotland's cause for freedom.

This woman appeared as smooth and polished as a pearl on the outside. Yet like a pearl, she had been formed out of grit and salt and struggle. And now she feared being crushed under his boot for having shown the fragility beneath her outward luster.

"Ye ken ye dinnae need to be afraid," he offered quietly. "Yer secrets are safe with me. *Ye* are safe with me."

She darted a glance at his face. She murmured something under her breath—Will couldn't be sure, but it sounded like *If only that were true.*

Her dark gaze lingered for a moment, dropping to his mouth, and of its own accord, his body warmed in response.

Eleanor ripped her eyes away and turned back to the door that adjoined their chambers. "I ought to return to the tournament. I'll make an excuse for you if you'd like, but remember what I said earlier about avoiding unwanted attention."

"Eleanor."

She yanked back the tapestry covering the door and reached for the handle, ignoring him. "You must play your part at tomorrow's events," she continued. "No more slinking back to your chamber to sulk and—"

"*Eleanor.*" He caught her by the waist, turning her to face him.

Damn, but his hands seemed made to rest in the soft inward curve there. A breath slipped between her lips at the contact. She stared up at him wide-eyed. She didn't pull away.

"I…" He swallowed. "I have been thinking about that kiss."

"Aye?"

Bloody hell. He wanted to tell her that he had barely slept the night before, knowing that she was just on the other side of the door. That he ached to taste her lips again. That he had been hard with wanting her—all of her.

But something else needed to be said instead.

"It cannot happen again."

Her brows dipped in surprise. "What?"

"It was a mistake."

Even as he forced the words out, his body betrayed him. His hands burned where they lingered on her waist. He dipped his head closer, letting her soft scent, of rosewater and sweet woman, wrap around him like a caress.

"Becoming…entangled could endanger us both," he continued, his voice husky. "And it would confuse things in an already complicated situation."

She drew back her chin slightly, blinking. He didn't miss the hurt in the depths of her eyes before she shuttered them behind a mask of indifference. "Aye. Of course."

Spinning on her heels, she yanked the door open and darted through it, leaving him staring at the swishing tapestry in her wake. The door thudded close behind her.

With a muttered oath, Will's head sank against the tapestry. He listened for a moment, but the telltale sound of the bar being lowered did not come. Instead he heard a faint rustle of fabric. Eleanor was leaning on the other side of the door.

Will slid the tapestry aside and pressed one palm against the cool oak. God, how he wanted to pull the door open, haul Eleanor into his arms, and take that sweet mouth of hers in another kiss.

Something burned between them—something untamed and dangerous, like a wildfire that consumed an entire forest in its blaze. He had to keep this desire in check, lest it destroy them both.

At last, he heard her release a shaking breath,

followed by the swish of her skirts as she crossed her chamber and slipped out.

Yet Will remained standing before the door, struggling to cool the raging need burning him up inside.

And failing.

Chapter Sixteen

"Tell me again why we cannae simply charge at each other with lances. I thought that was the way these preening English courtiers liked to play at battle."

Eleanor glanced around to make sure no one had overheard Will, then cast him a pointed look. "Remember yourself, Will *Stewart*," she said.

He rolled his eyes, then put a false grin on his face. "Och, I do. I cannae imagine a better use of an entire day than horse racing, for naught is more important to me than the amusement of the King of England."

She almost snorted at the upward cant of his voice as he imitated a stuff-shirted nobleman. Fortunately, she managed to keep her features sober.

"The King does not like jousting," she informed him. "As the heir to the English throne, his father,

Edward I, would not permit him to participate with the other young men."

"And so because Edward cannae enjoy it, no one else can," Will finished, lifting a brow. "Sounds about right."

"He is very fond of horsemanship, however."

Will cast a dry look around. "Hence we are here, ready to serve at his pleasure."

They were once again gathered on the grassy flatlands below the palace. It was another brilliantly sunny day. The two dozen or so courtiers participating in the competition all stood about, checking their tack for the hundredth time. The King and Queen already sat on the platform not far away.

Though the race itself would only take a matter of minutes, it had been turned into an entire day's event, beginning with a parade and an inspection of the animals. The King himself had then picked the route, making sure the ground was dry along the way to protect the horses. Once that was settled, there had been much grooming, chest-puffing, and milling about.

Eleanor ran a hand down the shoulder of Will's giant bay stallion. "Are you sure you don't wish to use one of the King's coursers? Several of the others—"

"Nay, Fearghus can handle a wee race."

She eyed the enormous animal. He was longer of leg than many of the other men's horses, but he was also barrel-chested and heavy of hoof, unlike the sleek coursers designed for speed and agility. He was certainly more suited to jousting—or all-out warfare —than racing.

"At least this is preferable to archery, is it not?" she offered.

The brow above his eye patch lifted sardonically. "Aye, it is that."

"To the starting line!"

At the squire's call, the courtiers leapt into action. Making their final adjustments and inspections, they began mounting and leading their horses to a ribbon laid on the grass before the King's raised platform.

Eleanor turned to hurry back to the Queen's side, but she paused partway and glanced over her shoulder. Will was swinging easily into the saddle, his long, muscular legs flexing.

"Good luck."

He nodded to her, then tossed her a lopsided grin. "Unless I finish last, it will be an improvement on yesterday."

Fighting a smile, she tipped her head and continued on toward the platform. Clutching her skirts, she hoisted herself up and sat in her chair beside the Queen.

"He seems in finer spirits today than yesterday," Isabella commented casually, her eyes following Will as he nudged his stallion to the starting line. "I see you took my advice and...*soothed his pride.*"

Eleanor bit the inside of her cheek. She hated lying to Isabella, but it was safer to let her believe that she and Will were developing an affection for one another.

The fact was, Eleanor wasn't entirely sure what was happening between them. Since yesterday, when she'd told him of David and her past, she noticed a subtle softening in his demeanor toward her. He no longer glowered at her with cold suspicion. Instead, this morning he was...well, not warm, exactly. He was still rough-edged and brusque as ever. But he was at least attempting to play the part of a cheerful courtier, unlike yesterday. And he had even managed a few jests with her.

Still, whatever trust existed between them was as delicate as a single thread of spider's silk. With so many secrets remaining, it seemed too much to hope that their truce would hold.

And then there was the matter of his rebuke yesterday. When he'd mentioned their kiss, her heart had nearly leapt from her chest. The memory of it made her hot beneath her constricting gown. She'd thought he meant to kiss her again—only to be told it was an error that could not be repeated.

He was right, of course. Curse him. It was a

mistake to have kissed him. A mistake she could not seem to stop thinking about.

Eleanor gave the Queen a demure smile. "I am a lady, Highness. I'm sure I have no idea what you mean."

Isabella chuckled softly, shifting her attention back to the racers.

Unlike yesterday's archery competition, there were to be no rounds. Instead all two dozen competitors would take off at the sound of a horn and run the course as fast as possible. The first man across the finish line would not only win the event, but also move closer to winning the entire tournament.

The King had devised a point system to determine who would be crowned the victor of the whole tourney. Ten points to the winner of each event, five for second place, and three for third place.

To Eleanor's displeasure, Conrad had come in second in the archery event yesterday. Hugh Despenser had been third, and a nobleman named John Alderly had won. Will certainly didn't need to be crowned the tournament's champion, but a small, petty part of her at least wanted him to beat Conrad.

Her gaze landed on him as he took his place with the others. He was easy to pick out, sitting a head above the rest of the courtiers, his hair glinting with threads of gold in the sunlight. While the other horses shifted nervously under their riders, Fearghus stood like a boulder, clearly taking his cue from his steady master.

With everyone in their places, the squire hurried over to the base of the platform. He lifted a horn to his lips and looked at the King, who raised his hand. Edward paused, seeming to savor the anticipation, then jerked his hand down like a hammer. The squire blew into the horn and the horses exploded off the line, tearing away across the grass.

They rode as a pack at a dead gallop toward the tree line in the distance, the ground thundering in their wake. Eleanor sat up straight in order to keep her gaze locked on Will amongst the teeming throng of riders.

Only when they reached the edge of the forest and made a sharp turn to the right did their grouping begin to thin out. While some of the less capable courtiers had to rein in hard or cut a wide arc to make the turn, the more accomplished riders sliced a tight corner and shot ahead.

Will was among the front-runners. What his horse lacked in maneuverability or lightness, Will made up for in sheer skill. He leaned over the stallion's neck as the horse broke into a gallop for another straight stretch of the course.

They were to ride the length of the forest's eastern border, make another turn, then ride like hell for the ribbon line where they'd started. As the racers continued along the forest's long edge, the gap between those in the lead and those behind grew wider until a cluster of six were more than twenty strides ahead of the rest.

Eleanor squinted as they approached the farthest corner of the course. Will was at the back of the group of leaders. His stallion's strides seemed slower than the others, but his long legs allowed him to hold his ground, neither losing nor gaining on them.

They reached the second turn, and again Will demonstrated his mastery with the animal. Clods of dirt flew from the stallion's hooves as Will reined him into a tight corner. At Will's urging, the stallion charged out of the turn, and suddenly he was in the middle of the pack.

The Queen clapped her hands, grinning at the display of skill. Eleanor pressed her lips together, her heart thundering in her chest as fast as the horses' hooves.

The six horses in the lead now entered the final straightaway, charging toward the finish line. Two coursers shot out in front of the rest, jockeying for position, but after a few dozen paces, their energy flagged and they fell back. All the while, Will's stallion maintained a steady speed, consuming ground with his deceptively long gait.

Another one of the riders who'd been alongside Will in the middle of the pack began to fall away.

Half the distance remained to the ribbon, and now only two horses remained in front of Will.

The rider behind the leader made his play, digging his heels into his horse's flanks to spur one final surge of speed from him. The horse briefly moved ahead, challenging the leader. But then the leader made his own move, shooting forward for the final hundred paces.

The second horse began to fade, his energy spent. Will passed him, still driving his stallion at a steady, punishing gallop.

Beside the Queen, Edward leaned forward in his chair, his eyes riveted on the race. The leader had opened a several-stride lead over Will. Yet as the front-runner's speed began to fade, Will's stallion chipped away at the gap separating them.

The two horses thundered past the raised platform, sending up clumps of dirt and grass in their wake. The sheer speed and power of them stole Eleanor's breath.

By less than a neck, the rider ahead of Will, whom Eleanor now saw was Hugh Despenser, held onto his lead. Both horses streaked across the ribbon in the grass, then slowed gradually to a canter beyond the finish line.

The others in the leading group crossed the ribbon a moment later, but then a long gap followed while they waited for those in the rear to finish. Will and Despenser took the opportunity to trot toward the platform.

"A magnificent race!" the King beamed, rising from his chair.

Despenser grinned widely at Edward, but Will's gaze slid to Eleanor.

"Well done," she breathed. In response, a pleased curve tugged at his mouth.

The King spoke to Will, snagging his attention. "I believe if that race had been another ten paces, you would have won, Stewart."

"But alas, it was no'," Will said diplomatically.

"When you opted for that enormous steed, I thought you didn't stand a chance," the King went on, clearly still in the throes of excitement from the spectacle.

"Ye selected a rather long course, Highness." Will patted the stallion's sweat-damp neck. "I kenned Fearghus could outlast the rest—except for ye, Despenser."

Despenser dipped his russet head toward Will, though the arrogant smile still lingered on his lips.

At last, the rest of the riders began reaching the finish line. The King paused to watch them pass, clapping wanly for their effort. Conrad was among those at the back, having mismanaged the very first turn. His handsome features were twisted with frustration as he reined in his horse beyond the finish line and dismounted, pulling his steed toward the palace.

Once all the courtiers had completed the course and were gathering around the platform, Despenser drew Edward's attention. "As the victor, may I not claim a favor from the lady of my choosing?" he prodded.

Yesterday, John Alderly had requested—and received—an embroidered silk kerchief from Juliet, one of the Queen's other ladies-in-waiting. He had been courting her for several months, and his request earned him a blush from Juliet and a few vulgar jests from his fellow courtiers. It had all been quite amusing—and smiled upon by both the King and Queen.

Now, though, Eleanor stiffened, uncertain what Despenser meant to do with the opportunity.

"Of course," the King replied, waving a hand over the ladies on the platform. "You may select any—"

"The Queen." Despenser's cool gaze settled on Isabella. "I wish to have the Queen's favor."

The courtiers close enough to overhear applauded at Despenser's gesture, taking it as that of a gallant nobleman toward his honored sovereign.

But Eleanor knew better. She was close enough to see the cruel glint in his brown eyes. This was clearly some sort of challenge, for Despenser knew the

Queen would hate to give him aught, yet also that she could not refuse—not in front of everyone, including the King. Aye, Despenser was relishing the opportunity to exert subtle control over Isabella.

Defensive anger roiled in Eleanor's belly. Though Edward and Isabella had an understanding, an agreement that at least publicly they would treat each other with the respect due their positions not only as King and Queen but as husband and wife, Despenser did no such thing. He sought to twist the knife with Isabella whenever he could, reminding her that although she was Queen, she was surprisingly powerless compared to the King's favorite.

Isabella rose slowly to her feet, settling her rich purple silk skirts elegantly. Then she extended one bejeweled hand toward Despenser, silently making it plain that she would only grant Despenser the honor of kissing the back of her hand, no matter what favor he hoped to claim.

Despenser's lip curled in something closer to a sneer than a smile. Without even bothering to dismount and kneel before his Queen, he reined his horse alongside the raised platform. He looked dead in the eye for a long moment, his gaze cold, before leaning out of the saddle and taking her hand, brushing it with a kiss. Isabella turned her head away, not deigning to look at Despenser.

As Isabella drew her hand away, Eleanor noticed

a wet spot on the back of the Queen's hand. Despenser had no doubt left it intentionally, knowing that the Queen could not wipe her hand without being overtly rude. Nor could she discreetly wipe it on her skirts, for the silk would show the blot of moisture.

Again the courtiers applauded the gesture, clearly missing the taut discomfort of the exchange.

But Will didn't. Eleanor looked up to find his narrowed gaze shifting between the Queen and Despenser, keen and knowing.

Abruptly, he swung down from his saddle. "I hope ye dinnae consider me too presumptuous, yer Highnesses, but..." He cast his gaze about, searching for his next words. "But my horse...could use some encouragement."

The King blinked at Will. "What did you say?"

"Fearghus." Will cleared his throat. "He came so close to winning, Highness. I'd like to put a fire in him, inspire him for his next race. Mayhap the Queen would give him a wee pat? For good luck?"

Several of the nearby courtiers snickered at Will's uncouth request, but the King snorted in amusement. The snort turned into a deep laugh.

"I have never heard of such a thing," the King commented through his chuckles. "You are a most odd and entertaining sort, Stewart." Edward turned to the Queen. "What say you, my lady wife?"

Isabella released a confused breath. "Aye, I suppose I will pat your horse, Will."

Will guided Fearghus next to the platform. Eleanor watched, uncertain what he was about.

He extended a hand to the Queen. "I'll steady ye, Highness, so that ye may reach out to him."

Still bewildered, the Queen placed one of her hands in Will's, then stretched the other toward the horse.

"That's it. A wee stroke with the back of yer hand is sure to inspire the animal, Highness."

Realization struck Eleanor. Will held the Queen's left hand, leaving her right—which Despenser had kissed—free to wipe on the horse.

The Queen, too, seemed to understand him suddenly, for she started, then some of the tension eased from her neck. She reached for Fearghus, running the back of her damp hand along his sweat-soaked neck.

Eleanor doubted if anyone else noticed, but Will gave the reins in his free hand a subtle tweak. In response, Fearghus bobbed his head as if nodding in excitement.

The King laughed and clapped at that. "The beast is fond of you, Isabella."

Fighting a smile, the Queen drew back. "You may be right, husband." She fixed sparkling eyes on Will. "Thank you."

Will bowed over her other hand before releasing it. "Nay, thank ye, Highness. And apologies for Fearghus's sweat."

Seeing an opening, Eleanor shot to her feet and moved to the Queen's side. She pulled a linen kerchief from her sleeve and extended it. "Highness?" Now that the pretense was to wipe horse sweat from her hand rather than Despenser's kiss, the Queen could take the kerchief without slighting Edward's favorite.

As the King and Queen moved back to their seats, Eleanor lingered on the edge of the platform.

"Your manners are quite pretty all of a sudden," she murmured to Will.

He looked up at her, his blue-green eye flashing. "Ye'll find I am full of surprises."

She lowered her voice further. "Thank you for doing that."

"It pleases me to ken that I am beginning to win yer trust." His gaze darkened with a look that was both hungry and determined. "I want more of it. *All* of it."

Chapter Seventeen

Will dared a glance away from his opponent to assess the skies. Rain had threatened all morning. Now the ominous steel-gray clouds overhead appeared ready to break open at last.

Sensing his opponent winding up for another attack, Will jerked his attention back and braced his sword to block the blow.

He caught his attacker's dulled blade with his own, the force of the swing reverberating up his arms. Once he'd absorbed the attack, he pushed back against the other man's sword, sending him staggering away.

Will and the courtier—Sir Thomas Woodburough, Will thought his name was—circled each other slowly, both taking the opportunity to catch their breath and shake feeling back into their arms.

As on the previous two days of the King's mock tournament, the final event, sword combat, had started early, with plenty of fanfare and pageantry.

The competing courtiers had begun by choosing their swords from an array that were stored in the palace's garrison. Will had selected a long, heavy weapon that most closely matched the balance of his own sword, which was still locked away in the gatehouse.

Then they had been fitted with padded jacks for defense. The King had proclaimed that since this was a friendly tourney, all the blades would be dulled and the men would be spared from having to wear full armor. Still, a blow from one of the two-handed longswords the courtiers wielded, dulled or nay, could easily break ribs or damage organs without some padded protection.

The majority of the rest of the day had been filled with the earlier rounds of competition. The two dozen competing courtiers were paired up, then faced each other on the open expanse of grass before the King's platform. The winner of each match moved on to the next round.

The late morning had crawled by, for the King demanded that only one bout happen at a time so that he could draw out his amusement. Some matches were over in minutes, with one of the courtiers receiving such a sound beating or growing fatigued so quickly that he would be forced to concede. Others had dragged on, neither man yielding until one was unconscious.

Will had managed to advance into the late afternoon with relative ease. These courtiers were used to combat for show, but as soon as the first few minutes were over, they flagged quickly. Will, on the other hand, had been training for warfare for nearly a decade. Though he had grumbled many a time at Ansel Sutherland's relentless drills at the Bodyguard Corps' camp, the strength it had forged in his body could not be bought or faked by these pampered English noblemen.

Sir Thomas was the first one to give Will any real trouble. The man was of an age with Will, a bit softer around the middle, but clearly hale and adept with a sword. He was one of four competitors remaining. Once their bout concluded, Conrad de Russ would square off with Hugh Despenser. The winners of the two matches would face each other in the final bout.

Will brought his attention back to Sir Thomas. Before he could think about the next match, he still had to win this one. And Sir Thomas appeared to be ready to launch another bone-jarring attack.

The nobleman swung in a low arc, aiming for Will's thigh. If his sword had connected, not only would Will likely walk with a limp for several days, but he also would have been knocked onto his back and forced to admit defeat. He lowered his sword and blocked the strike, clenching his teeth against the jolting impact. But instead of retreating to wait for Sir Thomas's next attack, Will surged forward, ramming his shoulder into the man's torso.

Sir Thomas lost his balance and landed hard on his backside in the grass. Like lightning, Will darted forward, notching the blunt tip of his blade into the hollow at Sir Thomas's throat. For one heartbeat, Sir Thomas tensed as if he meant to resist, but then he let a breath go. With a muttered curse and a rueful grin, he tossed his sword onto the ground.

"I yield to the superior skill of my opponent," he said loud enough for those gathered to hear. The onlooking courtiers and those on the raised platform all broke into applause for both men. Will lowered the tip of his sword and extended a hand to Sir Thomas, who took it and hauled himself to his feet.

"Well fought, Stewart," he said, pounding Will on the back. "You may wield a sword like a savage, but you have the honor of an Englishman."

Will gritted out a smile at that, forcing a chuckle through his locked jaw. "Thank ye, Sir Thomas. Ye are most gracious in defeat."

He and the nobleman walked to the edge of the circle of courtiers surrounding the designated combat grounds. Sir Thomas peeled off, accepting the handshakes and words of consolation from the others, while Will moved beyond the circle alone. As he began unfastening his padded jack, he caught sight of Eleanor approaching.

She glided toward him like a swan, the snugly laced cream-colored gown she wore revealing every tantalizing curve. He tore his gaze away, shrugging out of the jack.

When she reached him, she extended a waterskin. With a nod, he accepted it and drank deeply.

"Despenser is favored to win," she commented into the silence. "And not just because of his connection with the King. He is a more skilled swordsman than Conrad."

To keep from staring at her, Will trained his gaze on the combat grounds. Conrad and Despenser had just stepped into the ring of courtiers, rolling their shoulders and eyeing one another. The King called out encouragement to Despenser from his seat on the raised platform.

"Are you well? I saw that hit Sir Thomas landed on your shoulder at the start of your bout."

"Aye, I am fine."

In truth, his shoulder still ached and was likely turning black and purple beneath his tunic, but it was naught to the discomfort of having Eleanor stand so close, looking up at him with those dark, keen eyes.

He had managed to avoid touching her for the last two days. The lack of contact should have strength-ened his resolve to keep a safe distance between them. Instead, the longer he fought to restrain himself, the weaker he felt. And whenever she drew near, all he wanted to do was pull her against him and take her curving lips in a kiss once more.

He craved her. There was no denying it.

Yet there was so much more at stake than satisfying his lust, he reminded himself for the hundredth time in the last few days. A disloyal spy was a very dangerous thing indeed.

After all she'd told him of her past and David, Will was no longer as certain as he'd once been that Eleanor's allegiances had shifted. But she still hid much. He was making inroads with her, learning more of her nature and gaining her trust. Mayhap soon she would confide everything to him of her own accord.

The last thing he needed was to lose his head over an infatuation with her and risk becoming blind to the truth.Or worse, come to trust her only to realize that he had been duped, just as he had once before.

Which meant he'd had to content himself with watching her from a distance. The King had held a feast after each of the tourney events. He'd observed her from behind a mug of ale, as he'd done on the night the King had arrived.

And when she would retire each evening, he returned to his own chamber. She hadn't barred the door adjoining their rooms again after telling him about David, but nor had she come to him. He was left to lie awake every night, stiff with wanting her and knowing she was only a few paces and one slab of oak away.

He jerked his mind from the images that rose at the possibility.

"Any new...*developments* with regard to our mutual friend? I eagerly await the opportunity to tell him of all the merry diversions we've had before the King departs Langley."

She stiffened at his veiled remark, her eyelashes flickering ever so slightly. Aye, this was what he needed—to keep his attention on his mission, not Eleanor's enthralling claim over him.

"More time is needed before we send word," she replied quietly.

He snorted softly, watching as the bout between Conrad and Despenser got underway.

"It seems everyone here believes we have naught but time to waste," he commented.

She lowered her voice even further, so that he had to lean toward her to make out her words. "If it matters, the situation is...advancing. I believe we are approaching a crossroads."

"Funny ye should mention that. When I was riding to Langley, I passed through many a crossroads and became quite familiar with a tradition ye have here in England. The heads and limbs of traitors are put on pikes for all to see at each corner. I believe it is meant as a reminder to the passerby no' to betray one's fidelity."

Her slim throat bobbed. "Indeed."

Guilt once again tugged at him. He didn't trust her completely, but nor did he wish to torture her with threats. It seemed that whenever he pushed her, she withdrew further behind her wall of secrets and silence. He needed her to come to him freely.

He released a breath. "As long as Edward remains here, he cannae launch a counterattack on Carlisle. Ye may have more time. But ye had better be right that yer plan is reaching a head—one that is in our mutual friend's best interest."

Just then, the heavens finally opened and fat raindrops began to splatter them. She blinked up at him through the rain, her eyes filled with more clouds than the sky. Her lips parted, but no words came out. She stood there struggling for a moment before he took pity on her.

"Go," he said gently. "Yer fine gown is getting wet."

She hesitated for a long moment, but at last she nodded. Ducking her head against the downpour, she hurried back to the shelter of the damask-covered platform.

Will forced his attention back to the match

between Conrad and Despenser. The two men were circling each other within the ring of courtiers. Conrad took a swing at Despenser, who managed to deflect the attack. Then Despenser began advancing on Conrad, pushing him back with a series of blows that Conrad just barely blocked.

Despenser did indeed appear to be the more adept fighter, as Eleanor had said, yet Conrad was fast on his feet. And he was nearly a match for Despenser's considerable strength.

Despenser paused in his hail of attacks, readjusting his grip as the rain intensified. Seeing an opening, Conrad lunged forward. Despenser retreated, but the ground beneath him had been churned to mud by the rain and their boots. Despenser slipped and landed awkwardly on his side. He shoved himself up to one knee, but before he could rise all the way, Conrad's blade came to rest against the side of his neck.

A gasp went through the courtiers at the unexpected turn of events. Despenser remained on one knee, his gaze darting to the King. Edward wore a frown, but he did not move or speak.

At last, Despenser dropped his sword. "I yield," he said grudgingly.

Hushed applause rose from the courtiers. Conrad grinned broadly and withdrew his sword. While Despenser slowly rose to his feet, Conrad's gaze slid to

Will. His smile deepened, his upper lip drawing back from his teeth as he continued to send Will a challenging stare.

Until a moment before, Will had been contemplating how to lose to Despenser while still giving Edward plenty of entertainment—and holding on to a shred of his own dignity. Though his pride hated the idea, he wasn't so foolish as to best the King's favorite.

Now it seemed he was to face Conrad in the final bout instead. There would be no holding back, no kowtowing to the King's favored man.

He let a smile that matched Conrad's come to his own face.

This he would enjoy.

Chapter Eighteen

W ill shrugged into his padded jack as he stepped into the combat circle. Someone handed him his sword. He took it, never breaking his stare with Conrad.

"Are you sure you don't wish to rest for a spell, de Russ?" one of the courtiers behind Conrad asked.

"Nay, I think not. My blood is already warm. Besides, the Scot won't beat himself—unless we return to archery, that is."

A low ripple of laughter passed through the gathered courtiers.

A day's worth of aches, bruises, and fatigue vanished from Will's limbs, to be replaced with single-minded loathing for the man he was about to battle.

Conrad swung his sword in a lazy circle by his side, assessing Will with sneering eyes.

"It must gall you," he commented, sauntering toward Will. "To come so close to winning yesterday's race, yet still wind up short."

"No' as much as it would have stung to come in nigh dead last," Will replied evenly.

Conrad's features flashed with annoyance before he regained control of them. "Aye, well, you have your horse to thank for your performance. Imagine that—your success is only because of the efforts of a beast. Whereas when you are on your own, as you were for the archery event…" He lifted one shoulder in a condescending shrug.

Will narrowed his good eye against the hammering rain. He tightened his grip as he lifted his sword to indicate he was ready.

"I am on my own today. Let us see how I fare, shall we?"

Without warning, Conrad darted forward, slashing at Will's left flank. Will batted his sword away, retreating a pace. His boots squelched and sucked in the mud. He would need to be more mindful of his surroundings than Despenser had been.

Will returned Conrad's attack with one of his own. He swung for his ribs, but Conrad deflected the strike. Keeping their swords locked, Will attempted to bind Conrad's blade, but his padded jack, which was rapidly becoming swollen with rainwater, restricted his movement. He was forced to disengage and retreat instead.

Conrad launched another assault, this time aiming for Will's right shoulder. It took him a fraction of a second longer to read the trajectory of the blade. He managed to block it—barely. The impact made his hilt shudder against his palms.

Conrad took a step back, giving them both a moment to assess each other. A slow smile curved his mouth.

"I have gathered something about you, Stewart."

"Oh?"

"Your eye."

He waved the tip of his sword at Will's eye patch. Will's shoulders stiffened.

"You cannot see as well on your right side because of it," Conrad continued. "You must have a blind spot, for you are slower to respond on that side."

Damn him to hell. If only Will could deny it. But it was true. Conrad had sussed out his weakness.

At Will's silence, Conrad grinned wider. "I'll make sure to take advantage of that."

With a quick step forward, Conrad hammered Will with three attacks in quick succession, all to his right side. Will retreated, catching each swing of Conrad's sword with his own just in the nick of time.

Abruptly, Conrad changed direction, hacking at Will's left arm. Will pivoted, shifting his sword across his body, but not fast enough. The blade edge of Conrad's sword slammed into his upper arm, sending him staggering to the side.

A stunned murmur traveled through the onlookers. Belatedly, Will realized it wasn't simply because of the speed and ferocity of Conrad's attack, nor his own poor reaction. In addition to the numbing pain of the blunt force of Conrad's strike, his skin felt hot and wet beneath his jack. When his gaze landed on his arm, he understood why.

The jack had been sliced through, the padded wool turning dark with blood.

Burning realization hit him. While he and the others had been fighting with dull-edged blades, Conrad had somehow managed to slip a sharpened weapon into the competition.

Will's gaze shot to the King. Edward sat on the edge of his chair, a jewel-encrusted wine goblet clutched in his hand and his gaze riveted on the fight. Everyone on the rain-drenched field seemed to hold their breath as they waited. Conrad had undeniably violated the rules of the competition, yet the King clearly did not want to call an end to the thrilling final event.

After an extended pause, Edward tipped his head in a subtle gesture to continue. Excited murmurs coursed through the courtiers. It seemed the "friendly" tourney had just gotten far more interesting.

Will muttered a curse. His gaze shifted to Eleanor. She sat rigid as a rock beside the Queen, her hand lifted in shock over her mouth. Her eyes were wide with fear.

Conrad must have followed the line of his stare, for he spoke in a low, taunting voice just for Will's ears.

"*When* I beat you into the mud where you belong, dog, I'll be sure to ask Lady Eleanor for her favor. Mayhap one she can fulfill on her hands and knees."

A cold, clarifying fury hit Will then. But not one directed at Conrad. Aye, the man was the vilest, most dishonorable of bastards. Yet Will only felt angry at himself.

He had allowed Conrad to prey on his emotions. Instead of maintaining his composure, he'd taken Conrad's bait about his eye and Eleanor. He'd let Conrad set the tenor of this bout, reacting rather than seizing control.

What was more, Will had been acting as though he was one of these English nobles. He'd taken their blows and delivered his own, all by their rules.

Bloody hell, he'd forgotten everything the Bruce had taught him. He'd met strength with strength, attack with attack, rather than fighting as a Scotsman did. All these years the Scots had battled the English, they'd learned to embrace their advantages—evasion, awareness of their surroundings, and the element of surprise. Rather than using force against force, they'd applied their wits to outmaneuver the English.

Ye have always been more than just a warrior, Will. The Bruce's words drifted back to him. *Yer mind has always been as sharp as yer sword.*

Will nearly snorted. At the moment, he held a blunted blade against Conrad's sharpened one. He wasn't sure what that implied about his wits, but he could contemplate it later.

Conrad was smirking at him, waiting for Will's reaction to his latest barb about Eleanor. Will glanced again at his sliced jack. The sleeve was frayed and red with his blood.

He held up a hand toward the King.

"A moment?"

Edward's brows knitted together, but he tilted his head in acquiescence.

Propping the tip of his sword in the mud, Will eased his cut arm out of its sleeve. The wound stung, but it wasn't deep enough to prevent him from wielding his sword with both hands.

Will stilled for a moment then. It was time to decide. With a nod to himself, he tugged at the jack, but instead of pulling it up over his shoulder once again, he shrugged out of it completely.

Surprise and confusion circulated through the

courtiers. Will ignored them, tossing the waterlogged jack into the mud at the edge of the circle. No more hiding behind padding that slowed him down and restrained his movements. Besides, while it had softened the other men's blows, it would do little to stop Conrad's blade.

Aye, it was time to fight without fear or protection —like a Scot.

"I've just had my own realization, de Russ," he commented, fixing Conrad with a cold stare.

Conrad flexed his hands on his sword hilt, watching Will warily. "Oh?"

"Ye were right before when ye said that I couldnae do aught to ye despite yer trespasses against Eleanor and yer insults to me. Ye are a nobleman and a courtier to the King of England. I cannae lift a finger against ye—*outside this circle*."

Conrad's dark brows dropped, and Will glimpsed a satisfying shadow cross the man's eyes.

"But in here," Will continued, lifting the tip of his sword to indicate the ring of courtiers surrounding the combat grounds. "In here, I can do as I've wished from the moment I laid eyes on ye. And all with the King's blessing."

Growling like a poked bear, Conrad launched himself at Will. Will steeled himself, but instead of blocking the attack and absorbing the blow, as he had been doing all day, he instead spun out of the way at the last possible moment. Thrown off balance, Conrad stumbled and nearly landed in the mud.

Regaining his footing, Conrad spun and attacked again, this time aiming for Will's knees. Will twisted away, but he didn't retreat. He sidestepped, keeping Conrad on his left side so that he could see him better.

Conrad launched another attack on Will's right shoulder, but because he had to cross Will's body, Will picked up the angle of the blow with plenty of time to evade it. This time, he stepped into Conrad, driving an elbow into his stomach.

Sputtering, Conrad retreated. He glared at Will. "Does your arm hurt, Stewart?" he rasped. "Is that why you are resorting to dirty tricks rather than using your sword? I suppose I shouldn't be surprised that a Scot—"

Will didn't wait for Conrad to finish. The English might prefer to stand about blathering in the middle of a fight, but the Scottish didn't. He darted forward, drawing back for a blow to Conrad's head.

Though the King had said all areas of one's opponent were fair game for this competition, all the courtiers had seemed to implicitly agree on hits only to the body. Whether that was because they didn't truly wish to hurt each other—or worse, mar their appearance—or because most of them had simply never had to end a fight as quickly and ruthlessly as possible, Will wasn't sure. However, he didn't intend to play by their courtly rules of conduct.

Conrad was so startled at the trajectory of Will's blade toward his face that he immediately flung his arms high. He readied his sword to deflect the attack, but the position left his legs completely exposed.

A heartbeat before making contact, Will jerked his blade lower. He swung the flat edge against the side of Conrad's knee, forcing his leg to crumple. Conrad flopped into a heap in the mud with a yelp. In an instant, Will stood over him, the tip of his sword hovering an inch in front of Conrad's face.

"Do ye yield?"

Conrad sat motionless for a long moment. Then abruptly he smacked away the blunted edge of Will's blade with his hand and leapt to his feet.

Dragging his sword from the mud, Conrad surged toward Will. But his steps were unsteady after Will's blow. Will dodged out of the way easily, letting Conrad stumble by.

"Enough with your games!" Conrad roared, staggering around to face Will once more. "Fight me, you bastard!"

He came at Will yet again, extending his blade as if to skewer Will through the gut. Will caught the sword with his own, twisting his wrists to deflect it. With his arms now free of the constricting padded jack, he bound Conrad's blade, pinning it to the ground.

Conrad could have retreated out of the bind, but the arrogant fool instead attempted to push against it. Will let him expend his energy for a moment, knowing that Conrad's brute force could never win out over his superior position in the bind.

Realizing that Conrad still would not disengage, Will closed the distance between them with a swift step. He loosed one hand from his sword hilt, cocked his fist, and drove it into Conrad's face.

God, he'd longed to do that for a while.

With a satisfying crack, Conrad's head snapped back and he tumbled into the mud.

Will moved over him, sword poised at his throat. "Do ye yield now?"

Conrad blinked up at him in a daze. Blood streamed from his nose down either side of his face. He lifted his sword slowly.

Will placed a muddy boot on Conrad's wrist, pinning both his arm and his sword down easily.

"How about now?"

The arrogant idiot thrashed under Will's foot. When that didn't work, Conrad spat blood at him, most of which fell back down onto his own face.

With a shake of his head, Will turned to the King. "Would ye have me beat the man until he's senseless, Highness, or might the match be called?"

The King rose to his feet. "It is over. Will Stewart is the victor." Yea

Stunned silence echoed after the King's proclamation. Will strode slowly out of the circle of courtiers, not looking back at Conrad.

Someone began clapping. The applause was taken up by another, then another, until all the courtiers clapped. Will passed many wide-eyed stares as he made his way toward the King's platform. Whispers followed him along with the applause—murmurs of shock at the outcome of the bout, and vows never to cross the savage, cunning Scotsman.

"A most impressive contest," the King breathed as Will reached the base of the platform. "Are you hurt, Stewart? My personal surgeon can see to your arm."

Will glanced at the cut. His tunic sleeve was red below the wound, but it had nearly stopped bleeding now. "Nay, Highness, but thank ye."

A grin broke out on Edward's face. "Truly magnificent. I doubt I have seen a more thrilling match since the King of Spain arranged for a tiger and a bear to fight each other on my last visit."

"I am glad to have entertained ye, Highness," Will replied, struggling to keep the tight annoyance from his voice.

"To fight with no armor against a sharpened blade," the King continued eagerly. "It was very bold of you, Stewart, and not at all—"

A commotion behind Will interrupted the King. The courtiers were murmuring in displeasure, one voice rising over the others.

"I did not yield!"

Conrad pushed through the wall of men, one hand clutching his sword and the other cupping his bloodied nose.

"I never yielded, Highness," he continued, his voice muffled and pinched from the nose-break. "I *do not* yield to this…this…"

"*I* ended the bout, de Russ." The King's voice was suddenly unamused. "Do you question my decision?"

Conrad's eyes widened above his cupped hand. "Nay, Highness, but——" Will turned to Conrad, and the man visibly shrank back under his hard stare. "——but he broke my nose!"

"Indeed, but only after you drew first blood," the King commented. His dark blue eyes narrowed then. "With a blade that was not permitted in the competition."

Now Conrad turned white as a sheet. "I-it was an accident, Highness. A mix-up of some sort, I assure you. I would never——"

"Did you use that blade for the entire competition?"

"A-aye, I must have," Conrad said, seizing on his next lie. "The guard in the garrison who distributed the swords must have given it to me."

The King pursed his lips, yet his eyes glittered with displeasure as he stared at Conrad for a moment.

"Which means you might have injured any number of my courtiers throughout the day. You fought Elbert de Lacey earlier, did you not? And Hugh Despenser."

Will saw the trap Edward had laid a moment before Conrad did. Conrad actually gasped as he realized what he'd done. He'd not only beaten the King's favorite, but now Edward believed he could have actually injured him as well—or worse. It seemed that although the King loved to be entertained above all else, he did not find his favorite facing a sharpened sword very amusing.

"Highness, I only struck with the flat of the blade in my earlier bouts, I swea—"

"Because you knew the sword was edged?"

"Nay, Highness, I—" Conrad's dark gaze darted rapidly about, looking for an ally. Finding none, he fixed a glare on Will. "Stewart has clearly earned your favor, Highness, but I would remind you that he is a *Scotsman*. You would side with him over an English nobleman?"

"He is a Scotsman who is loyal to *me*," Edward countered evenly.

"Who invited him to court, Highness? And how did he come to be engaged to Eleanor de Monteney? The man is not to be trusted, I'm sure of—"

A stone of fear solidified in the pit of Will's stomach. Just as Eleanor had warned, his presence had drawn suspicion onto both of them.

For his part, the King spoke over Conrad with thinned lips. "First you question my judgment to end the bout, and now you imply that I cannot be trusted to determine the loyalties of those who surround me?"

From the growing panic in Conrad's eyes, he was finally beginning to understand how badly he'd blundered. "Nay, Highness, I would never presume. I only meant to—"

To Will's relief, the King held up his hand as if the conversation bored him, yet Will didn't miss the tightness around his eyes and mouth. "I think you had best return to your holding in Kent, de Russ," he said coolly. "I'm sure something there requires your attention. *Now*."

With a dismissive wave, the King turned away from Conrad as if he no longer existed. Conrad stood, confounded and bleeding, for a long moment. But then he bowed stiffly and strode toward the palace, presumably to gather his things and depart before the King could lay displeased eyes on him again.

Will at last let himself look at Eleanor. She sat next to the Queen, attempting—and failing—to assume an air of mild disinterest in all that had just transpired. But in the faint pinch of her brows and the soft parting of her lips, he read a mixture of worry and relief.

Heat flared to life in the pit of his stomach, spreading through his veins until he blazed all over with the need to touch her.

Rationality and wisdom be damned. He could not fight this anymore. He no longer wanted to.

"May I receive the favor of Lady Eleanor in honor of my victory, Highness?" Will asked without taking his gaze from Eleanor.

The King chuckled, easing some of the tension that lingered after Conrad's departure. "Aye, of course, if she'll grant it."

Eleanor's eyes grew bigger. Beside her, the Queen's lips curved. She gave Eleanor a discreet nudge in the ribs to urge her to her feet.

Eleanor rose and moved to the edge of the sheltered platform. Will looked up at her through the rain.

"Will ye give me a kiss, milady?"

She swallowed. The King, who was settling back into his chair, chuckled again. A few of the nearest courtiers called their encouragement. Eleanor dropped her voice so that only he could hear her over their jests.

"I thought you said we shouldn't—"

"Is that an aye?"

Her gaze darted about. "Aye, but—"

Before she could finish, he wrapped his hands around her waist and hauled her off the covered platform. She squeaked in shock as he hoisted her up. He slipped one arm beneath her knees and the other around her back, pulling her against his chest.

Ducking his chin, he found her lips with his in a fierce, possessive kiss. The courtiers roared their approval at the blunt, possessive display, but they were little more than buzzing midges in Will's ears.

He lost himself in the kiss. Her lips were like silk, soft and yielding under his. His fingers sank into her, feeling the supple curve of her limbs beneath the fabric of her gown.

It was madness, of course, kissing her with such abandon, and in front of so many. Mayhap he'd given up fighting his need for her because his blood still ran hot from his bout with Conrad. Mayhap it was simply that he was only a man, and therefore his resistance was no match against the spell Eleanor had cast over him.

Whatever the case, he didn't care in this moment. All he knew was the feel of Eleanor's lips against his, her body cradled in his arms. Her hands had looped around his neck and she clung clumsily to him as their kiss stretched on.

When at last he pulled back, she was panting for breath. She blinked up at him through the rain, her eyes a dark sea of confusion and desire. She had felt it too—the mad, clawing need that bound them together, making the rest of the world fall away.

Slowly, he lifted her in his arms until her feet brushed the platform once more. Steadying her around the waist, he waited for her to find her legs. She wobbled several times before she seemed stable. Reluctantly, he let her go, retreating a pace into the downpour.

"A most fitting end to my little tournament," the King commented cheerfully. "Now, let us escape this incessant rain. A feast is in order!"

Chapter Nineteen

Outwardly, Eleanor had a smile for everyone that night at the feast. Inside, however, she wanted to scream with frustration—or cry out with elation. One of the two. Or both.

She should have been unabashedly happy, for she'd watched Conrad de Russ ride away from Langley less than an hour ago. Despite the fact that darkness had fallen and the rain still fell in sheets, the King had been unmistakable in his curt dismissal of the man.

Conrad would certainly stay away now, for he risked far worse than banishment for wielding a sharpened blade against the King's favorite. It was one less moving part Eleanor had to manage, and a relief to know that he could no longer harass her. Nevertheless, she found herself ill at ease.

The King and Despenser were in high spirits. Despenser, having finished third in the archery competition, first in the horse race, and third again in sword combat, had accrued the most points of all the courtiers. He'd been crowned victor of the tourney and thus King for the evening. He wore one of Edward's crowns and sat in the King's throne, sipping wine and laughing with Edward.

The Queen was displeased at the spectacle of it all, but she'd managed to go largely unnoticed by sitting at the far end of the high table, which was likely best for all involved. It had been Eleanor's job to keep her distracted with talk of the ride they might take tomorrow if the rain abated.

And Will sat at the table below the dais, as he did every night. But tonight, he neither glowered at her nor followed her with his piercing gaze. Nay, he gave her the back of his head, though she did not miss the tension in his shoulders.

There was the true source of her frustration. What the devil was she to make of that kiss? He'd said their first kiss had been a mistake. Yet there could be no mistaking his fierce, unequivocal desire when he'd hauled her into his arms and kissed her nigh senseless.

All that had ever existed between them was evasion and doubt, secrets and ambiguities. *Enough*. It was high time she confronted him and demanded an explanation for his behavior.

With an excuse and an apology for the Queen, Eleanor slipped from her seat and stepped down from the dais. Will must have sensed her approaching behind him, for he turned and fixed her with his eye, warm and sharp.

"We need to talk," she said through a forced smile. "Alone."

He rose slowly, then offered her his arm as if he truly was one of King Edward's gallant courtiers. She took it, allowing him to lead her from the great hall.

"Just how alone do ye want to be, lass?" he murmured as they stepped into one of the dim corridors.

Eleanor glanced back into the great hall. Most of the servants were dashing between the kitchens and the hall, their arms full with pitchers of ale and wine, trenchers, and silver platters of fish, lamb, mincemeat pies, puddings, fruit tarts, and other delicacies for the King's feast. Still, some might be lurking in the corridors.

"Let us retire to your chamber."

Something dark lurked under his gaze, which was keen as a fast-moving river. He dipped his head, then led her deeper down the corridor.

Eleanor held her tongue until they had entered his chamber and he'd closed the door firmly behind them. Then she spun on him.

"What the hell was that?"

"What?"

"You know what—that kiss." She let out a breath. "You said we should not do that again. And I agreed."

He turned to the hearth, where a few embers glowed orange. "Ye also agreed to let me kiss ye this afternoon." He dropped a log onto the coals and waited for it to catch. "Ye could have denied me."

"In front of the King? And all his courtiers? Nay, it would have—"

"Ye could have denied me," he repeated, facing her and stalking forward a step. "But ye didnae."

Eleanor went hot under the heavy velvet gown she wore. She refused to retreat, though. She lifted her chin so that she could hold his gaze.

"Was it for show, then?" she demanded, her voice coming out thinner than she would have liked. "For the benefit of the others and the amusement of the King?"

"Nay."

"Then why?"

"Let us speak plainly."

"How can I, when I cannot tell what the hell is going on? When I cannot even tell what I—"

She stopped herself before she blurted something truly foolish. He was standing too close for her to think straight. He had bathed after his day of fighting and mud and blood, but he hadn't bothered to shave. Dark gold stubble glinted on his hard jaw in the low light of the kindling fire. He smelled of soap and clean linen and male skin.

His gaze traced over her face slowly. "I am no' sure what this is, either. Nor do I ken fully why I kissed ye. Mayhap I dinnae care."

The air seemed to stick in her lungs. Anticipation prickled over her skin. It seemed they were finally going to face whatever it was that smoldered unspoken between them.

"I dinnae care if this is right or wrong anymore," he continued, his voice heavy and coarse as granite. "I dinnae care if it is mad to want ye, mad to risk so much just to have ye."

He took another step closer, until she could feel the heat of his large frame and her skirts swished against his legs.

His gaze bored into her like a hot iron. "Mayhap all I want is to fill yer head with the same madness ye've filled mine with. To drive ye as crazy as I have been since that night in the garden when ye kissed me."

Flames of need licked her from the inside out. *Oh God.* A thousand rational thoughts flew from her mind, leaving her empty except for the hungry ache throbbing within her.

"Tell me the truth for once, Eleanor," he rasped, holding her captive with his stare. "Do ye feel the same? Do ye want me, too?"

The stone wall of resolve within her—to resist him, to resist *this*—began to crumble. She had been strong for too long. Alone. With only her fortitude to keep her warm at night.

But then Will Sinclair had come crashing into her life, upending all her control, all her carefully laid plans. He'd thrown her mission, all she'd worked for these last four years, in danger, his knowing gaze puncturing her defenses.

And he'd awakened her, like the blazing sun against a frozen land. She felt as though she'd been hibernating since David's death, protecting herself from the risk of opening to another again.

But she couldn't hold back any longer. Couldn't lie to herself, or to him. Not about what blazed between them.

She held his stare, letting the shield behind her eyes lower. "*Aye.*"

In an instant, he had her in his arms. His kiss was rough, his stubble rasping against her chin. He was no longer the charming, well-mannered courtier he played before the others. Nay, he was all hard planes and coarse edges—just the way she preferred him.

His tongue found hers, tangling in a heated caress. With a moan of surrender, she opened deeper, letting him invade her senses. He must have sensed her yielding, for his fingers sank into her possessively.

She clutched at him, no longer trusting her legs to

hold her up. Belatedly, she realized that he was maneuvering them both toward the bed. But instead of urging her onto the feather mattress, he backed her against one of the thick, polished oak posters.

The wood was solid at her back, but not as solid as Will's powerful form in front of her. His hands began to roam, trailing down her sides and over her waist. She could feel the heat of them even through her velvet gown.

Abruptly, he lifted her arms over her head and pinned them against the poster in one large hand. She gasped, feeling exposed and vulnerable. Yet it only fanned the flames of desire within her to be at this fierce, intoxicating man's mercy.

She was trusting him with her body—*with her heart*, a voice whispered in the back of her mind. The danger of doing so—of all that could be gained, and all that could be destroyed—sent her head spinning and set her blood on fire.

"This is no game," she breathed, meeting his gaze.

He held her there for a long moment, her hands restrained above her and his gaze riveting her in place.

"Nay, it isnae," he ground out. "We are far beyond that now."

Without breaking his stare, his free hand slid up from her waist to her breast. He cupped her in his callus-roughened palm. But he held back. Was he waiting for her to halt him? She never would.

Wordlessly, she arched into the hand on her breasts, testing the strength of his grip on her wrists. His hold clamped tighter, but his other hand obliged her. He circled the peak of her breast with one thumb, drawing a gasp from her. Even through her thick gown, sensation shot from her pearled nipple to the ache between her legs.

Her head fell back against the poster, but still she held his unrelenting gaze. With his thumb moving over her breast, he pressed the length of his body into her. She could feel the unmistakable evidence of his arousal. He was long and rigid against her stomach. She pushed back against him, loving the hard fusion of their bodies even through their clothes.

With a muttered oath, Will broke their stare first. His chin lurched down so that he could claim her mouth with his once more. His kiss was demanding, hard. Her lips would likely be swollen and rosy afterward. To repay the favor, she nipped his lower lip with her teeth, as he had done to her in the garden.

That drew a growl from him. Suddenly his hand vanished from her breast. A heartbeat later, he was rucking up her skirts. Cool air hit her stocking-clad calves. His hand closed behind her knee and hoisted her leg up the outside of one of his thighs. The position allowed him to wedge the hard column of his manhood at the crux of her legs.

Eleanor writhed against him, mindless now for aught beyond the need building between them.

"Dinnae," Will hissed, gripping her hip and pinning it against the poster. "Else I'll take ye here and now, hard and fast."

A moan slipped from her throat at the prospect. This was like naught she had ever experienced before. It was wild and raw, completely unrestrained by reason or propriety.

"I would rather taste ye first," he continued, his voice low and rough. "And fill ye slowly until ye are begging me. Claim ye completely."

As if to prove his words, he released her hands and sank between her legs. Shoving her skirts out of the way, he brought his mouth to the juncture of her thighs.

Though her hands were now free, Eleanor clutched desperately at the poster over her head. If she hadn't, she would have landed in a heap at the first flick of his tongue.

He teased her for a moment, grazing her sex then nipping her thigh. But soon enough, he was laving and stroking, delving deep.

When her legs began to quaver, he jerked to his feet, yanking off his tunic in the same motion. She felt her eyes go wide as she was met with the powerful expanse of his naked torso.

He seemed to be made of gold-dipped steel, limned as he was by the firelight. His shoulders were roped with muscle, his stomach banded with it.

His skin bore several scars, some pink, some white. A red line as long as her forefinger scored his left arm where Conrad had cut him earlier that day. It didn't appear to bother him, however. In fact, his gaze was fastened on her, seemingly oblivious to his bare skin and the marks upon it.

"Let me see ye."

She reached behind her back for the laces cinching her gown, but her fingers were clumsy and leaden. Gripping her hips, he turned her so that she faced the poster. She clutched the oak, holding her breath at the feel of him unlacing her gown.

When the ties came loose, he slid his hands between the velvet and her chemise. Gooseflesh erupted across her skin at his hot touch. He eased the garment off her shoulders and let it fall to the ground in a heavy pile. Then he turned her to face him once more.

Taking hold of the delicate linen, he glided it over her head and let it land with her gown. Then he allowed himself look at her.

Raw hunger burned in his blue-green eye as it swept her. "Ye are so damned beautiful."

She moved to him then. She didn't need any more flowery words of praise from him. All she wanted was what he'd promised—to fill her. *Claim* her.

She slid her palms down the stark planes of his stomach until she reached the fastening of his breeches. While she worked, he backed her up slowly until her legs bumped into the mattress. She eased herself down, pulling him after her. With a quick tug, he shucked his breeches and kicked them aside even as he lowered himself over her.

The tip of his cock came to rest low on her belly. It was velvet-soft yet hard as iron, big enough to make her throat bob.

He stilled, holding himself above her and pinioning her with his gaze.

"We cannae go back after this, aye?"

"I know."

"Are ye sure?"

She drew a breath. "Aye."

Keeping his gaze steady, he reached between them and took hold of himself. He positioned his cock at her entrance. She lifted her hips to him in a silent plea.

Just as he'd promised, he took her slowly, inch by torturous inch. By the time he filled her to the hilt, they were both panting.

A muscle leapt in Will's jaw as he held himself still, giving her time to adjust to his size. When he began to move at last, Eleanor could not stop the moans that tore from her throat. He drove slow at first, letting her feel every inch of him. But soon Eleanor's knees shook around his hips. She rolled beneath him, urging him faster.

His restraint seemed to snap then. With a growl, he clamped his hands on her hips, taking control. He thrust hard and deep, sending her spiraling higher toward ecstasy. She needed this. She needed to lose herself in him. Naught else mattered but this moment. There was naught but pleasure left.

Her release slammed into her like a breaking wave, crashing and swirling and tumbling her over and over. She cried out, her nails digging into Will's back. He rode out her pleasure, driving hard and fast while she quaked beneath him.

When the surge of ecstasy began to ebb, he thrust harder still for two heartbeats, then growled and withdrew from her, spending his seed onto the bed linens.

He remained over her, gasping for breath, his head falling between his shoulders.

"That was…"

Incredible. Stunning. The most intense experience of her life. And mayhap a grave mistake.

"Aye," was all she could say in response. It was all of those things and more, tangled together in a knot she didn't want to pick apart just yet.

Exhaustion pulled at her. She drew him down beside her, resting a hand over his hammering heart.

What had they just done? And what would it mean in the light of day come morning?

No answers came before blessed sleep tugged her under.

Chapter Twenty

Will stirred awake sometime later. The fire had died and his chamber was cast in darkness.

Without thinking, he stretched his hand across the bed—only to meet cool linen sheets.

Had it all been a dream? Nay, for the scent of Eleanor's skin still lingered on the pillow beside him. He had taken her right here. And she had taken him.

The intensity of what they'd shared had left him shaken. He'd been relieved when she'd softened into sleep beside him so quickly—so *trustingly*. It had given him some time to chew on what had happened. But he was just as conflicted now as he had been before unconsciousness had overcome him.

They were playing a dangerous game. Nay, as

she'd said, this wasn't a game any longer. It was their very lives they gambled with now.

Indeed, his life was in her hands. If she betrayed him... It sickened him to contemplate it, but he couldn't ignore the possibility. Yet her life was also in his hands. She had entrusted him with the truth about David and how she'd become a spy. And she'd given herself to him with a vulnerability and honesty that had stolen his breath.

One way or another, they were bound together now—their fates, their lives, and mayhap even their hearts.

He stared up at the canopy over his bed for a long while, waiting for her to return. She must have slipped off to her room to refresh herself or use her chamber pot. But as time stretched on, niggling doubt crept in. Where was she?

Slowly, he dragged himself from the bed. He fumbled in the dark for his breeches and tunic. Her clothes were no longer piled on the floor with his.

With a hand extended before him, he found the tapestry-covered door leading to her chamber. He tried the handle. The door swung open, unbarred.

The shutters on her window were cracked, letting in a single beam of moonlight. It revealed an empty chamber. Her bed was still made and naught was amiss. The little bottles and vials on her dressing table were still in place. Her clothes were nowhere to be seen.

Nor was she.

Will padded silently to the door that led from her chamber into the corridor. It opened on silent hinges. Unease pricked him as he glanced both directions down the dark corridor. Where the hell had she gone?

He checked to make sure his dagger was still tucked into his boot, then slipped into the passageway. He crept toward the great hall, uncertain what would bring her there at this time of night, but it was a starting point.

Once he reached the hall, he glanced inside but remained in the shadows of the corridor. The servants and quite a few of the courtiers slept on the floor. It seemed that even a palace the size of Langley did not contain enough chambers to accommodate as large a retinue as King Edward traveled with. Several snores rose from those in the hall, but there was no sign of Eleanor.

Will made his way back down the corridor, contemplating ducking his head into the Queen's solar or even her wing of private chambers, but some instinct carried him toward the gardens instead.

Cautiously, he slipped out into the cool, damp night. The storm from that afternoon had blown away, revealing a heavy-hanging moon and a black sky pricked with dazzling stars. The ground was still wet from the earlier rains, filling his nose with the scents of wet earth and plant life.

He stalked into the deep shadows along the inside of the curtain wall, wending his way around the perimeter of the garden. As he passed the King's menagerie, two glowing gold eyes fixed on him from below. The lion was restless tonight, pacing his cage, his tail twitching. Will could relate.

The lion's eyes followed Will as he snuck by, wary and sharp as unsheathed blades. Just as Will reached the edge of the row of plum trees along the back wall, his gaze snagged on a movement in the opposite corner of the gardens.

In the shadows surrounding the rear entrance to the kitchens, a black-cloaked figure emerged. A second figure materialized a few feet away, joining the first. *Eleanor*.

Though she had a hood drawn up over her dark hair, he recognized her mouth and chin where the moonlight touched her.

The cloaked figure said something to her, but Will couldn't make it out. She responded, her lips moving swiftly yet her words not reaching him. Then the first figure reached into his cloak and began to withdraw something.

Will tensed, fearing the worst. But if the man was drawing a dagger or another weapon on Eleanor, there was naught he could do from this distance.

Yet when the moonlight landed on the figure's hand, he held only a folded square of parchment.

A missive.

Eleanor accepted it, immediately tucking it away into the folds of her midnight blue cloak. The two exchanged another quick word, and then the figure dissolved once more into the shadows.

Eleanor's gaze darted around the gardens. Will froze as her eyes swept over him. His heart hammered wildly, but he was deep enough into the darkness cast by the wall to be invisible to her.

She hurried back toward the entrance to the palace's private chambers, still darting furtive glances over her shoulder as she went.

Will could have gone to her in that moment. He could have stepped from the shadows and called her name, or surged forward and grabbed her before she could escape into the corridor. He could demand an explanation from her.

But he already knew what she would say. *Trust me.* Or mayhap *I need more time.* Sour bile curdled in his stomach. What the hell was she about? And had he made a terrible error in believing her?

Instead of showing himself, he waited until she had disappeared into the corridor leading to the wing of private chambers. Only then did he emerge from the shadows. He stalked across the garden, slipping inside after her.

But the corridor was already empty. She had either hurried much farther down the passageway, or she'd snuck into one of the many chambers lining it.

Will glanced to either side. There were literally dozens of rooms just within a few paces of each other. He could barge into each one, demanding to know if she was inside. Or he could admit that she'd gotten away.

He strode slowly back to his own chamber, his mind a churning maelstrom. Mayhap the black-cloaked figure was her contact within the Bruce's network. Aye, mayhap she had finally resumed her reports about Edward's movements.

But she hadn't been sending a missive, he reminded himself—she'd been receiving one. He couldn't be sure if that was unusual. Mayhap from time to time someone from the Bruce's cause contacted her with a directive. Yet neither she nor Sabine nor the Bruce had ever mentioned that they'd tried to contact her after she'd gone silent. It seemed that Eleanor's communications only flowed in one direction.

Besides, why wouldn't she have told Will? Of course, she had to maintain secrecy from all the others in the castle. That would explain the hood and the midnight rendezvous in the shadows of the garden. But Will knew she was a spy. Hell, he'd been badgering her since the moment he'd met her about her sudden silence. Telling him would have gotten him off her back and engendered more of his trust.

Instead she was slinking out of his bed in the dark of night, meeting with a stranger to receive a missive.

This must have something to do with the plan she refused to reveal to him. That knowledge was like a spear to the gut. After what they'd just shared, she still didn't trust him.

When he reached his chamber, he crossed to her room and checked it once more. She was still missing. He returned to his bed, but sleep eluded him for a long time. Her scent clung to the sheets, taunting him.

He had been all too willing to forget himself—forget the lesson he'd learned the hard way—just to imagine that she was his for a moment. He thought he was finally coming to know her, mysterious and guarded and vulnerable all at once.

But it seemed he knew naught.

Chapter Twenty-One

E leanor stifled a yawn behind her hand. She had
barely slept last night. Between the passionate,
reckless lovemaking she'd shared with Will, meeting
the messenger in the garden, and sitting with the
Queen as she read the missive, Eleanor felt as though
her lids were leaden and her head were filled with
rocks.

She could have snuck back to her own chamber in
the wee hours of the morning, but she'd stayed with
the Queen instead, talking over and over their plan.
Though the Queen had been frayed and uneasy after
reading the missive, they both would have fared better
with sleep instead. But the truth was, Eleanor was
avoiding Will.

That was why she and Isabella now sat before the
Queen's roses despite the fact that dawn had only

broken a quarter of an hour ago. Somehow in the haze of a sleepless night, it had seemed better to hide behind the Queen's skirts than face questions about what last night had meant.

And then there was the matter that loomed over everything. Roger Mortimer's missive just might be the final stroke that would set her and the Queen into motion. And what lay ahead of them could prove to be both their ruin. Eleanor wouldn't bring the same onto Will.

It seemed, though, that she could not avoid him forever. He came striding from the keep, his gaze landing on them. Even from this distance, she could see his eye narrow.

He was dazzling and fierce in the early morning light. His dark gold locks were unbound and fell in thick waves nearly to his broad shoulders. He wore his usual plain tunic, breeches, and boots, yet the way he carried himself underneath—with lethal grace and barely-tethered strength—set him apart from any man she'd ever laid eyes on.

Once again, she was reminded of the lion in the King's menagerie, for Will seemed caged here at the palace, just as the beast was. What might he be like unleashed and free of the bounds of court life?

"Highness." He gave the Queen a shallow bow as he came to a halt before the bench where they sat. Then his gaze shifted to Eleanor. "There ye are. I didnae see ye...breaking yer fast this morning in the great hall."

It seemed she was safe from an honest interrogation, at least in the Queen's presence. But from the hard look in Will's eye, he still wanted answers.

"Such a fine morning shouldn't be wasted indoors," she replied airily.

"Indeed. And what a lovely place to enjoy it." His gaze skewered her. "The garden's pleasures should be appreciated any time, day or *night*. Dinnae ye agree, Lady Eleanor?"

One of Eleanor's eyelids twitched. She hastily plastered on a smile, but inside, her stomach seized with fear. She'd assumed his obvious foul mood this morning was because she'd slipped from his bed after their lovemaking and had been hiding out since. But was it possible he'd seen her last night?

"What an eventful day it was yesterday," she blurted, desperate to change the subject. "If only every day could be filled with such diversion."

"Nay, I think I've had enough of amusements and games," he replied darkly.

Eleanor opened her mouth, fumbling for a response, but none came. Blessedly, she was saved from continuing the barbed conversation when the King swept into the garden from the great hall.

He looked rather worse for the wear after his night of feasting and drinking with Despenser.

Though his blue velvet cape and red silk tunic and hoes were pristine as ever, dark circles lay beneath his eyes and his brow was pinched.

Barely glancing at Will and Eleanor, he fixed his clouded blue gaze on Isabella. "A moment with my Queen, if you please."

Eleanor instantly jerked to her feet. She dipped into a quick curtsy before taking Will by the wrist and pulling him deeper into the gardens.

But just as abruptly, she changed directions, darting behind a dense shrub that divided the roses from the rest of the gardens. She tugged Will with her so sharply that he bumped into her.

"What the bloody hell are ye—"

"Shh." She placed a finger over her lips, then used it to point back toward the King and Queen through the hedge.

He shook his head slowly, his gaze cold on her. "Och, I see. After shirking yer mission these past several months, *now* ye intend to get back to spying, do ye? Tell me, was receiving a missive in the gardens last night part of yer mission as well?"

Eleanor swallowed hard. He *had* seen her. Blast it all. She couldn't face his questions anymore—not after what they'd shared last night. And not when their lives—nay, the very fate of both England and Scotland—hung in the balance now.

"Apparently ye *have* been sending and receiving

missives these last few months," he continued in a low, harsh voice. "Just no' for the Bruce's cause. What are ye about, Eleanor? If ye dinnae——"

Just then, the King's voice drifted to them through the hedge. Reluctantly, Will clicked his teeth together, cutting off the rest of what he'd been saying. It seemed even now, filled with anger and suspicion for her, he recognized that their larger mission took precedence.

"...leaving this morning," the King was saying. "I must visit Wallingford, then Berkeley."

"And will you take away my guards, as you threatened before?" the Queen asked tightly.

"I must gather more men, Isabella. I cannot let this Scottish challenge at Carlisle go unanswered. It would make me appear weak and cowardly."

Beside her, Will stiffened at the mention of Carlisle. For the thousandth time since coming to court, Eleanor cursed Edward's blind pride. He would never let go of this foolish insistence on seeing his father's dream of crushing the Scots through. Which meant he would never end this war—unless he was made to.

"You would leave me here without protection, then?" Isabella demanded.

The King sighed. "Langley is only a day's ride north of London. This is hardly the volatile Borderlands."

"That is what you said about Tynemouth Priory. You said I would be safe there, that the fighting would never reach England. And then you *abandoned* me to an advancing army of Scots."

"Come with me, then," the King snapped. He fell silent for a long moment before continuing, his voice lower now. "You could travel with my itinerant court, as you used to. You would be surrounded by soldiers at all times. And we might…mend things between us. Come, Isabella. Stop moping behind Langley's walls. Join me by my side as my Queen."

Isabella hesitated. Finally, she murmured, "Will Hugh Despenser remain at your side as well?"

The King breathed a curse. "Of course. You know what he means to me. He is one of the only ones I can trust amongst these grasping nobles."

"How can you not see that he is using you to gain power and wealth?" Isabella bit out. "Funneling royal funds through him, all the gifts of land and titles— including Wallingford Castle, which was mine by rights for life. Edward, you have put your trust in a charlatan."

The King's voice rose with anger. "Hugh has remained by my side through all these years of rebellion and turmoil. The rebel nobles would have taken him away from me, just as they took Piers. *My* nobles —my own *cousin*—would have seen my head on a pike and the Earl of Lancaster in my throne. But

Hugh stood with me against them all. He cares for me."

"I have cared for you, too, Edward. And look where it has gotten me."

"No more of this, Isabella. Lancaster and his rebels failed to force Hugh from my side. So will you. You can remain here and sulk if you wish, or you can accept him graciously, as you once did with Piers."

"*Accept* him?" the Queen hissed. "Nay, I think not, for Piers Gaveston never forbade me from seeing my own children, as Despenser has." "If you would only sign the pledge of loyalty to Hugh, then you would be permitted—"

"First you entrust our children—*your* sons and daughters, Edward—to Despenser's family. Then he decides I am some sort of threat to his power, so the two of you demand that I sign a loyalty pledge—*I* the Queen of England, sign a pledge to *him*, a lesser Earl —or else I will never be allowed to see my own children again. I will not tolerate such treatment any longer. I will—" Isabella exhaled hard, cutting herself off.

"Enough." Edward's voice was full of ice now. "I only thought to extend you an opportunity to rejoin my traveling court. The kindness was clearly misplaced."

"I find that Langley provides the peace and tranquility I have so sorely longed for of late," Isabella responded stiffly. "Thank you for the offer, husband, but I plan on staying here indefinitely."

From the swish of fabric and the slamming of a door a few moments after, Edward had stormed back to the keep without another word. Yet judging by the long silence that stretched afterward, the Queen remained mutely rooted to the bench.

Eleanor dared a glance at Will. His features were stony, his mouth set in a grim line. Now he knew just how deep the rift between the Queen and Edward had grown over the years. But he couldn't understand how significant that conversation had been.

He turned to her, opening his mouth to no doubt demand answers from her, but then Isabella's unsteady voice filtered through the hedge.

"Eleanor. A word, please."

Eleanor slid around Will and strode back to the Queen. Isabella sat rigid-backed on the bench overlooking the roses, her hands clasped into white knots in her lap.

As Eleanor lowered herself onto the bench beside her, the Queen spoke hurriedly.

"The time to act is now. Roger will be ready for—"

Eleanor clamped one hand over the Queen's and brought a finger to her lips.

Good God, had Will heard all of that? The Queen didn't know that Eleanor and Will had been eavesdropping, yet Eleanor was acutely aware that Will could likely make out every word from his position behind the hedge.

"Aye, Highness, we can visit the royal library if you wish," Eleanor said loudly.

Isabella blinked in confusion, then her gaze slid behind Eleanor to the gardens beyond. Eleanor nodded slowly.

"When might we depart?" the Queen asked, lifting her voice to match Eleanor's.

"Arrangements would have to be made. Mayhap we could depart for the Tower of London in a matter of a few days?" Eleanor dropped into a whisper. "*Tonight.*"

Isabella fixed her with a searching look. "Do you trust your fiancé with this?" she breathed. "Would you bring him with us?"

Eleanor's heart felt as though it were being torn in two. There wasn't enough time to think. After so many months of biding and waiting, suddenly everything was happening at once.

Will had vowed that if she betrayed him, his trust would be lost forever. Could she risk losing him by withholding the truth yet again? Or was it more dangerous for him to know all?

Remember David.

Speaking the truth had been his ruin. She could never let herself forget that. No matter what happened to her, she could not let Will come to harm.

"Nay." She squeezed her eyes shut for a moment. "I do not want to involve him in this."

The Queen clutched her hand and squeezed it, her gaze shining with a tempest of emotion.

"I had best see the King off. Then mayhap we can discuss a trip to the royal library in more detail." She gave Eleanor a solemn nod and mouthed the word *tonight*.

Oh God. The time of reckoning had finally arrived. The fates of two nations hung suspended like an executioner's sword over her head. She could only pray that she would survive this. And that somehow, some way, Will could forgive her.

Chapter Twenty-Two

T he rest of the day was spent in a frenzy of preparations for the King's departure from Langley.

Trunks were stuffed with silks and velvets, then loaded onto wagons. Supplies were gathered from every corner of the palace. Horses were saddled and bridled. And the hundreds of squires, grooms, servants, and courtiers who trailed after the King all scrambled hither and thither in an attempt not to be left behind.

Because of the chaos, Will hadn't been able to get Eleanor alone to ask her what the bloody hell was going on.

First the Queen said she intended to stay at Langley indefinitely, then mere moments later she was planning a trip to the royal library? Something far more devious was afoot, Will knew. In the unguarded seconds before Eleanor could quiet her, Isabella had let slip a few precious, mysterious words.

The time to act is now. Roger will be ready…

Who the hell was Roger? Ready for what? And what exactly would Isabella and Eleanor be acting upon?

There was too much to parse in that one snippet of information, not to mention all that had passed between the King and Queen in the garden.

As the sun slanted toward late afternoon and the tail end of Edward's enormous retinue drew away in the distance, Will found Eleanor in the stables, checking on one of the Queen's more spirited horses.

"…ensure that buckle doesn't bother her anymore, Tom."

Will stepped between Eleanor and the stable lad she was speaking with, pinning her with his stare. "A word, milady?"

Eleanor's dark brows lifted briefly in surprise, but then to Will's confusion, sadness flickered across her eyes.

"Aye. Mayhap we could take a ride."

Will hesitated, but couldn't read any ulterior motive behind her suggestion. "If ye wish."

They waited in heavy silence as Tom saddled Fearghus along with a gentle mare named Satin for Eleanor. Once the animals were ready, he lifted her into her saddle, cursing the tingle in his hands from that simple touch.

Wordlessly, they rode out through the gates and over the drawbridge.

Eleanor seemed to have a destination in mind, so he let her lead them down the grassy rise upon which the palace sat and across the open expanse toward the woods. She slowed once they crossed into the trees, letting her mare pick her footing over the mossy ground.

Wide-leafed oaks blotted out the late afternoon sunlight, except where it broke through in slanting yellow shafts to gild the forest floor. The air hung thick with the scents of loamy earth and plant life. Unlike the palace garden, which was neat and orderly, the forest had been allowed to grow dense and wild.

Instinctively, Will's shoulders relaxed somewhat. He could almost imagine he was at home in some Highland woodland here.

Would Eleanor like the Highlands? That thought had arisen seemingly from nowhere, yet the prospect made something in his chest lurch. What would it be like to take her to Dundale? Would she marvel at the raw beauty of the untamed landscape? Stand in awe before the formidable keep that was all his? Would the place tug at her, calling her back, as it did him now?

It was a foolish fancy, of course. Too many secrets and lies lay between them. No idyllic future was in store for them. How could this possibly end in aught but disaster of one kind or another?

Eleanor reined in at the edge of a small brook that cut through the ferns and tree roots. Sliding down from the saddle, she gave her horse a long tether so that it could drink from the stream.

Then to Will's surprise, Eleanor knelt in a puddle of green brocade skirts and drank too. She cupped her hands in the swift-moving water and lifted a palmful to her mouth. His own mouth went dry as he watched the water bead on her lips.

She glanced up to catch him staring.

"Is it truly so shocking to see me drink from a stream?"

He grunted. "I didnae think English ladies did such a thing."

"You forget—I grew up in the Borderlands, not at court. I used to spend every moment I could out of doors, running wild as the feral boars that lived in the glen near our keep, or so my mother used to say." She glanced down at her pooled gown with a weak smile. "That was more than one lifetime ago."

Once again, Will found himself thrown off-kilter by Eleanor's mood. She knew he meant to ask her what she was plotting with the Queen. He would have expected her to be cagey, or cold as stone—aught other than the quiet sadness that had stolen over her.

Slowly, he dismounted and tethered his horse beside hers. "Ye ken why I wanted to talk."

She rose and moved away from the brook. He trailed her to a large boulder that was half-covered with lush moss. She settled herself on it, not looking at him.

"The Queen wishes to go to the royal library to select a few books for herself. She is a great enthusiast when it comes to reading, and she—"

"We both ken that isnae true. What are ye really about, Eleanor?"

When she lifted her head, her angelic features were drawn with pain. "You also know what I must say."

Will cursed. "I'm going with ye, then. Whatever ye have planned, I'll no' let ye face it alone."

She closed her eyes for a long moment. "Can we discuss it tomorrow morning? I am too tired to do battle with you now."

"Then dinnae fight me anymore, lass." He crouched before her so that he could look up into her face. "Tell me the truth."

Sudden tears lit her eyes. She brought her hand up to cup his cheek. "You know why I can't."

Hot frustration surged in him. "Ye think ye are protecting me, aye? But ye are so afraid of losing someone again that ye are only protecting yerself."

"Mayhap you're right," she whispered. "Mayhap I am being selfish. All I know is that I can't lose you."

"Mayhap ye already have," he spat. "I willnae keep putting my trust in ye if ye never do the same."

Her throat bobbed. "I know. You do not trust easily." Her hand touched the black cloth strap holding his eyepatch in place. "Because of this?"

He stood up abruptly, breaking their contact. "Ye truly want to ken what happened, do ye?"

"Aye."

Spinning, he fixed her with a hard stare. Deep in his heart, he knew he couldn't keep aught from her. Not now. Not when he had come to care so much for her, fool that he was.

"It was nearly six years past," he began. "I was assigned to protect an English widow, Lillian Fitzhugh, whose husband was a man of some import in England's war against Scotland."

"In what way?"

"He was the master mason commissioned to build the curtain wall around the town of Berwick. Someone got the idea that mayhap the wall had a design flaw, a weakness that could be used against the English. Richard, Lillian's husband, was tortured and killed in search of that information. When he produced naught, they went after Lillian."

"And the Bruce wanted her kept safe," Eleanor surmised.

"Aye. He doesnae like involving innocents in this war, but I believe he also hoped that if there *was* a flaw to be exploited, she would share it with the Scots, given the fact that it had been the English who'd killed her husband so brutally. So he sent a member of his Bodyguard Corps to protect her—me. But there was another player in motion, one I didnae ken about."

Eleanor's brow furrowed, but she waited silently for him to go on.

"His name was Kirk MacLeod. He worked for a bounty hunter organization called the Order of the Shadow. He'd been hired to find and capture Lillian, then bring her to his employer so that she could be tortured like her dead husband."

Will's hands clenched by his sides. "Lillian and I were tucked away in a remote corner of the Highlands, but Kirk still managed to find us. He put two daggers in me." He touched one shoulder, then the other. "But I wouldnae give up so easily. I had sworn to protect Lillian—with my life if I had to. So Kirk... put me down. He slashed my eye with another one of his daggers. While I lay in a pool of my own blood, he kidnapped Lillian."

Eleanor pulled in a breath. "But he left you alive?"

Will snorted bitterly. "Only because of a hidden allegiance I discovered later. It turned out the Bruce had recruited Kirk to work in secret for the Scottish cause. Kirk had been directed to infiltrate the Order of the Shadow. He was to gather information so that the organization could be destroyed from within."

"So when he attacked you…" Eleanor shook her head in confusion. "When he took Lillian away…"

"He was actually a member of the Bodyguard Corps the whole time," he finished.

"Have you…have you seen the man since then?"

"Nigh every damn day," Will ground out through locked teeth. "When his mission was complete and the Order was obliterated, he and Lillian—who had fallen in love and wed by then—moved to the camp where I lived and trained with the others in the Corps."

Eleanor chose her next words carefully. "And have you managed to forgive him?"

"Why the hell would I?"

She blinked at him. "Because it has been nearly six years, as you said. And because you and he are on the same side."

"Ye dinnae understand," he rasped. "The Corps is *family*. The King entrusts us with the lives of those most valuable to him, and so we in turn must trust each other unequivocally. Kirk betrayed that trust. And I told ye before—my trust, once lost, is lost forever."

"I am sorry, Will, but…but he *saved* you," she beseeched. "He might have killed you to keep up the ruse that he was a member of the Order of the

Shadow. Instead he left you alive, and in a manner that thrust you out of harm's way."

"He left me maimed for life," Will snapped. "Aye, I didnae ken when he attacked that he was a fellow Corpsman. But *he* kenned it. He withheld that information from me. And he chose to take my eye, even though I was supposed to be his family."

She opened her mouth but he barreled on.

"And I could have died, Eleanor. A fever gripped me for a fortnight afterward. I was lucky. But even though I lived, I am forever changed. Ye saw me in the archery competition. Before Kirk cut me, I was training to become one of the most elite warriors in all of Scotland. Now I cannae shoot, and the gap in my vision on the right side makes me a liability. He took that from me."

She fell silent, her dark gaze searching him.

"Now do ye see why I am loath to trust *blindly*?" He gestured toward his eyepatch, but his face bore no traces of humor at his grim pun.

"I wasn't there," she began carefully. "And I don't know fully what you suffered. But I do know what it's like to hold someone else's fate in your hands and make the wrong decision, even when you are doing your damnedest to make the right one."

"This isnae the same as what happened to David. Yer mistake was borne of naiveté and innocent trust. Kirk acted with full knowledge against me."

"Aye, he took your eye knowingly. But mayhap he also knew it was the only way to shield you from greater danger. When I look at you, Will, I see a man who is alive despite being hurt. Wronged. Yet also a man who has been protected from worse."

He huffed a mirthless breath. "Like ye are protecting me now?"

"Aye, mayhap."

She rose from the boulder then, going to him. As if he were a wild animal, she reached for him with gentle hands.

"You've carried your anger, your resentment, for a long time now," she murmured. "Mayhap it is time to let it go."

When her small palms landed on his chest, it felt as though his heart fractured and fell to pieces.

"Damn ye, lass."

"For what?"

He swallowed against a ragged throat. "For making me *want* to trust ye. For making me care more than I should for ye."

Her lashes shuddered with pain and sadness, her lips parting on an exhalation. "If I am damned for making you care, then so are you, for you have undone me just as surely."

Rising on her toes, she brushed her lips against the vulnerable pulse at the base of his neck. Then she kissed the underside of his jaw, his chin, his cheek.

"Let us be damned together," she murmured against his skin.

By the time her lips hovered over his, he knew he was already lost. With a curse, he abandoned his last shred of reason and claimed her mouth in an aching kiss.

Chapter Twenty-Three

Eleanor felt herself falling headlong into the torrent of dangerous emotion she had fought so hard to resist.

She met Will's fierce kiss, unable to pull herself back and no longer caring. This was insanity, kissing him, caring for him. *Loving him.*

It was unlike aught she had ever known. Her love for David had been sweet and slow-building, the first love of a girl, not a woman grown. But what burned between Eleanor and Will was mad and wild and perilous. They might both be consumed by the raging heat that kept dragging them back together.

But it was so much more than lust. He'd shown her his pain, his scars, his fears. And she'd shown him hers, yet despite that, he still looked at her as though he longed to pull her into his arms and never let go.

She wasn't the gentle, innocent girl she'd once been anymore. She'd been forged and reshaped into something stronger, sharper, like iron wrought into steel. It would be no easy feat for a man to love who she was now. But the savage longing in Will's kiss made her hope that mayhap he could.

Until she left him, that was.

He might never know the truth of the plan she'd staked her life upon. He might never know what was in her heart.

But in this moment, at least, she was in his arms, their mouths joined as one, and love beating like a pulse inside her. It would all be dashed come morning, yet for a few blessed hours, it could still be perfect.

His hands were rough on her, tugging at the laces running down her back, clutching the fine brocade in fistfuls. His fingers sank into her hips to draw her closer. Her own hands went wild in response, delving into his unbound hair and scoring his scalp.

He growled like a feral animal. With a swift jerk, he removed the plaid from his shoulders and snapped it open. He let it drop on the soft forest floor, then urged her onto it.

Will kissed down her neck and to the exposed flesh above her gown's scooped neckline. Meanwhile, one hand fumbled under her skirts, skimming over her silk stockings and to her bare thighs.

A shiver that had naught to do with the cool forest

air stole over her. Instinctively, she parted her knees to his touch. When his fingers brushed against her curls, she pulled in a ragged breath. He stroked into her damp heat, teasing that spot that drove her to mindlessness.

But before she lost herself to pleasure, she needed more of him. All of him.

Wrapping her arms around his neck, she pulled him down to the plaid beside her.

"I need you inside me."

"Come here to me then, lass."

Grasping her hips, he rolled to his back. He brought her on top of him, settling her knees on either side of his lean hips. As she yanked her tangled skirts from between them, he gripped the gown at her shoulders. With a swift tug, he dragged it down, exposing her breasts.

The gasp that slipped from her lips at the touch of the cool air quickly turned to a moan as he closed his mouth over one peak. Her head lolled back as he laved first one breast and then the other, leaving them wet and puckered.

Even as he continued giving her breasts sweet torture with his tongue, he reached between them and fumbled with the ties on his breeches. When his hard cock sprang free, she could not contain the wanton need burning her up. She ground her sex against him, sliding along the stiff length and drawing a groan from them both.

Apparently unable to endure her teasing any longer, Will gripped her hips in a viselike hold and stilled her. He shifted her until his cock was poised at her entrance. But then, she laid staying hands on his chest.

"Let me see you."

Tentatively, she reached for the patch covering his right eye. He stiffened beneath her, but he did not stop her as she eased the patch away.

Staring blankly at her from beneath the black cloth was his clouded, milky eye. A scar, white now, pinched the skin both above and below the eye into a tight line. Even as she felt his other eye boring into her, this one remained fixed and void of sight.

She wondered fleetingly what the eye had once looked like. It would have been a match to his other, the blue-green color of troubled water, yet clear and sharp like a jewel.

Just as briefly as the image occurred to her, however, she cast it aside. Her heart ached for him and for what he'd been through. He was not perfect. He was no longer the man he'd been when he'd had the use of both eyes. He had suffered. Lost.

Yet she did not want that other man with a perfect face. She wanted him as he was now, scarred, hardened by his past, yet choosing to lay himself bare in this moment, only for her.

She touched his cheek, feeling the burn of raw emotion behind her eyes. She shifted her gaze to his good eye and found him watching her, not with his normal wary, keen stare, but with a look that was unguarded. Vulnerable.

Ravenous.

Holding her gaze, he pulled her slowly down onto his length, filling her, stretching her, taking her completely.

By the time he was seated fully inside her, every one of Eleanor's breaths was a moan. She dropped her head until her brow rested on his, their panting breaths mingling.

He began moving her by her hips. He lifted her unhurriedly so that he drew out of her, then brought her back down with a hard tug. When he was buried to the hilt, he ground his hips upward, sending pleasure thundering through her.

She found and matched his rhythm, lifting, lowering, and rolling with him deep inside. He dragged his head off the plaid and captured a nipple in his mouth once more. His tongue and lips sent frissons of fire between her breasts and her core.

Her thighs began to quake as release edged closer. She rode him harder, faster, losing the rhythm, losing everything but the feel of him around her, inside her, everywhere.

He must have sensed her urgency, for he slid a hand between them and pressed against that blazing point of need just above where they were joined.

That sent her flying over the edge and into ecstasy. With a stuttering cry, she shattered into a thousand shards of light. He came hard after her, growling and groaning. But this time he didn't pull away. Nay, he thrust up into her with fierce abandon, spending inside her.

They soared together for what felt like a never-ending moment. But then reality began to edge back in. Distantly, she became aware of the passage of one heartbeat, then another, then another, reminding her that time would not stop for them.

To the thud of their hammering hearts, Eleanor slowly came back into herself. She sagged over him, her face coming to rest against the strong column of his neck. She inhaled deeply, letting his scent brand itself on her senses.

After a long while, he eased her gown back over her shoulders and pulled her down alongside him. His hands were gentle on her hair, yet she could sense that he had retreated somewhat. And that he waited for her to pull away in turn.

Her heart broke then, for she could not speak the

words he longed to hear. He must have known it, too, for he didn't bother asking her once more what she had planned.

Reluctantly, she pushed herself out of his arms and up to a seat so that she could look into his face. Sometime while she had been lying against him, he'd shifted his eyepatch back into place. He looked at her now with sad resignation.

She fumbled for something—anything—she could say to soften the dreaded wall that was rising between them once more. "I know this is not nearly enough, but...the enemy of your enemy just might be your friend."

"Ye speak in riddles again. What does that mean?"

She shook her head, unable to say more through her rapidly cinching throat.

"And what of us?" he asked, his voice like the crunch of gravel underfoot. "Are we enemies, then, Eleanor?"

"Nay," she breathed. "I am not your enemy. Please...do not ever forget that."

He shook his head slowly. "Wherever ye are going, whatever ye are doing, I'm going with ye."

She closed her eyes for a terrible heartbeat, willing the lie out of her mouth. "We can discuss it in the morning."

After a long moment, he turned away from her and began straightening his clothes. They rose and retrieved their horses in silence, then rode back to the palace in the fading light.

Chapter Twenty-Four

A s the first rays of morning light slipped under the shutters, Will awoke in his bed.

His empty bed.

Though they had made love the previous afternoon, a secret part of him had hoped that Eleanor would come to him again in the night. But after a somber, quiet meal in the great hall, she had retired for the evening and had remained in her chamber all night.

He had waited, staring up at the velvet canopy over his bed, longing for the sound of the adjoining door opening and Eleanor slipping past the tapestry and into his room. But she never came, and sleep had eventually claimed him.

Mayhap he was blinded by his feelings for her, but he believed he understood more clearly than ever why she continued to evade his demands for information. She thought she was protecting him.

Like Kirk had.

The thought tumbled over like a pebble in his mind, but to his surprise, it did not elicit the surge of fury he would have expected. That was her doing. As she'd said, he'd been bitter about what had happened to his eye for a long time now. He'd clung to his anger, letting it fester like an untended wound for six long years.

But what if she was right? What if he accepted Kirk's many apologies, accepted the fact that he'd acted as best he could in a terrible situation to save Will from even more harm?

And what if he accepted that he was no longer the warrior he'd once been, nor the warrior he might have become with a second eye, but rather the warrior he was today, scarred and reduced but also honed by all that he'd been through?

The concept was jarring after so many years spent harboring resentment and shame over what had happened. It felt as though he was trying to wield a sword with his left hand rather than his right. But as he'd learned after losing the use of his eye, the body could be trained to adjust, compensate, and ultimately recover. Mayhap the mind could, too.

Still, he dreaded what awaited him this morning. Though Eleanor had spurred him to reconsider his anger toward Kirk, it could not change matters between them. She had held back the truth from him, even after what they'd shared in the woods. He needed to speak with her, and he would not be put off any longer.

He rose and dressed, then knocked softly on the door that connected their chambers. He received no answer, so after a moment's pause, he tried the handle. The door swung open—she hadn't barred it to him last night. Yet her chamber was empty and dim, the shutters drawn tight and the bed already made.

He exited through her door and strode toward the great hall. The hall was strangely quiet now that the King and his enormous retinue had departed. The whole palace felt deserted, with only the remaining skeleton crew of servants, and even fewer guards than when Will had arrived.

He tried the gardens next, but Eleanor wasn't there either, so he circled back through the wing of private chambers. Mayhap Eleanor and the Queen had already departed for a morning ride.

Or mayhap…

He shoved the lurking doubt away. Eleanor had said it would take several days to make preparations for a visit to the royal library—or whatever trip they were truly planning.

As he approached the door to the Queen's solar, one of the other ladies-in-waiting slipped out.

"Ye there."

The lass nigh jumped out of her skin at the sound of Will's voice booming down the corridor.

"A-aye, milord?" she said, smoothing her hands over her rounded hips and staring at him with wide eyes.

"Marietta, isnae it?"

"Aye, milord. What can I help you with?"

He came to a halt and jutted his chin toward the solar door. "Is Lady Eleanor within?"

She blinked at him in confusion. "Nay, she is with the Queen."

A spear of icy trepidation sliced Will's gut. "And where is the Queen?"

Mariette took a step back, and belatedly Will realized that he'd growled the question.

"They departed, milord. For the royal library. I thought you already knew of their plans for a trip."

Bloody hell and damnation.

They had already left. And Eleanor had flat-out *lied* to him. She had led him to believe—

Nay, he couldn't dwell on her betrayal now. He needed to find her—and wring the truth from her at last, for he was damn sure she didn't actually intend to spend the day quietly reading in a library.

"When did they leave?" he ground out.

"Oh, several hours before dawn, milord. The Queen hoped to reach the library by this evening so that she could retire to the Palace of Westminster for the night."

"And how many others went with her?"

Marietta's dark brows drew together. "Well, Lady Eleanor, of course, but the Queen didn't request the presence of any of the other ladies. And mayhap ten guards."

This was all sorts of wrong. From what he'd overheard Eleanor say to the Queen in the gardens yesterday morn, Will knew the royal library was housed in the Tower of London. The Tower was indeed a full day's ride from Langley, and if the Queen was heading there, it would make sense for her to stay at the nearby Palace of Westminster.

But given what he knew of the Queen's fears after the Battle of Old Byland, she never would have traveled with fewer than three dozen soldiers to protect her.

Mayhap she was aware of the strain it would put on Langley's already depleted forces to remove so many men for her little excursion. But that was assuming she and Eleanor were truly making the innocent decision to visit the royal library. Yet Will would stake his life on the instinct that they were up to something far more underhanded.

"Which way did they ride out?" he demanded, his mind swirling.

Marietta looked confused. "The library lies to the south, milor—"

"I didnae ask which way the library lies. I asked which way they rode out."

Marietta took another step back, bumping into the opposite corridor wall. "I…"

Damn it all. He had terrified the poor lady-in-waiting so much that she looked ready to faint.

"Forgive me, milady," he said through gritted teeth, "but I hoped ye might have seen them depart with yer own eyes."

"N-nay, milord. I am sorry, but I did not."

Will hissed a curse that made Marietta jump. "Thank ye, milady. That is all."

She practically ran in the opposite direction away from him. When he was alone, Will breathed another colorful oath. He charged toward the outer courtyard, his mind in turmoil. He would have his horse saddled and then set out after them.

But where the bloody hell had they gone? He could ride south toward London, but given all of Eleanor's lies, there was no reason to believe that her wee tale about taking the Queen to the royal library was true. Aye, they could still be headed south—or they could be traveling in literally any other direction.

He spun on his heels, retracing his steps back toward the private chambers. He needed more information, a clue, however small, of what their true intentions were.

While he walked, he picked over everything Eleanor had ever said to him.

What I am working toward has been months—years—in the making.

She'd claimed it was all for the greater good of Scotland, but he'd been smart enough not to trust her word blindly—that was, until he'd bedded her and lost all his wits.

If it matters, the situation is…advancing. I believe we are approaching a crossroads.

Aye, she had been maneuvering long before he'd arrived, including meeting with that cloaked messenger in the dead of night and receiving a missive. If she had been approaching a crossroads before, it appeared that now she'd picked her direction and was riding toward her fate.

The enemy of your enemy just might be your friend.

What the hell did that mean? She'd seemed desperate to reveal all to him yesterday afternoon when they'd shared an intimacy Will had never known before. Was it a warning? Or a clue?

Scotland's enemy was King Edward. Edward's enemies were…the French? As far as Will knew, things were tense between Edward and France's King Charles, but they weren't all-out adversaries.

The nobles who'd rebelled against Edward, then? But they had all been hanged or beheaded at traitors, including the King's cousin, the Earl of Lancaster.

Conrad de Russ? Though the man had left angry and humiliated, Eleanor had said he was a lesser noble with little coin or land and even less power.

He found himself standing before her chamber door, no closer to understanding her mysterious schemes. He entered, closing the door tight behind him. Just as it had been earlier, the room was shadowed and still.

His feet carried him to the armoire on one wall. Her dresses hung like colorful pennants inside. It seemed that wherever she'd gone, she hadn't taken any of her fine gowns.

He moved to the trunk at the foot of her bed. It contained a few folded blankets and some spare linen chemises—naught that illuminated her true purpose. He rifled through the bottles and vials atop her dressing table, but they revealed naught also.

As he turned away from the table, his gaze caught on one of the tapestries hanging on the wall. The tapestry portrayed what appeared to be a forest nymph leaning down from a branch to kiss a bedraggled-looking knight below. But what snagged his attention wasn't the romantic scene. Rather, it was what the tapestry covered.

Behind the lower left-hand corner of the weave,

nearly to the floor, was a crack in the mortar between the wall's stones. Will fell to his knees and yanked the tapestry aside. He ran a finger along the crack, then skimmed his hand over the wall.

One of the stones stood out ever so slightly in relief from the others. The mortar was fractured all the way around it. Gripping the stone with his finger-tips, he gave it a wiggle.

It was loose.

With swift dexterity, he worked the stone out of its slot and set it aside. Then he reached into the hole where it had been.

His fingers brushed parchment.

Closing his hand, he pulled out a stack of missives, each unfolded and nested into the next. Heart hammering in his ears, he began with the one on the bottom. It was dated more than a year ago and written in a strong, masculine hand.

My dearest love, it began.

Will's stomach plummeted. Last spring when the missive had been scrawled, David had already been dead for roughly three years. Another man had called Eleanor his dearest love, then.

The missive went on to speak of how difficult the writer found it to be apart from her, but that they *fought for their beloved England—together, someday, if God is kind*, the man wrote, which made their separation bearable.

It was signed simply *R*.

The next was much the same, beginning with flowery language about how R loathed to be forced from Eleanor's side, but that he was lucky to be alive. *Memories of your beauty haunt me, my darling. I imagine that I can taste your lips upon mine, feel your heated skin, your cries of pleasure ringing in my*—

Abruptly, Will realized he had crumpled the missive in his fist. Could R stand for Conrad de Russ? Eleanor had said she'd been using him for information for over a year. The timeline matched. But she'd also claimed that they'd never shared intimacies. Was that a lie? Or had she been involved with yet another man, this mystery R?

Will hurriedly read the rest of the missives. They were filled with more words of longing, and more praise for Eleanor's beauty, wit, and strength. R wrote of being imprisoned somewhere, but that he hadn't stopped fighting to be free so that they could be reunited once more. And so that they could bring about a better and stronger England together.

As he read the final missive, he realized that it must have been the one Eleanor had received in the garden only two nights past. *Your missives have kept me alive these long months. I await you, my love, with fear for your safety, but courage in my heart. We will fight for England together at last. When the time is right, come to me. I am ready.*

The parchment slid out of Will's suddenly slack fingers.

The time to act is now. Roger will be ready...

The Queen had spoken those words to Eleanor in the garden only yesterday.

R was Roger—Roger *who*, Will did not know. But the Queen seemed to know of Eleanor's affair with the man. The missive, plus the King's departure, apparently created the opening that Roger and Eleanor had been waiting for. Under the pretense of going to the royal library, Isabella was actually assisting Eleanor to meet with Roger.

The time to act is now. The time to fight for England together, as Roger had written so many times.

Realization after realization hit Will in the chest like rapidly fired arrows. Eleanor had lied to him— about the visit to the library, and that they would discuss whether he would come along this morning. She'd known yesterday as she'd taken him inside her, then lain in his arms with her head over his heart, that she would leave in the dead of night, like a thief, before he would awake this morn.

And she'd lied about this affair with Roger. She had told Will she cared for him. She'd wrung his secrets from him with tender guile, and all the while she'd been carrying on with Roger.

Fool that he was, Will had believed her when she'd cried his name in pleasure. And when she'd cursed him for making her come to care for him, as he'd come to care for her. *As he'd come to love her.*

Damn him to hell and back. He had been caught unawares yet again, just like before. As with Kirk, he'd been betrayed by the one who had vowed allegiance to him, who was supposed to be on his side.

But this wasn't just about Will's deceived heart. It was so much worse than that. The biggest lie of them all had been that she was loyal to Scotland. The truth was, all this time she had been working secretly on some scheme with Roger "for the benefit of England's future," as he'd written more than once.

I am not your enemy. Her words from yesterday twisted his stomach. Another lie.

And like a fool, he'd believed her. Trusted her. Fallen in love with her.

Bile rising in the back of his throat, Will shoved the thought aside. He could feel sorry for himself later. Now, he needed to find her.

A snippet from one of the earlier missives tugged at his mind. He rifled through the sheets of parchment in search of it. It was when Roger had been lamenting his imprisonment. He quickly scanned one of the missives. Aye, this had been it.

It has been eight months since I have laid eyes on you, dearest love, and four since I was brought to the Tower.

Could he mean...the Tower of London?

The pieces shifted into place in his mind. He'd

assumed that the Queen's excuse to visit the royal library in the Tower had been just that—a ruse to explain Eleanor and her departure, naught more.

But what if they were indeed going to the Tower? Not for books, which was cover enough to get them inside, but to reunite Eleanor with Roger, who was imprisoned there? Judging from the closeness that existed between Isabella and Eleanor, the Queen would do such a thing—lie and deceive for Eleanor's sake. Especially if it was in the best interest of England, her adopted country.

Will thrust the missives back into their hiding place and shoved the stone in its slot. He'd seen enough. London was a full day's ride from Langley. Assuming they'd left several hours before dawn, as Marietta had said, they only had a half a day of riding on him at best.

As he stormed toward the stables, he steeled himself for what awaited him. *Sword*

Eleanor had turned against Scotland.

Mayhap it was her love of Roger that had bent her allegiances back toward England, as her love of David had drawn her toward the Bruce's cause. Or mayhap her loyalty to the Queen, and therefore England, trumped her devotion to Scotland. That would make even more sense given the fact that she'd nearly been killed fleeing the Scottish army after Old Byland.

Whatever the case, there could be no doubt of her betrayal now. And the Bruce had made it clear what Will ought to do if he discovered she'd turned traitor.

To save his mission—and mayhap to save all of Scotland—he had to find her.

And then he had to kill her.

Chapter Twenty-Five

Will urged Fearghus faster. He was rapidly losing daylight, and with it, his ability to track the Queen's retinue.

When he'd left Langley, he'd known to ride south, but because it hadn't rained for the last few days, the ground was firm enough to reveal only minimal tracks. He could have ridden straight to the Tower, but he still hoped to catch Eleanor out in the open before she could reach London. Or Roger.

He'd been forced to ride in a line that cut diagonally across the landscape, slicing back and forth as he searched for signs of the retinue's passing. A half-dozen miles beyond the palace, he'd finally picked up their trail and urged Fearghus into a gallop.

Now he could only pray that he reached them

before they made it to the Tower. Or before night fell completely.

Though Eleanor and the Queen took nigh daily rides, an hour-long jaunt for fresh air was far different than a full day's journey. To accommodate Isabella's comforts, they may have been forced to travel slower than a retinue of a dozen riders without a Queen and a noblewoman present would have.

At least, that was Will's hope. Otherwise, he might be too late to stop whatever Eleanor had planned.

Just off the road ahead, a stand of dark trees rose from the blue-gray twilight. Will slowed Fearghus. He squinted at the hard-packed dirt beneath him. Individual hoof prints were becoming almost impossible to pick out, but the grass alongside the road had been flattened recently. The trail of compressed grass led toward the copse of trees.

His pulse hammering, Will dismounted slowly and pulled Fearghus off the road. The stallion was well trained enough not to wander off. Nor would he bolt if violence erupted.

Will closed his hand around his sword hilt to keep the scabbard from thudding against his legs as he moved closer. God, it had felt good to retrieve the weapon from Langley's guardhouse as he'd departed. The feel of it wrapped in his hand sent a familiar calm through him even as he slinked toward the stand of yew trees.

Even before he'd reached the outer edge of the trees, voices drifted toward him. He recognized John, one of Isabella's most trusted guards, immediately.

"…believe we should press on, Highness."

"How much farther to Westminster?" the Queen asked, her voice weary.

"It is still at least two hours away, Highness."

"It cannot be safe to remain out here for the night," she replied, fear now edging her tone. "My own fatigue does not matter. We must continue."

"We are nearly there," came a reassuring murmur. Will froze, instantly recognizing Eleanor's voice. "Just a little more discomfort, Highness, and the journey will be over."

He had to swallow several times to rid his mouth of the bitter bile that rose up the back of his throat. To his disgust, his heart still responded to the sound of her voice, lurching painfully. Damn him for ever trusting her. And for letting himself fall in love with her.

Forcing his feet to move once more, he slipped behind a wide-trunked yew, then eased his good eye around it to assess the situation.

The entire party of a dozen had dismounted. The Queen and Eleanor stood in the middle, the Queen's fists pressing into her lower back where she likely ached from the day's ride. Ten guards circled them, waiting for the Queen's word.

All the guards had swords hanging from their hips, and he could make out a few crossbows strapped to the saddles of their horses as well.

He bit down on a curse. There was no way to soften it—the odds against him were more than steep. He would have the element of surprise, but even before he'd lost his eye, he would have been hard-pressed to take on ten trained, armed men, English or nay, by himself.

He only needed to get to Eleanor, he reminded himself. He didn't need to fell every one of the guards. In fact, the thought of killing the men turned his stomach. They were innocent—well, as innocent as men who served King Edward could be.

In truth, they served Isabella, whom he would never harm. It had become abundantly clear at Langley that she had no sway over Edward or his decisions. He could not bring himself to kill a Queen, let alone a blameless woman.

Eleanor, on the other hand…

His grip tightened on his sword hilt. If killing her would stop whatever plot she'd concocted with Roger for England's benefit, then he could not hesitate. She had the potential to do far more harm to Scotland than the ineffectual schemes of King Edward ever had. She was far too clever and cunning. Worse, as a spy, she had been privy to secrets that could destroy not only the Bruce's network of information gatherers, but the entire cause itself.

A realization slowly crept over him. He likely wouldn't make it out of this alive. He could probably incapacitate several of the guards before they would cut him down. Hopefully he could reach Eleanor and put a stop to her. But even if he was successful, he would be killed, either with the immediate mercy of a blade, or the slow, torturous death of a traitor.

He closed his eye for a moment, his ears filling with the rapid thud of his pulse. This was what he had trained for. This was what he'd pledged himself to when he'd joined the Bodyguard Corps—to defend Scotland from her enemies, with his sword, with his wits, and with his life if he had to.

He was proud to die for the cause if it meant a safer future for Scotland.

Slowly, so as not to make a sound, he slid his sword free of its scabbard.

God, forgive and keep me. For Scotland.

With a deep breath, he surged forward. *

Chapter Twenty-Six

"Let me aid you, Highness." Eleanor fitted the Queen's riding boot into her stirrup, then gripped her forearm and helped boost her into the saddle.

Isabella's strength had been flagging since late afternoon. Still, they had made it this far. And the Queen was determined to reach London in what was likely a combination of dread at being exposed after dark and anticipation at what awaited them at the Tower.

"Only a little longer," she said, dropping her voice just for the Queen. "And then you will see Roger and we will—"

A heavy thud sounded behind her. The Queen's gaze shot over her head and a scream tore from her throat.

Eleanor spun to find that the shadows had come alive. A man materialized from the darkness, a sword grasped in his hands. He stood over one of the guards, who lay motionless at his feet.

Oh God, nay.

Will.

A scream of warning rose in her throat, but whether it was for the guards or Will, she never knew, for it died when the remaining guards lunged for him.

Will dodged to one side, blocking the swing of a sword. Then he darted forward, bringing the pommel of his hilt down onto one of the guard's heads. The man fell into a heap, but the onslaught did not slow.

Will moved like a wolf through the shadows as he battled against the guards, light on his feet with his shoulders slightly hunched over the sword he clutched with both hands. She'd seen him fight before, but never like this. In the King's tourney he had been restrained, deliberate. Even when he'd fought Conrad, he had withheld some of his strength and deadly speed.

Not anymore. His sword flashed and darted like a striking viper. The blade was one with the fluid, lethal movements of his body.

Yet she realized that he hadn't given any of the guards a fatal blow. Two lay on the ground, unconscious. Just then, his blade sliced one of the guards' thighs, forcing the man down with the others. He wasn't aiming for their necks or torsos.

A realization hit her.

He isn't here to kill them. He could have already killed three of the men if he had intended to.

Something had gone terribly wrong for Will to even be here. She'd known he would be furious when he woke that morning to discover that she and the Queen had left. She'd lied and misled him, at the cost of his trust. But she hadn't expected him to track them down and attack.

A second realization crashed through her on the heels of the first.

He is here to kill me.

She staggered backward, bumping into Isabella's horse. The animal, like its rider, was terrified. The horse sidestepped and snorted, its ears swiveling. The Queen's eyes were so wide that Eleanor could see white all around them.

"Steady!" she cried to both the horse and the Queen. Isabella was clearly conflicted—she looked ready to spur the horse into a gallop to get away from the attack as fast as possible, but some rational part of her fear-clouded mind must have also understood that if the guards bested Will, she was safer remaining close to them.

Eleanor's head snapped back to the battle. She had to find a way to speak to Will before the guards killed him. Whatever he believed, she needed to mend it. She had betrayed his trust and deceived him, but if he thought the worst of her...

A fourth guard sagged to the ground as Will drove his hilt into the man's gut, then punched him in the face. But just as Will spun back to the others, one of the guards lunged forward on his right.

At Will's delayed response, a horrible comprehension filled her. The guard moved in Will's blind spot.

He shifted to block the blow at the last moment, but it was too late. The blade plunged into his shoulder. He roared in pain and jerked backward off the blade.

"Nay!" Without thinking, Eleanor surged into motion. But it felt as though her feet were moving through thick mud. She couldn't get to him fast enough.

Will's gaze shifted to her then. In the heartbeat that he hesitated, the remaining guards swarmed him. One man wrested the sword from his grasp while the others grabbed for his arms and legs, dragging him to the ground.

John raised his sword overhead as the others held Will pinned down.

Time slowed. A horrible image flashed through Eleanor's mind—Will, lying in a pool of his own blood, his piercing blue-green eye open and unseeing in death.

It was happening again. It seemed Eleanor was doomed to meet the fate she had feared the most—losing the man she loved a second time—on the path she'd sought to avoid it.

Nay, nay, nay!

Just as the sword descended toward Will's neck, Eleanor flung herself the last several feet separating them. She landed on top of his chest, her body sprawled out over his like a shield.

But she was not made of metal. She drew one final breath, waiting for the sword to pierce her flesh instead of Will's.

"Stop!"

Eleanor felt a whoosh of air from the descending sword against her upturned cheek, but the bite of the blade never came.

"Stop, John!" the Queen shrieked again.

Eleanor opened her eyes to find John staring down at her in stunned horror, the sword poised mere inches from her face. He remained frozen in shock for a long moment, but then he dropped the tip of the sword into the forest floor with shaking hands and sagged backward.

"Do not harm him." Eleanor's voice came out a ragged plea, but the rest of the guards did not move. "He is here for me, not the Queen."

Isabella gasped. "Is that true, Will Stewart?"

From beneath her, she could feel Will drawing a pained breath. "Aye, Highness."

"I can explain aught," Eleanor implored. "Please, you don't understand, Will, I—"

"I willnae listen to any more of yer lies!" he roared. He struggled against the guards' grip, but they held fast.

Eleanor pushed herself partway up so that she could meet his furious gaze. Dark blood leaked over his tunic from the wound in his shoulder. He lay panting like an enraged bull, his body pulled taut beneath her.

"*Please,*" Eleanor said, though she wasn't sure if she was speaking to the Queen, the guards, or Will. "Let me explain."

She tried John first. "Have the guards release him. I must speak with him."

His brows drawing together and down, John turned to the Queen.

"He isn't a danger to you, Highness," she said, shifting her attention to Isabella as well. "He doesn't understand..." Darting a glance at the guards, who had been kept in the dark, she chose her words carefully. "He doesn't understand what we hope to accomplish in visiting the Tower. I kept it from him for the safety of us all. But I would tell him now so that he doesn't have reason to doubt us."

Isabella stared at her in desperate silence for a

long moment. "And you think…" she began slowly. "You believe if you tell him, he will agree with what we seek to do?"

"Aye, Highness."

"He garnered the King's approval," Isabella continued, her gaze shifting warily to Will. "He may not accept——"

"Nay, he will. I trust him, Highness."

At that, a low growl issued from Will's throat.

The Queen hesitated for several seconds. At last, she gave herself a small shake and a nod. "Very well. Release him."

The guards were slow to obey her order, but they had no choice. Reluctantly, they eased their grip on him and began retreating a few paces.

Eleanor shifted off him, coming to crouch on the ground by his side. Her limbs shook with what had just happened—and what might have happened. But most of all, she trembled for what lay ahead. Somehow she had to convince Will that—

"I cannae fail," he murmured. "I willnae."

He moved like lightning, his hand flying to his boot. The dagger he kept there flashed before her eyes an instant before he pressed it to her throat.

The Queen screamed wordlessly and John shouted. The guards took a step forward, but there was naught they could do with the dagger resting against her neck.

Will yanked her back against his chest, his heavy arm clamping around her and holding her immobile. Then he began dragging her up, first to her knees and then to her feet.

Eleanor swallowed against the blade. It was cold, but the metal was rapidly warming from contact with her skin.

"This doesnae concern ye anymore, Highness," he said, his voice low and rough. "Leave. Now. All of ye."

"Nay!" Isabella cried.

Like a ship on the distant horizon of the sea, an idea, small and blurry, crossed Eleanor's mind. The idea drew closer, taking a more distinct shape as it did.

"Aye," she said softly to the Queen.

"What?"

"Aye," she repeated. "Go, please, Highness."

"And leave you alone with a knife to your throat? Nay, Eleanor, I—"

"It is the only way. I have to make Will understand. And I cannot speak all before the guards. You must leave me here, Highness."

Isabella faltered, her eyes filling with tears.

"Go to the Tower with all haste," Eleanor continued. "I will meet you there."

The Queen shook her head. "But what if—"

"If I live through this night, I will find my way to your side, Isabella. If not—" Her throat closed and she had to swallow several times before she could speak again. "If not, see the plan through without me. Too much depends on this for it to be destroyed now, because of me."

"Eleanor…"

"Please, Isabella."

The Queen held her gaze as silence fell between them. Eleanor's vision blurred with unshed tears. Finally, Isabella spoke. "I will see you very soon, my dearest friend." She slid a hard stare at Will for another long moment before she turned to the guards, nodding.

Muttering curses for Will, the guards retreated. They gathered up their unconscious and injured comrades and mounted, reining into a tight circle around the Queen. With a final, long look over her shoulder, the Queen spurred her horse into motion. In a matter of moments, they were swallowed by the night.

Leaving her alone with Will.

"It was a kindness to spare her from seeing this," he said flatly. Drawing a ragged breath, he angled the sharp edge of the dagger against her throat.

Oh God. This was it.

"Please, Will," she cried. "Listen to me. I beg of you."

"Damn ye, lass." His voice broke. "Dinnae make this harder than it already is. We both ken I cannae let ye live to carry out whatever ye have planned with Roger."

Shock cut through her terror. How did he know Roger's name? And what did he believe she was about?

"Just hear me out," she pleaded. "Curse it all, I should have told you already, but I was so afraid. Let me speak the truth—all of it—now."

When he hesitated, she slowly lifted her hand to his where he held the dagger. She laid gentle fingertips on the back of his hand. Her heart broke into a hundred shards at the feel of his warm, rough skin.

"*Please*," she choked out. Tears began to slip unchecked down her cheeks. "We are alone now. I cannot overpower you. If you hear all that I have to say and still do not believe me, th-then you can k-kill me."

He remained motionless and silent in response. Time stretched. She felt something warm and wet on her shoulder blade and realized it was his blood soaking through her riding gown. Would her blood be spilled as well?

Abruptly, he yanked the dagger away from her throat and spun her around.

Eleanor gasped in relief and would have crumpled to the ground, but he held her shoulders in a viselike grip. He leveled her with a cold, heartless stare.

"Start talking."

Chapter Twenty-Seven

D amn him to hell and back. He still loved her. And he was still caught in her web, for instead of ending this swiftly once and for all, he was going to let her spin more lies.

But at her gentle touch, his resolve had shattered. He was weak, and a fool. But he could not kill her without giving her one last chance to speak.

"Begin with who the bloody hell Roger is," he said, imbuing his voice with ice.

"How do you know his name?"

His gut twisted with disgust. Of course. More dodging from her. But she wouldn't evade him this time—not when he laid everything bare and let her try to answer for it.

"I found his love notes to ye," he practically spat. "I must commend ye—ye hid them well, but while I was searching yer chamber for information, I noticed the loose stone. He is clearly verra taken with ye, Eleanor—as ye must be with him, given how much ye've risked to go to him. But I suppose it is worth it when ye are fighting for *England's* future together."

"Love notes…to *me*?" Eleanor's dark eyes widened in horror. "Nay, nay. Oh God, no wonder you think—"

"Dinnae deny it. I read them all. It is obvious that ye have been using me this whole time. And lying about yer loyalty to Scotland."

"His name is Roger Mortimer," she blurted. "And he is not my lover. He is the Queen's."

Will opened his mouth, but as her words sank in, he found himself speechless. "Wh…"

She let a shaky exhalation go. Dashing the tears from her cheeks with her palms, she fixed him with an intent look. "I should start further back."

"A-aye, ye should."

"Two years past, the Queen became acquainted with Roger Mortimer. Well, reacquainted. She had met him a few times before, for he is—*was*—one of Edward's nobles. He was a powerful earl with several holdings along the Welsh marches. Yet in the same way that Edward's lords along the Scottish border became disaffected by his incompetence, so too did Mortimer begin to lose faith in the King. To make matters worse, Edward had begun granting some of

Mortimer's holdings—holdings that were meant to be his for life—to Hugh Despenser."

Will stood in stunned silence. If he hadn't been so shocked, he might have been able to see where Eleanor was going with this, but as it was, all he could do was listen and try to fit the pieces together.

"Mortimer visited the Queen, hoping to petition her to speak to Edward on his behalf," Eleanor continued. "But even then, things were strained between Isabella and Edward. You see, Edward had done to Isabella what he was doing to Mortimer. He'd given Wallingford Castle—which was one of his wedding gifts to the Queen and meant to remain in her sole possession forever—to Despenser as well."

Eleanor shook her head, her lips tightening as she went on.

"Isabella had just delivered Edward's fourth child. Because she'd been in her confinement and unable to travel with him, Edward turned his attention even more fully to Despenser. She felt abandoned, forgotten by the man she'd devoted her life to, and set aside for another. While Edward was away, she and Roger…they formed a connection. He was attentive and kind where Edward had been distracted and absent."

Slowly, Will's wits were beginning to return. His thoughts swimming, he bent and tucked his dagger back in his boot.

"This was all in 1321?"

"Aye. Unrest was growing across England. Many nobles felt as Mortimer did."

"Including the Earl of Lancaster and his rebels."

Eleanor nodded. "Exactly. Mortimer joined the uprising of nobles against the King. He fought with Lancaster to dethrone Edward for his recklessness regarding Despenser and his ineptitude when it came to the conflict with Scotland."

"But Lancaster's rebellion failed last year," Will said.

"Aye, and most of the rebels were given a traitor's death. Mortimer was captured and condemned to execution. But the Queen worked through back channels to have his sentence commuted to life imprisonment in the Tower of London—with my help."

Despite the still-incomplete description of events, suspicion instantly spiked in the pit of Will's stomach. "Why would ye do that?"

Eleanor drew in a ragged breath, seeming to steel herself for what she had to say next. "Because I believed the Queen was on the verge of acting in a way that would ultimately benefit Scotland. Because I hoped that by throwing my support behind her, I could inch her toward a path that would eventually end this war once and for all."

Will digested her words for a long moment. "Ye mean ye set the Queen on a course against Edward?"

Eleanor swallowed. "Aye."

He swiped a hand over his face. "Bloody hell, lass. That is bold—or mad."

"Indeed," she breathed. "Either way, it was incredibly dangerous. But I saw an opportunity to aid the cause in a far greater capacity than simply sending missives with a snippet of information here or there."

"*The enemy of yer enemy might just be yer friend,*" he said slowly. "Ye meant the Queen. She has become Edward's enemy, and ye believed she could be used to Scotland's ends."

"I never sought to *use* her," Eleanor replied, her shoulders stiffening. "She truly has become a friend over the years I've served her. But I saw how she was changing in the face of Edward's mistreatment of her. By the time she fell in love with Roger, she had already turned away from Edward. Once we had ensured that Roger would be spared the King's wrath for the uprising, I encouraged her to maintain their connection through secret correspondence."

"The missives I found," he murmured, another piece shifting into place. "But why were they hidden in yer chamber?"

"The Queen refused to burn them, for they were all she had of Mortimer. Yet if they were discovered in her possession, she could be hanged for adultery. So I offered to keep them for her, knowing that if they were found, it would be I who would appear to be having an affair. And if someone were to uncover who R was, and what we had planned, I would be given a traitor's death instead of the Queen."

Will nodded slowly, then frowned in thought. "So the Queen and Roger continued their communications. But then somewhere along the way, something changed, didnae it? Matters became more…serious."

"Aye. After Old Byland—Edward's abandonment, the deaths of her squires and ladies-in-waiting, and our narrow escape from death ourselves—I knew naught could ever be repaired between Isabella and Edward. She had forsaken him for good. I saw an opening to guide her toward a new course of action."

"And what exactly did ye do to encourage her on this new course?"

Eleanor snorted softly. "Hardly aught. Mortimer had already laid the groundwork for me. He had written to her many times about joining him in the fight for control of England."

"Aye, I remember from the missives."

"It was something they'd spoken about in person as well. He never gave up on the principles behind the nobles' uprising, and she understood better than anyone else just how harmful Edward's rule had been to England. They both had to be careful with what they put in writing, despite the secrecy with which the missives were conducted. Still, they knew what it meant to speak of a new future for England.

Mortimer was asking the Queen to join him in an all-out rebellion against Edward."

"*Bloody hell.*" He raked a hand through his hair. "And ye...ye helped nudge her toward it."

"I did."

"But ye never told the Bruce—or anyone else within the cause—any of this in yer communications. Why?"

Eleanor sank to the ground then, her simple brown riding skirts pooling around her.

"I was afraid." She looked up at him, her eyes shimmering with unshed tears. "*So* afraid, Will."

He knelt in front of her, silently urging her on.

"After Old Byland, everything was in chaos. The Queen no longer believed herself safe, even on English soil. Though we do not speak of it, neither of us will ever forget that night, when we came so close to death."

A shiver stole over her. She clamped her teeth together to keep them from chattering for a moment before going on.

"And afterward, when our plan began to take shape, matters were incredibly delicate. Things between Edward and Isabella were growing worse. The King was on edge, the Queen was desperate to keep away from him, and what was left of their affection had eroded for good. Knowing the Queen as I did, I could envision the scheme with Mortimer in its entirety, and I saw a path for its success—to Scotland's benefit. But I feared that if I tried to convey it in my missives, it would come off as mad. Or worse, traitorous."

"Ye were working in secret as the Queen of England's ally—aye, I can see how that might appear suspicious," he said, his voice tinged with wryness.

A ghost of a smile flickered across her lips before she grew sober again.

"What was more, the Queen required much of me—companionship and consolation, but also support and guidance when it came to Mortimer. She knew she loved him and wanted him freed, but the prospect of launching a full-blown uprising with him terrified her, especially after what had happened to the nobles who'd rebelled against Edward. Lancaster was the King's own cousin, and he was beheaded at Edward's feet like a common thief."

"So ye fell silent."

"A decision that was confirmed with Andrew Harclay's execution. He was one of the King's most esteemed nobles until a few months past, when his treaty with the Bruce was discovered."

Damn. Will hadn't considered how terrifying Harclay's death would be to a woman working as a spy within Edward's court.

One minute Harclay had been championed by Edward for his role in defeating Lancaster's rebellion, and the next, he was drawn and quartered, his limbs displayed in every corner of England to remind its people what happened to traitors.

Tears once again began sliding down her cheeks. "I feared at every turn that I would be uncovered as a spy and meet the fate of a traitor. Edward seems rather foolish from the outside, always seeking amusement and sport for diversion. But when he feels he has been betrayed, he is ruthless. Both the Queen and I have lived in constant fear these last several months that we will be found out."

Will closed his eyes as another realization hit him. "And then I arrived, drawing attention to ye and giving others reason to be suspicious—all the while accusing ye of being a traitor to Scotland."

To his surprise, she laughed weakly. "Aye. You turned my whole world upside down, Will Sinclair. But I cannot regret that you came into my life."

His chest squeezed nigh painfully at that. God, how he wanted to reach for her, take her into his arms, and never let her go.

But he could not give in to that desire just yet. There were still a few unanswered questions.

"Ye told me often that ye'd been working on this scheme for months. Why are ye finally acting now?"

"Matters had been building to a breaking point for quite some time. Mortimer didn't want to delay, but the Queen still feared a misstep would cost us all our heads. Yet Edward's arrival at Langley pushed her over the edge. The final straw was his decision to remove some of her guards. It reminded her of Old Byland all over again—of being abandoned and unprotected."

Will let out a long breath. "And that is why ye told me to hold off on alerting the Bruce to the fact that Edward was raising another army. Ye hoped that the Queen would act before Edward got himself organized for a counterattack on Carlisle."

She nodded in confirmation. "It broke my heart that the Queen had to endure so much, but it was necessary for her to reach the point of being willing to act. And she will—assuming she can see the plan through once she reaches the Tower."

"And what exactly *is* the plan?"

Eleanor met his gaze. "We are going to break Mortimer out of the Tower."

This was madness, but given the rest of what she'd just told him, he could do naught but accept it. "And then?"

"Mortimer will go to France. Isabella has arranged for him to stay under her family's protection at the royal palace in Paris. He'll be untouchable there. Then she will wait, bide her time, and look for an opening to join him, while he will be busy gathering an army willing to stand against Edward. And then they will attack."

Will breathed a string of oaths, but he ran out of words before he had recovered from the shock of that audacious plan. A look at Eleanor's hard-set face told him she was in earnest. Aye, it was insane, and far-fetched, and improbable. But it was also clever, and strategically ingenious—and it had already been set in motion.

"What makes ye believe that outrageous plan will work?"

"Because I know the Queen," Eleanor replied evenly. "She may appear to be little more than smiles and fine gowns and jewels, but she is strong. And smart. And made of steel beneath all the silks and velvets."

She hesitated then.

"But it is more than that. I believe in this plan because I believe in the power of love."

Will's heart leapt into his throat at that word. "Aye?"

"Isabella loves not only Mortimer, but England itself," Eleanor said quietly. "She spoke the truth when she called it her adopted homeland. She cares for the country and its people, and hates the suffering and harm Edward has caused—including through his endless war against the Scots. She has vowed to see the conflict ended, for she recognizes that it hurts England as much as Scotland."

"And ye think her love of Mortimer and England will be enough?" *Children*

Eleanor's gaze traveled slowly up to his. "I, more than most, understand just how powerful love can be. It was what drew me into Scotland's fight for freedom in the first place. It is why I lied and kept so many secrets from you, yet also why I am telling you all this. And I suspect it is why I am still alive right now."

Will went completely still. "What are ye saying, lass?"

She drew in an unsteady breath. Time seemed to stretch as she worked up the courage to speak. And when she did, the words hit him like a battering ram to the chest.

"That I love you, Will."

Chapter Twenty-Eight

It felt as though the whole world went quiet as Eleanor waited for Will to say something in response to her declaration of love.

At last, he spoke. "I dinnae understand."

Her stomach plummeted. Tears pooled in her eyes. She fought against them even as the realization that her love didn't matter tore her in two. "Can you not?"

"Nay, I cannae. For I love ye too."

Confusion swamped her. "You…you love me, too?" she mumbled through an emotion-tight throat.

"Aye. Yet I dinnae understand how ye could love me in return when I have done naught but doubt ye."

She stared at him in stunned silence for a long time before she found her voice again.

"You have challenged me, aye, and battled me,

and refused to let me pull away. But I gave you reason to doubt me. I have been hiding so much for so long, Will. From the Queen, from everyone at court, from you—even from myself."

With a shaking hand, she reached out to him, her fingertips brushing his cheek.

"I didn't trust you at first with the knowledge of what I had planned. But then…then I began falling in love with you. And I was so afraid—for my own life, aye, but for yours as well. I feared that what had happened to David would happen to you, and the more I fell in love with you, the more terrified I became."

"Eleanor…"

Nay, she had to get the words out before her strength failed her.

"You were right when you called me a coward and accused me of trying to protect myself just as much as I've been trying to protect you. I could accept the risk of a traitor's death for myself, but not for you. I couldn't bear the thought of losing you." Her voice wobbled and broke then. "Not when I l-love you so much."

Abruptly, he rocked forward and pulled her into a rough embrace. An overwhelmed moan lodged in her throat at the feel of his strong, warm arms wrapping tight around her.

"Eleanor, my love, my heart," he murmured

against her hair. "I have been afraid, too. Afraid to lose you, and afraid to face the truth—that I still loved ye even when I believed ye'd turned traitor. I still loved ye even when I thought ye'd betrayed me and all I stand for. I thought I was a man of honor, a man of conviction, but ye've reduced me to naught more than a fool in love."

She made a sound against his neck that was somewhere between a laugh and a sob.

"I've run from you over and over, and yet you've kissed my heels as I've fled. I do not deserve you. I do not deserve this happiness in the midst of so much turmoil and destruction."

"Nay, Eleanor, ye do. Ye have borne so much, yet ye have been loyal all this time. And ye have taught me so much."

"I have?" she asked tentatively.

"Aye, lass. Loving ye has been like pressing my heart through a sieve."

"That sounds painful."

"Och, well, aye, but it has also been clarifying. I was full of anger and shame when I met ye. But in coming to love ye, it is as if all the detritus, all the hate and resentment and suspicion, was shaken to the surface where it could be sifted out. And now all that is left are the best parts of me—the parts that ken how to love ye."

She drew back then so that she could look up at

him. But before she met his gaze, her eyes snagged on his shoulder. His blood appeared nigh black in the rapidly falling night. It seeped over his chest, darkening his tunic in a wide circle.

"Your shoulder," she gasped.

He gave her a half-smile. "It is naught but a scratch."

"You were run through, Will."

"Aye, but I am a Highlander, lass. I can take more than that wee poke."

Yet his attempt to experimentally roll his shoulder resulted in a wince and a grunt.

"Let me look at it."

Grudgingly, he eased his arm out of its sleeve— accompanied by a few more grunts and curses. She squinted in the low light at the wound. "It is still bleeding, but it appears clean and smooth-edged."

"Ye'll have to bind it then. We cannae waste time fumbling about in the dark with stitches if we are to catch up with the Queen."

Her eyes shot to his. "You mean...you mean to let me go to her?"

"Nay. I mean for *us* to go to her. I'm coming with ye."

Suddenly uncaring of his injury, she launched herself at him. Her mouth collided with his in a hard, fierce kiss. He met her rough need with his own, kissing her back with wild abandon.

This was how it should have always been between them—forming an plan and then riding into danger. *Together.* If they somehow lived through this, Eleanor was never letting him go or pushing him away again.

When she looped her arms around his shoulders to pull him closer, however, he hissed an oath against her lips, bringing her back to herself. She pulled back, panting from their kiss.

"Now, tell me what the two of ye had planned while ye bind this damn wound," he said.

Reluctantly, Eleanor released him. She reached under her skirts and ripped a long strip of linen from her chemise. Then she carefully lifted his arm so that she could begin winding the material around his injured shoulder.

"We had hoped to reach the Palace of Westminster before dark, but we traveled slower than anticipated. The plan had been to leave the guards at the palace, then slip out later tonight and make our way to the Tower."

Will frowned "Without any protection?"

"It would be a risk, but a calculated one. The Queen didn't wish to involve any of her guards in the scheme in case we were caught. They would be killed without mercy, even if they had no part in our plot. Besides, there can be no eyes or ears for the second portion of the plan."

"Which is?"

"Easy enough to begin with," Eleanor said. "As the Queen, Isabella will have no difficulty getting inside the Tower. The royal library is housed right next to the White Tower, the innermost keep within the stronghold. Political prisoners—including Mortimer—are kept there."

"What of the guards watching the prisoners?"

One side of Eleanor's mouth lifted. "The Tower of London is thought to be all but impenetrable, but the fact is, the Queen has the right to go wherever she wants. The hardest part for anyone else trying to break into the Tower is the easiest for her. Once we reach the White Tower, only a few guards and the Constable will stand between us and Mortimer's cell."

He lifted one brow at her. "Queen or nay, it still isnae naught for two women to get around a Constable and several guards."

"Not when the Constable will be sound asleep."

"Oh?"

"It has all been arranged. A servant who has been paid handsomely—by someone who has already disappeared into the French countryside at the Queen's urging—will slip a draught into the Constable's wine tonight. He takes his meals quite regularly, by the strokes of the bells in the fortress's Bell Tower. He will be unconscious no more than fifteen minutes after the bells for Compline are struck."

Eleanor glanced at the dark blue-gray sky overhead. "In fact, he should already be snoring in the private chamber where he dines if all is going according to plan."

She finished wrapping Will's shoulder and tied the ends of linen in a tight knot.

"Then we wait until the bells of Matins are rung," she continued, "after which we will have one quarter of an hour when the guards change over and no one will be posted in front of Mortimer's cell. In that time, we must reach Mortimer and get him out of the Tower. A ship awaits in the Thames for him."

Will blew out an astonished breath through his teeth. She cast him a glance under quirked brows.

"I told you this was months in the making, and that there were many delicate and interconnected moving parts."

"Aye. I should ken better by now no' to underestimate ye, lass. All the same…"

She frowned. "What?"

"I willnae let ye and the Queen go to the Tower alone. As ye say, there are many intertwined steps—and if one thing goes wrong, ye could both be in real danger."

"What do you have in mind, then?"

"I'm going in with ye. Call me yer personal bodyguard, or the Queen's. The Queen neednae try to protect me if things go sideways, for I have already pledged my life to Scotland's cause. If I die in a scheme to bring peace to Scotland at last, then so be it."

Emotion suddenly seized her throat in a crushing grip. "Will…"

"Dinnae fash, lass. I dinnae have a death wish. If things go wrong, I plan to fight us to safety. Ye may need a bit of brute strength and sharpened steel on yer side."

She touched his face gently. "And your wits. You are more than just a warrior, Will."

His gaze softened on her for a moment. Then he shoved his arm back into the sleeve of his tunic with a wince.

But when he bent and reached for the dagger in his boot once more, Eleanor sucked in a breath. Had she somehow failed to convince him, even after all she'd told him? Had he only been pretending when he'd said he loved her?

She jerked back in shock as he pulled the dagger free. It took an extra heartbeat for her stunned mind to register than he'd removed not only the blade, but the sheath in which it lay as well.

Slowly, he extended the sheathed dagger toward her, his features suddenly clouded.

"I…I may never forgive myself for drawing this on ye, Eleanor. I thought…well, ye ken what I thought. The worst."

For what felt like the hundredth time in the last

day, Eleanor's throat closed and tears burned behind her eyes. "You do not have to—"

"I want ye to have this," he said, nodded toward the dagger. "In case…in case something doesnae go as planned tonight. And if I am ever such a blind arse as I have been of late, I want ye to use it against me."

Given how grave the situation that lay before them was, the laugh that bubbled up from Eleanor's chest was entirely inappropriate. But she could not stop it from slipping out.

"Should I expect you to give me reason to use it, Will Sinclair?"

A wry smile tugged at his mouth. "Nay, but ye never can be too careful with us Highlanders. We are an untamed, dunderheaded lot at times."

With another breathed chuckle, she accepted the dagger and tucked it into her own boot.

He rose then, giving her his hand to help her to her feet. "We had best find the Queen. This night will be a busy one, and yer plans willnae wait on us."

Chapter Twenty-Nine

They overshot London to the east, cutting a wide arc to avoid not only the city wall, but the sprawl of houses and shops that spilled outside it. When the bluish-white blot of the Tower rose in the distance, Will and Eleanor reined their horses to a walk.

A quarter of a mile north of the Tower, Will made out a dark clump of mounted riders. He positioned Fearghus in front of Eleanor and her mare, approaching cautiously. But as he drew nearer, he made out the splash of the Queen's scarlet skirts, dark as blood in the low light. He called to them so as not to catch them by surprise for a second time that night.

Will halted Fearghus outside the circle of guards around the Queen, but Eleanor rode straight to her.

She reined alongside Isabella and leaned out of her saddle to give the Queen a fierce hug.

"I knew you would return to me," the Queen said, her voice tight with emotion.

Will, however, did not receive such a warm welcome. The guards glowered at him, several closing their hands around the swords on their hips.

Eleanor pulled back from the Queen's embrace.

"He can be trusted," she said, then turned back to the Queen, adding quietly, "He knows all."

Will remained motionless, eyeing the guards in case one of them decided to act anyway. The Queen's soft words drifted to him.

"Are you sure, Eleanor?"

"I love him, Isabella," Eleanor murmured in response. "And he loves me. He stands with us in this endeavor—and he is coming with us."

The Queen's gaze slid to Will, and he unconsciously straightened in the saddle, despite the twinge of pain in his shoulder.

"That is no small matter. You more than anyone understand what this means." She shifted a knowing look to Eleanor, then raised her voice, addressing the guards.

"Leave us, please."

John made a surprised noise. "But, Highness—"

"Go to Westminster and wait for us outside the gates, in the forests just north of the river," she continued, imbuing her tone with all the calm authority of a Queen. "Tell no one of our excursion to the Tower, nor of our encounter earlier with my most trusted personal guard, Will Stewart. Understood?"

Her orders might have stunned them, but the guards' loyalty to Isabella was unquestionable.

"Aye, Highness," they said in crisp unison. At John's signal, the guards spurred into motion. They were quickly swallowed by the night.

Isabella turned to Will and Eleanor then. "Someday I hope to hear the full story," she said. "But Matins is nearly upon us. There is no time to waste."

"Lead the way, Highness," Will said, giving her a nod.

It was hard to keep their horses at a walk, for the animals could sense their riders' nerves as they approached the Tower.

As they drew nearer, the stronghold seemed to grow in size, looming over them ominously. The entire fortress was surrounded by a moat that had been cut to let the Thames flow around it, making approach that much more difficult. Thick whitewashed stone walls made a massive, multi-sided enclosure around the fortress, with a singular column, the White Tower, rising from the middle. Each corner of the wall held an elevated guard tower with arrow slits and spy holes so that an attack from any side could be obliterated.

But they weren't attacking, Will reminded himself.

If all went according to Eleanor's plan, they would be able to walk right in with little more than a word from the Queen.

The Queen led them southward along the Tower's eastern side. Just when Will was convinced there was no way through the moat and wall, she turned toward a small, thin bridge Will hadn't noticed before. The bridge spanned a narrow part of the moat and ended in a heavy portcullis laid into the wall.

A dark head filled one of the small gatehouse windows.

"Halt," came the sharp order.

Will pulled in a breath and held it, his pulse filling his ears.

"You address your Queen," Isabella said smoothly, reining in her horse just on the near side of the bridge.

Will caught a breathed curse right before a clatter and thump emitted from the gatehouse. Then the head returned to the window.

"F-forgive me, Highness. I did not recognize you in the dark."

"You are forgiven. But please make haste with the portcullis. The night threatens rain and I am eager to reach the sanctuary of my library."

"Of course, Highness. Right away, Highness."

The guard's head disappeared and a heartbeat later, the portcullis groaned and began to rise. Over the squeaks and moans of the rusty gate, a bell rang sharp and loud nearby.

Isabella darted a glance at Eleanor, who gave her a single, solemn nod. The striking of Matins. They now had one quarter of an hour to find Mortimer and get him out of the Tower while the guards changed over.

The Queen held her spine straight and her chin slightly lifted in the cool, regal manner of her position. But this close, Will could see her hands locked in a whitened grip on her reins as she urged her horse onto the bridge.

The bridge was so narrow that they had to cross one at a time. Eleanor followed the Queen, and Will brought up the rear. He glanced over his shoulder as he crossed, half-expecting to see an entire English army bearing down on them, but only shadows greeted his gaze.

The back of his neck prickled as he rode under the spiked metal portcullis. Once he'd cleared the portcullis and moved into the stronghold's outer ward, the guard began lowering the gate once more.

Will nearly gave a rueful snort. He'd been so concerned about getting into the Tower that he hadn't considered how much worse it was to be locked inside. They were prisoners now, no different than Mortimer. He could only pray getting out alive would be as easy as getting in.

As the Queen dismounted, the guard who'd opened the portcullis came scurrying down from the gatehouse. He bowed deeply to the Queen, but as he straightened, his confused gaze landed on Eleanor and Will.

"My lady-in-waiting and my personal guard," the Queen said, waving dismissively at them.

The Queen's oddly small retinue might have seemed strange to the guard, but he couldn't question his sovereign.

"Of course, Highness. May I see to your horses?"

"Keep them saddled, please. I am looking for something very particular in the library. I doubt we will be long."

The guard bowed again and gathered up their reins one at a time. The Queen glided away toward one of the smaller towers attached to the massive White Tower in the middle of the ward. Eleanor and Will fell in behind her.

But once they reached the shadows at the base of the whitewashed stone structure, the Queen abruptly changed direction. She darted off to the left, toward a wooden door inlaid into the base of the looming White Tower.

She reached for the handle, but Will shot forward and covered it with his hand first.

"If something...unexpected awaits ye on the other side of this door, Highness..."

"I am the Queen," she said, though her voice wobbled with nerves.

"Aye, but all the same. Let me go first."

She swallowed and nodded, smoothing her skirts with shaking hands. Eleanor looped her arm with the Queen's and gave it a reassuring squeeze.

To Will's amazement, Eleanor's only indication of nervousness was a faint tightness around her eyes and mouth. Then again, mayhap he shouldn't have been surprised. Eleanor had lived and worked in the heart of danger every day for the last four years. No wonder she was as cool as a Highland loch, at least on the surface.

His muscles tightening in preparation, Will eased open the door. Inside was a vestibule lit with torches set into iron wall sconces. A spiral staircase led both up and down to the left. Ahead was a long, dim corridor lined with doors. To the right, a door was ajar, warm light spilling out of it.

The Queen stepped in behind Will and nodded toward the partially open door.

"The Constable's chambers," she whispered.

Eleanor closed the outer door silently while Will moved forward. He cracked the Constable's door open further, thanking the saints for the well-oiled hinges.

His gaze fell on a large wooden desk in the center of the chamber. A man sat in the chair behind the desk, though Will couldn't make out his features, for he was slumped forward, his cheek resting on the desk's oak surface and his hand flopped partway into a bowl of stew beside him. A wine glass rested next to the stew, half full of glittering ruby liquid. The man's breathing was slow, steady, and deep.

"I'd say the servant used enough of the draught," he murmured, shooting Eleanor a lifted brow.

She appeared tempted to roll her eyes at him for an instant, but instead pointed at the Constable. "His key ring."

Eleanor watched the door while Will padded on silent feet toward the unconscious Constable. He found a heavy iron key ring on the man's thick middle. As he unhooked the ring from the Constable's belt, the keys gave a heavy jangle. Will froze. The Constable snuffled in his sleep, smacking his lips a few times, but then fell still once more.

Easing back toward the door, Will eyed the keys.

"Do ye ken where Mortimer is being held, and which of these will free him?"

The Queen's brows pinched together. "He was originally imprisoned in one of the upper chambers. As for the keys, I do not know."

"There's only one way to find out." Will slipped around Eleanor and out the door, giving the vestibule and corridor a quick scan before motioning the women to follow.

Closing his hand around the hilt of his sword, he began climbing the stairs. When he reached the first landing, he held up a hand to stay the Queen and Eleanor, then glanced down the row of wooden doors with small iron grates inlaid in them. He hesitated. He would have looked into each holding cell himself, but belatedly, he realized he had no idea what Roger Mortimer looked like.

He fixed the Queen with a look, then pointed wordlessly toward the doors. She nodded in understanding, then crept to the first door, her skirts clutched in her fists. Standing on her toes to see through the grate, she glanced inside. Fortunately, a torch rested in a sconce opposite the doors. She must have had enough light to recognize that Roger wasn't inside, for she swiftly moved on to the next one.

As she moved farther down the row, a noise sounded on the stairs.

Footsteps. Coming down from above, from the sound of them. The Queen spun back to Will, her blue eyes round and filled with terror. With a jerking wave, he motioned her farther down the row and into the shadows. Her skirts gave a muted swish as she hurried away.

Eleanor, who had been standing in the landing's opening to the stairs, darted toward Will. The footsteps drew closer. There wasn't enough time for them to follow the Queen into the shadows without their movements being seen through the archway that opened to the landing.

Without thinking, he yanked Eleanor against his chest, then spun so that her back came up flush against the stone wall opposite the doors. He plastered himself against her, trying to cover her as much as possible.

Her gown was a subdued brown unlikely to draw an unsuspecting eye, yet her scooping neckline revealed an expanse of creamy skin that stood out like a beacon in the dim corridor. At least his breeches and tunic were dark like the stone wall behind her. What was more, if whoever approached saw them, Will would willingly take a blade in his back if it bought Eleanor and the Queen time to escape.

Be still, he mouthed, holding her tight gaze with his own. She blinked slowly in acknowledgement.

"*There was a maid this other day, and she would needs go forth to play…*"

A low, gravelly voice mumbled the words to the tavern song. The singing grew nearer with the footfalls.

"*And as she walked she sighed and said, I am afraid to die a maid…*"

At that, the approaching guard snorted to himself.

"*And if you please, fair maid, to stay, a little while, with me to play…*"

The guard's boots clacked on the stone landing

and echoed down the corridor in which they stood frozen. Will held his breath, his shoulders knotting in anticipation of the guard's surprised shout when his gaze fell on them.

"*I took this maiden then aside, and led her where she was not spied…*"

The guard's voice drew farther down the stairs, his soft chuckle at the bawdy tune drifting up to them. His footsteps grew faint as he continued on.

As one, Will and Eleanor released a ragged exhalation. He stepped back, searching her with his gaze.

"All right?" he said, more a breath than a whisper.

She nodded, though he didn't miss the way her throat bobbed on a hard swallow.

The Queen tiptoed out of the shadows then, her face pale with nervousness. She pointed toward the row of doors, then shook her head to indicate Mortimer wasn't in any of them.

"Ye still have yer dagger?" Will whispered to Eleanor.

She nodded in confirmation. His hand once again wrapping around his sword hilt, he lifted his chin toward the stairs to indicate that they could continue.

He took the lead once more, with the Queen behind him. He hated making Eleanor bring up the rear, but at least she had a weapon if danger came from below.

They reached two more landings similar to the

first. A quick check by the Queen still did not uncover Mortimer's holding cell, though.

Will could practically feel time draining away like sand through an hourglass. If Eleanor's information had been correct, they likely only had a handful of minutes remaining while the guards changed over. Where the hell was Mortimer?

They wound their way up and up the spiraling stairs until abruptly the stairs ended—not on another landing, but at a single wooden door. No torch was mounted on the wall, so the only light came from the dim glow of a torch farther down the stairs.

Will motioned the Queen forward to peer into the iron grate set into the door. He took up a position facing the stairs so that he stood in front of both women. Out of the periphery of his good eye, he could see the Queen rise on tiptoe as she had before the other doors and squint into the darkness inside.

All was silent for a long moment. Then suddenly the Queen gasped and sagged against the door. Eleanor wrapped an arm around her, keeping her from collapsing completely on the stone floor.

"Roger," the Queen breathed. "Oh God, it is him."

"…Isabella?" the voice on the other side of the door croaked weakly.

The Queen began to weep. Eleanor tried to soothe and shush her.

Will rushed to them, yanking the heavy key ring out.

"Hush now," he ordered quietly. "Ye must fortify yerself, Highness. We must still get him out of here."

With Eleanor's help, the Queen rose shakily, choking back her sobs with a fist over her mouth. She lifted her head and took a steadying breath. Eleanor was right—the woman was made of far stronger stuff than silks and velvets.

Will jammed the first of the keys into the rusty lock on the door. He winced at the scraping noise that echoed harshly off the stones. The key didn't match the lock. He moved on to the next one, jingling it lightly to test its fit.

As he worked, a ghostly face appeared on the other side of the iron grate. The man inside—Roger Mortimer—had long, greasy hair and a dark, unkempt beard. His blue-gray eyes were wide and haunted as he stared out through the grate.

"W-what…what is happening? Isabella, is it really you?"

"Aye, Roger, I am here. It is finally time."

Mortimer breathed his thanks to God, his dry voice wobbling.

Will moved on to the next key, then the next. He was halfway through the ring already with no luck.

As he fumbled with the ring, Eleanor's hand

clamped over his in a white-knuckled grasp. He glanced at her, stilling for a moment.

When he did, he heard it.

More footsteps. Coming up the stairs. And a soft, tuneless whistling.

The Queen must have heard it too, for she pulled in an almost soundless gasp. Mortimer instantly fell silent as well.

Bloody hell and damnation.

There was nowhere to go, nowhere to hide.

They were good and trapped—and about to be caught.

Chapter Thirty

Will's mind tumbled and churned like the waters of a raging river. There had to be some way to escape the approaching guard.

They could try to scramble back to one of the landings farther down, but judging from the loud echoing of the guard's footsteps, they would run into him before they would reach the nearest landing.

Will could attack, but there was no way to ensure the guard wouldn't be able to raise a cry of alarm before Will could incapacitate him. And what few precious moments of concealment they had left were rapidly draining away.

So he made a split-second decision. He slammed the next key into the lock. It would not slide in. He tried the next.

"Will…" Eleanor breathed, her gaze darting between him and the stairs.

He fumbled with yet another key. No luck. He moved on to the second-to-last key on the ring. Still no.

This was it. One last chance. The guard's shadow stretched long on the stones curving around the stairs. It reached for them like a black hand.

With a *thunk* and a heavy click, the key slid home and turned in the lock. Will yanked open the door, but instead of dragging Mortimer out, he shoved both the Queen and Eleanor in. He tugged on the key where it now sat buried in the lock, but the cursed iron would not glide out again.

To hell with it. Will flung himself into the cell, leaving the key in the lock, the ring dangling below it. He pulled the door closed behind him just as the guard's shadow crossed over the little grated window.

Only the faintest light slanted into the cell through the grate. Inside, he could make out a straw pallet in one corner, a bucket in another, and a single slit in the stones that let in cold night air and weak starlight. That was all.

The Queen clung to Mortimer, who was dressed in a dirty tunic and breeches that hung from his lean frame. Eleanor stood beside them. She reached out and put a hand on Will's arm. Her fingers trembled.

Will squeezed the hilt of his sword until he could

feel his pulse in his palm. He willed his heartbeat to quiet so that he could hear the guard better.

The man's whistling drifted up the stairwell and through the grate, seeming to pierce the silence like a knife. As the guard's footsteps neared the top of the stairs, the whistling stopped, to be replaced with heavy panting.

The guard grumbled something about so many damned steps. He huffed when he reached the top, his boots shuffling across the stones.

But then he fell abruptly silent. Will dared a look through the iron grate. The guard's eyes were fixed on the shadows around the door—where the Constable's key ring swung gently from the lock.

"What the bloody—"

Will surged forward, throwing his entire weight against the door. The door swung out and slammed into the guard, knocking him back against the opposite stone wall.

Darting forward, Will grabbed the guard even before he'd fully recovered. He looped an arm around the man's neck, squeezing with all his strength. The guard thrashed and clawed at Will's arm, a gurgling sound emitting from his throat where no air could pass. He fumbled for the sword on his hip, but before he could draw it, he began to go slack in Will's hold.

Will counted slowly as the guard sagged against him, careful to ensure that the man would remain alive but unconscious. At last, he loosened the choke-hold. Then he dragged the limp guard toward the cell door, wincing at his injured shoulder's protest under the man's hefty weight.

When he nudged the door open with his boot, he was met with the wide-eyed stares of Eleanor, the Queen, and Mortimer. Eleanor was the first to recover. She leapt into action, holding the door open for him as he pulled the guard inside.

"Trade clothes with the guard, Mortimer," Will grunted, lowering the man onto the cell's stone floor.

Mortimer's mouth sagged at the sound of Will's Scottish accent, but after a heartbeat of staring, he began stripping off his dirty tunic.

"Do not misunderstand, I am very glad to see you all," he said as he began untying the guard's cloak. "But may I ask—who are these people, Isabella?"

"This is my lady-in-waiting, Eleanor," the Queen replied. "The one who has helped us so much these many months."

Despite the fact that he was standing half-naked in a dirty cell, Mortimer executed a hasty but formal bow to Eleanor. "Then I am in your debt, milady." His sharp eyes shifted to Will. "And the Scot?"

"He is my fiancé," Eleanor said before the Queen could reply. "And an ally to the Queen and your cause."

"I wouldnae go quite that far," Will said smoothly,

assessing Mortimer. "More like I am the enemy of yer enemy."

The Queen's head snapped around to him. She fixed him with a puzzled, searching look. "I get the impression that I do not know nearly enough about you, Will Stewart."

"Aye, Highness."

She opened her mouth, but seemed to change her mind about what she was going to say. Her eyes turned knowing. "I am in no position to turn away someone who would help me—even if he is more the 'enemy of my enemy' than an outright ally. I take it your true allegiance in fact lies with Scotland?"

He lifted a brow at her, but didn't say more. The Queen turned to Eleanor.

"I also suspect you and I will have much to discuss someday, Eleanor. I wonder…" The Queen gave herself a little shake. "But that must wait." She fixed concerned eyes on Mortimer. "Are you well, my love? Have they treated you poorly?"

"At least I can say I am alive—thanks to you, Isabella."

"I arranged extra payment for one of your guards to ensure that you were fed every day. Please tell me he did."

"Aye," Mortimer said, sounding one hundred years old all of a sudden. "I fared better than most. Albert saw that I received something most days. And he was the one who passed on your missives and brought me writing supplies on occasion." He glanced down at the unconscious guard on the floor and scowled. "Henrick, however, preferred to torment me."

"Let us reminisce elsewhere," Will urged. "Another guard may be on his way."

Mortimer hastily finished dressing in the guard's clothing. When he was done, he wore King Edward's livery—a red tunic with three golden lions rampant on the chest, dark breeches, plus a royal blue wool cloak to cut the chill within the tower. He looked rather bedraggled with his unshorn hair and beard, and the clothes were loose on him, but he would pass for a guard in the dark.

"What now?" Mortimer asked, stamping into the guard's boots.

"Now we get out of this damn place and pray we arenae noticed," Will said.

"I have arranged for a ship to be on the Thames, beneath the London Bridge," the Queen added. "It will take you straight to France, Roger."

"And what of Henrick and the rest of the guards?" Mortimer asked, lifting his chin toward the unconscious man.

"We'll leave him in here. Someone will find him eventually—hopefully at first light when we are long gone."

"But Will." Eleanor fixed him with worried eyes. "He saw you. They'll be able to piece together Mortimer's escape."

"Aye, he saw me—and only me. Who kens who I could be—an Englishman, a Scot... Besides, they willnae necessarily connect a single man's actions with the Queen's visit to her library. The night is long. Any number of things could have happened during the hours of darkness."

When Eleanor continued to frown in concern, Will added, "Dinnae fash, lass. I have no plans to linger in London to be identified."

Her knitted brow eased slightly and she gave him a wordless nod.

Will was the first to slide his head out of the cell, listening for a moment in the doorway for sounds of more guards approaching. But all was quiet in the tower now. He stepped out, giving the betraying key a swift jerk to remove it from the lock. Then he motioned the others to follow as he began to descend the stairs.

When he reached the bottom, he paused again, darting a gaze down the corridor. The changing of the guards must have been complete, for no one roamed the corridor or the vestibule.

The door to the Constable's chamber remained ajar, so Will slipped inside. The Constable still slept on his face, his hand resting in his stew. Will crept toward him, refastening the key ring to his belt. Let the Constable and the guards puzzle that out when they awoke in the morning to find Henrick inside the uppermost cell and Mortimer gone.

Once they exited the tower, Mortimer drew up the hood on his cloak. Will ducked his head, falling in behind the women alongside Mortimer to appear like a guard. The Queen resumed her normal regal air, gliding across the inner ward toward the gate through which they'd entered.

They found their horses tethered to a post below the gatehouse, saddled and ready, just as the Queen had instructed. Mortimer took Eleanor's horse, and Will pulled her up in front of him atop Fearghus's broad back.

"Open the gate, if you please," the Queen called up to the gatehouse.

The same guard appeared, ducking a quick bow to the Queen. "Of course, Highness. Did you find what you were looking for?"

"I did, thank you." Then she cleverly added, "One of your men has agreed to escort me to the Palace of Westminster." She waved casually at Mortimer. "He likely won't return tonight."

"Very good, Highness." The guard gave Mortimer a curt nod, which Mortimer returned from the depths of his hood.

Will waited with drawn breath as the guard lifted

the portcullis. He followed the Queen and Mortimer through the gate and across the narrow bridge. Miraculously, no shout of alarm went up behind them. The bells did not erupt in clangs of warning. They had somehow managed to penetrate the Tower of London and make it out alive.

The Queen led them west along the river. The river's edge had been built up with a stone embankment several feet high to protect the town against flooding. Their horses' hooves clacked loudly on the stones, making Will wince, but all of London seemed to be battened down and sleeping.

Ahead, London Bridge emerged over the dark waters of the Thames. The stone structure was massive. Any other time, Will would have grudgingly marveled at the English feat. Nearly two dozen arches spanned the wide river. The bridge atop the arches was lined with shops, houses, and a chapel from the looks of it. There was even a wooden drawbridge set into the main bridge to accommodate tall-masted ships that needed to pass through.

True to the Queen's word, a small cog ship lurked in the shadows beneath the archway on the close side of the river. The sail was lowered and it appeared to be anchored as if it were any other cargo ship harbored for the night, yet it was clearly waiting for something—for *them*—under the bridge.

They reined to a halt in the shadows beneath the

archway. The Queen scanned the ship, but all was quiet.

"*C'est une bonne soirée pour faire de la voile.*"

Will sifted through his rudimentary knowledge of French. *It's a good night for a sail.* It must have been some sort of code phrase the Queen had pre-arranged with the ship's crew.

A dark head appeared from belowdeck.

"*Oui, ma Reine,*" came the hushed reply.

The man lowered a wooden plank over the ship's gunwale, setting its other end down on the stone embankment upon which their horses stood.

Slowly, Mortimer and the Queen dismounted.

"I cannot believe I have just regained you, only to lose you again so soon," the Queen said, her voice tight with emotion.

Mortimer took both of her hands and held them against his chest. "My freedom will not be complete until you join me in Paris, my love."

"I do not know when that will be," the Queen choked out. "If only we had more time…"

Eleanor glanced up at Will, a question and an entreaty in her dark eyes.

"We dinnae have time to waste, Highness," he said reluctantly. His gaze shifted between the forlorn lovers and he nearly muttered a curse. "But a moment willnae be our ruin."

Still holding the Queen's hands, Mortimer walked

slowly to the plank. They climbed together, halting at the top and falling into a fierce embrace.

Eleanor slipped from Will's lap and moved to gather up the reins of the Queen and Mortimer's horses. Will discreetly averted his gaze from the Queen and Mortimer, looking out over the black waters of the Thames.

For several long moments, the only sounds were the soft lapping of the river against the stone embankment and the lovers' murmurs of devotion and reassurance.

But a sharp gasp cut through the hushed night. Will's head snapped around. His gaze landed on the source of the sound, yet his mind refused to comprehend what he saw.

Nay. It wasn't possible.

And yet the nightmare did not disappear into smoke and shadow. It was real.

Conrad de Russ held Eleanor around the waist—with a knife at her throat.

Chapter Thirty-One

Instinctively, Eleanor strained away from the blade at her throat. But with Conrad holding her against him, her head bumped into his chest. When she tried to twist to the side, the knife pressed harder into her skin.

She froze then, her heartbeat thundering in her ears and her head spinning with fear. How could this be happening? It was the second time in one night that she'd had a knife to her throat. But unlike the first time, she doubted this encounter would end in declarations of love.

Fate seemed to be toying with her yet again. Just when everything had finally fallen into place, disaster struck once more. She had Will's love. They had escaped the Tower with Mortimer. All she had worked for these long, lonely, difficult years had at last come to fruition. Yet somehow Conrad was here, his arm clamped around her waist, his voice like a tightly pulled bowstring next to her ear.

"Don't even think about it, Stewart," he said to Will.

Will's hand had darted to the sword at his hip the instant his gaze had landed on Eleanor, but now he stilled. Yet Fearghus stepped nervously and tossed his head. The normally steady and impeccably trained stallion was clearly responding to his rider's sudden panic.

Just then, the Queen gasped from the top of the gangplank. "Lord de Russ, what are you—"

"Silence!"

The Queen was so stunned at the shouted order that her words cut off even as her mouth remained open.

Will's gaze locked on Eleanor. "Easy, lass," he said as if she were a trapped animal. "Ye'll be all right, I promise."

Eleanor tried to nod, but the dagger forced her to remain motionless.

Conrad began edging along the embankment between the ship and the horses, angling back toward the Tower.

"I knew it," he hissed, ignoring Will's words to Eleanor. "I knew you were a disloyal Scottish barbarian."

Will slowly threw his leg over Fearghus's back and began to dismount.

"I warned you not to move, Scot," Conrad snapped. He gave Eleanor a jerk, which caused the knife to pinch into the skin at her throat. A whimper slipped from her lips.

Will landed on his feet but held up his hands to show he wasn't making a move against Conrad.

"I only wanted to stand eye to eye with ye," he said, his voice low and soft, "so that ye would ken I speak the truth when I say if ye so much as leave a scratch on her, I will tear ye into wee pieces with my bare hands and feed ye to the fish."

Conrad rasped a laugh. "I clearly chose my hostage well. You are so protective of her—both of you," he added, jerking his head toward the Queen, "that I knew you would be at my mercy just as much as she is."

"What is yer plan here, de Russ?" Will asked.

"I should ask you the same question." He paused in his sidestepping and lifted his chin toward where the Queen and Mortimer stood frozen on the gangplank. "It seems I have come upon quite the seditious plot. I was right to follow you, Stewart."

Will's brows dropped. "Ye what?"

Conrad snorted softly. "I always had a suspicion about you. Something was off. It made little sense that Eleanor's parents would arrange a union with another

Lowlander after the scandal caused by her first fiancé. What was his name? Daniel Mac-something-or-other?"

"Maxwell," Eleanor breathed, fury burning up her throat. "David Maxwell."

Conrad didn't acknowledge that she'd spoken. Instead, he continued on, addressing Will.

"You fooled Edward into trusting you, but I knew better. You Scots are a savage, animalistic lot, but one thing that can be said for your kind is that you are loyal. I never believed you would turn away from your precious pretender King and join the English cause against your own."

Conrad inched past Will, giving him as wide a berth as was possible given the limited width of the stone embankment. His back was now to the river, his boots on the lip of the wall, and Eleanor held in front of him like a shield. Will still remained rooted beside Fearghus, but he had pivoted subtly with Conrad so that he remained facing him head-on.

Distantly, Eleanor realized that Will was angling so that Conrad was slightly more on his left side—in front of his good eye. Was he planning some sort of counterattack? The surge of hope in her chest was quickly swallowed by desolation. There was no way Will could draw his sword and close the distance between them before Conrad could slit her throat.

"I knew you were up to something, scheming your

way into everyone's good graces—and between this bitch's legs." He gave Eleanor another hard shake, making her teeth rattle.

Her hands clamped down on the arm that held the dagger, desperate to keep it from piercing her neck. Yet Conrad was far too strong. She couldn't pull his arm away. All she could do was cling to it and pray she would have half a heartbeat's warning in the flexing of his forearm before he drove the dagger into her throat.

Her vision blurred at the thought. Would these be her last few breaths on this earth? Was this what David's final moments were like—filled with helpless terror and panic?

She blinked rapidly, forcing her eyes to focus on Will. If she was to die, let him be the last thing she ever saw.

His gaze was fixed on Conrad, his good eye blazing with rage like a blue-green fire. Every inch of his tall, strong body was drawn taut, like a wolf about to pounce, yet held motionless by an invisible leash. He was the most fearsome, breathtaking being she had ever beheld.

"…so when the King sent me away, I didn't go far," Conrad was saying. "I saw Isabella and Eleanor ride out in the dead of night, but I did not bother with them. It was you I was after."

He chuckled to himself in disbelief before going on.

"To my good fortune, I noticed you setting out after them. I meant to get you alone and draw answers from you under my sword. But I am glad I bided my time. For in continuing to follow and watch you, I have stumbled upon something far grander than I gave you credit for, Stewart."

Conrad waved dramatically with the dagger before returning it to Eleanor's throat.

"I never expected Isabella and Eleanor to be part of your schemes. Yet here we are—the Queen of England, her lady-in-waiting, and a double-crossing Scot, all caught in the act of freeing the traitor Roger Mortimer."

"Lord de Russ, please—"

"I told you to be silent, *Highness*," Conrad snapped at the Queen, his voice dripping with venom.

"What do ye mean to do then, de Russ?" Will asked levelly. "Ye've seen us. Ye have Eleanor. What is yer play?"

"I mean to go to the Tower," Conrad replied. Eleanor could tell from his tone that he wore a smug smile. "Alert the guards to what has transpired this night."

"If ye want to take someone to the Tower, take me," Will ground out. "I am the one they'll want. I'm the one who should hang for this."

Tears flooded Eleanor's eyes. "Will, nay," she moaned softly. She could not let him die. Even if she had to give her life for his.

"Oh, they'll do far more than hang you, Scot," Conrad said. "But I don't need to put a blade to your throat to ensure that you'll be drawn and quartered like the animal you are. I only need Eleanor."

Conrad gave another cold, giddy laugh, speaking more to himself now. "And to think—I once believe I needed to marry the bitch to secure a favorable position for myself. But now I only need her as bait to lure you traitors. When Edward learns that I have not only recaptured Mortimer but uncovered his own wife's betrayal, he will likely drown me in coin and lands."

"Leave Eleanor out of this," Will growled.

"Why?" Conrad demanded. "She has clearly played some part in this treachery. Besides, neither you nor the Queen can stop me as long as I have her. You can't so much as touch me, for if you do, Eleanor's blood will be on your hands. You'll do exactly as I say, or else…"

The muscles in Conrad's forearm clenched beneath Eleanor's hands as he ran the flat side of the blade along her throat slowly. Then he angled the dagger so that the sharp edge once again puckered her skin.

Will held up his hands in a desperate plea. "*Dinnae.* Just tell us what ye want us to do."

Conrad began sidestepping along the edge of the embankment once more. "You'll follow me—all of you," he said, jerking his head toward the Queen and Mortimer. "Stay back ten paces. Do not try aught. Do not seek help. Do not draw closer, or fall back, or reach for a weapon. If you do, she dies."

Through the storm of terror swirling inside her, a realization struck Eleanor like a lightning bolt. She was Conrad's leverage. As long as he held her, Will and the Queen would be forced to do whatever he said—even if it led them to their own deaths.

But if he no longer had her in his grasp...

If she screamed, he would likely stab her, though Conrad might just be clever enough to keep her alive. If she struggled, kicked, and scratched him, raised Conrad's ire, he might do something foolish and kill her.

Then he would have naught. It would mean Will and the Queen's safety. Their lives.

Their lives for mine.

Everything went quiet inside her head then. *God,* how she wanted to live—with Will. Her heart was full to overflowing with love for him, yet they'd had so little chance for happiness.

And her chest ached at the thought of being taken from the Queen now, when there was so much left to say. Isabella likely knew that Eleanor had kept many secrets, but Eleanor owed her a full explanation. She was Eleanor's dearest friend—her only friend. If only there was time to tell her everything.

It felt as though her heart were splintering with the knowledge of what she needed to do. Aye, she didn't want to die. But if that was the price to save them, so be it.

"…and once Edward learns of this—of all I've done," Conrad was saying, "I'll be the richest—"

Eleanor bucked against him, ramming her hip back into his. Conrad stumbled and the blade wavered in front of her face for an instant before he brought it back to her throat.

"You bitch," he hissed at her.

She ignored him, stomping on one of his feet. He snarled in anger.

"Eleanor!" Will bellowed, his voice edging with fear. "What are ye doing?"

Saving you.

She rammed her head back, catching Conrad's chin with her skull. In retaliation, he dug the dagger deeper into her throat. Burning pain hit her, followed by wet warmth against her skin.

The Queen screamed wordlessly off to her left. Eleanor fixed her gaze on Will. His good eye was wide with panic, his mouth opening for a roar of fury.

This was it.

I love you, Will.

She closed her eyes and surrendered to death.

Chapter Thirty-Two

E leanor waited for the rush of her life's blood over her chest.

Yet through the hazy chaos of shouts and screams, a realization forked through her.

Conrad hadn't cut deep. The flow of blood down her neck was a trickle rather than a river. He had managed to restrain himself and foil her plan.

She'd failed.

"Stupid whore," Conrad yelled at her. His arm closed so tightly around her waist that she came off her feet. She thrashed and kicked but could not make solid contact with him.

"Eleanor!" Will shouted again, his gaze desperate on her. "Ye cannae fight him. He has a *dagger* and ye dinnae."

Despair swamped her. Will was right. She was

helpless. She couldn't free herself. She couldn't even make Conrad kill her.

"He'll kill ye with that _dagger_ if ye keep struggling," Will went on, his gaze searing into her.

Comprehension hit her like a punch to the stomach. _The dagger._ She still had Will's dagger in her boot.

Her eyes widened. Will nodded a fraction of an inch, then his gaze darted to the sword on his hip before returning to her.

"…thought you could outsmart me," Conrad sneered. He still held her aloft as he continued edging along the embankment. "But I won't be outmaneuvered this time. You won't—"

There was no more time to lose. Conrad was already three paces away from Will, and the distance was growing.

Her gaze locked on Will. His whole body seemed to tense.

Now.

Eleanor jerked her knees into her chest, gripping Conrad's forearm for leverage. She let go with one hand and fumbled for the dagger tucked inside her boot. The blade came free with a smooth hiss. In the same motion, she plunged it into the arm around her waist.

Conrad yelped in surprise, his grip on her faltering. Calling forth every last drop of her strength, Eleanor wrenched back the arm that held the dagger poised against her neck. Then she twisted to the side, torqueing against his hold.

Just as she broke free, she felt a whisper of air on her face. It was Will's sword rushing past her. He had somehow managed to yank his sword free and close the distance between them in a single heartbeat.

Time seemed to slow then. Will's blade cut through the night like a beam of moonlight. Conrad's eyes went wide with shock an instant before the tip met his chest. The sword drove through him as if he wasn't even there, skewering him and nearly lifting him off his feet.

Will did not stop until the blade was buried to the hilt in Conrad's chest. He stood mere inches from the man, his narrowed eye holding Conrad's rounded ones. "I am a man of my word," Will growled, giving the blade a sharp twist.

Conrad pulled in a breath, but the sound turned wet and thick. Blood bubbled up his throat and out his mouth. Will stepped back, jerking the blade free of Conrad's heart. Conrad's dark eyes were already clouding over in death. His body hung like a suspended puppet for a long moment, then he toppled backward off the stone embankment and into the Thames.

He landed with a loud splash face-up, his life's blood leeching out around him. It was black as ink in the night-dark river. His eyes remained open but unseeing now in death. The waters took him, pulling his body further downriver, away into the current and the darkness.

Eleanor swayed on her feet, all her strength evaporating. She staggered on quaking legs, veering dangerously toward the edge of the embankment.

Suddenly Will's sword clattered to the stones. He yanked her back from the precipice and into the safety of his arms. She sagged against him, a sob rising in her throat.

"Eleanor!" The Queen dashed down the gangplank and to her side, Mortimer following after. "Good God, he nearly—" Isabella swallowed back some of the hysteria in her voice. "You saved her, Will. You saved my dearest Eleanor."

Eleanor lifted her head from Will's chest. Belatedly, she realized that tears were streaming down her face. With one arm wrapped around Will's solid torso, she reached the other out and took the Queen's hand. They stood like that for a long time, Eleanor crying and shaking in Will's embrace, and squeezing her friend's hand in reassurance.

At last, Mortimer cleared his throat discreetly. Eleanor drew in a ragged breath and reluctantly released both of them.

"If I could, I would halt the very sun so that we might have more time together, my love, but the dawn will not wait for us," he said to the Queen, his gaze heavy with sadness.

It was true. The sky was already turning from black to azure with the distant approach of dawn.

The Queen's face drew tight with barely-controlled anguish. She took Mortimer's arm and they slowly made their way back to the gangplank. As before, they paused at the top, their heads dipping together for a few pained words of parting. Then they lingered in a slow kiss until it was Will's turn to clear his throat.

"We must be away, Highness," he said quietly.

Isabella gave Mortimer one last, long kiss before pulling back, lifting a hand to dash away her tears. She glided down the gangplank, every inch a Queen even in her grief.

Will helped first Isabella and then Eleanor mount before swinging into his own saddle. But the Queen did not urge her horse into motion. Instead, she sat rooted, watching as the cog's small crew hurriedly lifted the anchor and raised the sail.

The ship drifted out from beneath the bridge's stone archway before it caught the gentle breeze coming down the river. The sail filled and the ship glided into motion across the dark waters of the Thames.

Only when the ship had been swallowed by the

night did Isabella straighten her spine and take up her reins.

"Once Roger reaches Paris, I will find a way to get word to him," she said quietly. "Then I will bide my time until the moment presents itself for me to join him. And then the real work will begin."

The thought of a Queen and her lover raising an army against her King-husband appeared on the outside so preposterous that had the situation been any different, Eleanor would have given up all hope long ago. But Isabella wasn't just any Queen. She very well might be strong enough to survive what lay ahead —and mayhap even succeed.

"We must go to Westminster, at least for appearances," the Queen continued evenly."We cannot stay long, though. By dawn, we'll ride back to Langley with my retinue. The longer we linger in London, the greater the danger to us all of being discovered."

"Agreed," Will said grimly. "But I must ask, Highness... Do ye truly believe Mortimer will be safe in France?"

"I would never send him there if I had any doubts. My brother the King has vowed to protect him, though I do not believe Edward would ever look for Mortimer in my family's palace in Paris, let alone France. And even if he did, Edward has neither the ability nor the desire to wage war against France. The last thing he needs is another enemy."

Will's brows lowered, then a keen spark lit his eye. "Thank ye, Highness."

"For what?"

"Ye've just given me an idea."

"Oh?"

"Aye." His gaze shifted to Eleanor, his features softening ever so slightly. "A way we can advance our shared cause even further. Together."

As they spurred their horses into motion, Eleanor's heart swelled until it felt as though it would burst from her chest. There would be no more secrets between them anymore, no more lies and obfuscation.

Aye, they could face everything that lay ahead— they could face *anything*.

Together.

Chapter Thirty-Three

"Where the bloody hell is he?"

Will sat, silent and motionless, while Edward blustered further down the high table. Out of the corner of his eye, he saw Eleanor and Isabella exchange a look, but neither spoke.

Life at Langley had been strangely quiet and uneventful for the last fortnight—until the King had returned. News of Mortimer's mysterious escape from the Tower of London had traveled like wildfire over England, reaching the King at Wallingford Castle a few days past.

He had charged back to Langley, his five-hundred-man retinue scrambling after him, to partake of the peace and calm of his favorite residence—and to seek answers.

But thus far, none had emerged.

"How can a wanted man—a man who is a known traitor to his King and country—simply vanish for an entire fortnight?" Edward demanded of no one in particular.

Hugh Despenser sat tight-lipped on Edward's right side at the high table in Langley's great hall. The Queen kept her gaze demurely averted. Eleanor and Will, who had been placed on the Queen's left side, held their tongues to avoid the King's notice. The courtiers, squires, and servants seated at the tables below the raised dais kept their conversations hushed. The King's displeasure was palpable, and no one wanted to be caught up in the storm of angry words.

The King turned to Despenser. "Mortimer and his allies would have seen you stripped of your lands and titles, Hugh—and would have locked me away and taken my throne for themselves. I want him dead or alive."

"Aye, I know," Despenser replied, consciously lowering his voice. "And we'll find him, Edward. It is only a matter of ti—"

"I want the search efforts doubled," the King snapped. "Tripled." He pounded his fist on the table and abruptly shoved out of his chair. He began pacing on the raised dais like the caged lion he kept in the menagerie. "Increase them tenfold if necessary. He must be somewhere."

Edward swiped an agitated hand over his golden

hair. He kept pacing, his velvet, ermine-trimmed robes swishing around him. Despenser fell silent once more, sipping dourly from a jewel-encrusted goblet.

This might be Will's best opportunity. He glanced at Eleanor, lifting his brow. She knew what he meant to do. Once they'd ridden back to Langley from London, he'd explained his plan to her. She feared he ran the risk of overstepping with the King, but given the possibility of success, the risk was worth it.

Eleanor assessed the King quickly, then returned her gaze to Will. Though her chestnut eyes tightened with worry, she gave him a slight nod.

It was time to make his move. Drawing a steeling breath, Will straightened in his chair. As the King made another turn in his pacing, Will cleared his throat to gain his attention.

Edward's agitated blue eyes landed on Will.

"Forgive me, Highness, but any new word on how Mortimer escaped?"

The Queen's shoulders tensed ever so slightly, but the King didn't seem to notice, so distracted was he by his own fury.

He released a breath. "Nay. The trouble is, those rebels he allied with are like weeds. Every time you think you've pulled out the last roots, another one springs up. I have worked for over a year to eradicate each and every one of them, but some of those traitors may still be out there. Any one of them must have helped him break out."

"And what of Conrad de Russ?" Will prodded. He and Eleanor had discussed this strategy as well. De Russ's disappearance hadn't gone unnoticed. His name swirled around England in connection with Mortimer's escape. "Any news of him?"

Edward's face darkened. "The bastard is still missing. And given the terms under which he was sent from my presence, his betrayal seems likely. I never liked the man. He was always scraping and slithering about..." The King waved an annoyed hand. "Mayhap he wished to have vengeance on me for sending him away. Mayhap he thought he could harm me by loosing Mortimer into the world."

In typical fashion, the King could only see the situation as it related to him rather than his country as a whole. He saw personal vendettas and conspiracies everywhere, yet he had not noticed the far larger implications of a new mounting rebellion happening right under his nose—from within his own palace.

The Queen sipped her wine placidly, seeming to ignore the entire conversation, yet Will knew she would be relieved that Edward suspected naught. The King could search every inch of England for Mortimer and the mysterious man who'd freed him from the Tower, but his efforts would be fruitless thanks to his own blind pride.

"Yer anger is more than justified, Highness," Will said gravely. "As is yer determination to find Mortimer. The greatest danger to a King often comes from within—from his own nobles, his own countrymen. Such threats cannae be allowed to stand. In fact, I wonder…"

Will pretended that an idea was coming to him. He eased back in his chair, his gaze wandering away from the King.

"What is it, Stewart?" Edward demanded testily.

Will blinked and refocused on the King. "Och, naught. Merely a possible course of action to aid in yer search for Mortimer."

The King sat down heavily in his chair once more. "Then speak, man."

Shaking his head wryly, Will fixed Edward with an uncertain look. "It would be preposterous coming from me, a Scot, Highness. I cannae voice the idea without appearing a traitor myself."

"Spit it out, Stewart. Naught is more important than finding Mortimer."

Will dragged out the King's anticipation by busying himself with repositioning his chair. He scooted back from the table and hauled the heavy wooden chair closer to the King's. When at last he faced Edward only a few feet away, he leaned forward, propping his elbows on the chair's arms.

"It is just…well, this matter with that scoundrel

Mortimer ought to receive the full force of yer might. Such plots against ye, the most powerful man in the kingdom, cannae be ignored. As ye say, naught is more important that finding and weeding out traitors. And yet...I cannae help noticing that yer attention has been divided, Highness."

"What?" The King's voice was sharp, yet his brows were drawn in concern. He waited for Will to go on.

This was it. Will had Edward hooked. Now he just had to pull him in.

Will sighed, feigning reluctance once more. "It may no' be my place to say, Highness, but...but these bloody defiant Scots under Robert the Bruce have consumed much of yer energy. I cannae help wondering if ye might find Mortimer sooner and end this rebel scheming once and for all if ye could give yer full focus to the task."

"You are suggesting that the King of England abandon his conquest of the barbarian Scots?" Despenser asked, his tone barbed.

"Nay, milord, Highness," Will said quickly, addressing them both. "No' abandon. As ye ken, I fully support yer efforts against the Bruce and his unruly countrymen. They must be brought to heel— eventually. I am merely suggesting that for the time being, ye...*shift* yer attentions to the most pressing of matters. The last thing ye need is another enemy."

As Will repeated the words Isabella had used a fortnight past along the Thames, the Queen's gaze flashed to him.

Eleanor had apprised Isabella of Will's plan. The Queen, too, had considered it dangerous, but as she'd told Will, naught would ever be accomplished without some risk. Her bright eyes were knowing as they fixed on Will for an instant before returning to the table before her.

Edward sat back in his chair, his hand absently fiddling with the fur trimming on his robes.

"In a perfect world," Will went on, sensing the King's receptiveness, "there would be endless men, supplies, and hours in the day to see all of yer objectives tackled at once. But of course ye are King here in the real world, Highness, where men like ye must make difficult decisions about what is most important."

The King absorbed Will's flattery with a tilt of his head, acknowledging his agreement. Good God, this was the man who had brought so much destruction and suffering to Scotland—a man of immense power, but enfeebled character. A man easily swayed by words of praise yet without the will or ability to live up to them.

Edward pursed his lips in thought. "And you think I ought to *shift* my agenda toward finding Mortimer?"

"The fact that a man who raised arms against ye

and challenged yer claim to the throne, along with Lancaster and the other rebels, now roams England freely is surely the most urgent matter, Highness," Will said solemnly. "Just think—what if he manages to find others who remain loyal to his rebellion? What if he—"

"Enough," Edward said, running an agitated hand over his face. "I agree, the threat is real. But I am loath to lose ground against the Scots. They are like wild dogs—you give them a single scrap and they tear your hand off for more. No offense, Stewart."

Will forced a chuckle through clenched teeth. "None taken, Highness. I ken my countrymen's nature all too well, and ye are right. But I cannae help noticing that ye are sending men and resources to the border which could instead be used to comb every inch of England for Mortimer. I hear the Scots continue to harass Carlisle. Where would they drag ye to next, Highness?"

The King scowled at that. "Indeed, I do not like that they have set and controlled my priorities for so long."

"Exactly," Will said, seizing on the opening. "Ye need to set yer own agenda, Highness, no' be led around by the Scots like their wee dog."

When Edward slammed his fist into the tabletop again, Will feared he'd gone too far. He held his tongue, watching keenly and waiting for an indication that it was safe to speak again.

"As I said, I ken my countrymen's nature," he continued casually. "Like petulant bairns, they dinnae like being told nay. They buck and strain against control, yet left to their own devices, they have little ability to manage themselves."

Will leaned further forward in his chair. "Mayhap it would be good for ye to give them a taste of home rule. It would be amusing to watch how quickly they'll turn on each other and tear their own country apart. And of course Scotland isnae going anywhere. When the problem with Mortimer is resolved, ye may return where ye left off with the Scots."

Edward eyed Will under lowered brows. "And how exactly would I accomplish that? If I withdraw my soldiers from the border, those savages will only pour into England, raiding and razing aught they encounter."

Will settled back in his chair as if to contemplate that. Inside, though, his chest thumped wildly with his impending victory. He was nearly there. Just one more seed to plant.

"Och, ye're right. I suppose ye'd need a treaty of some sort—one that allowed ye to withdraw and focus yer efforts on finding Mortimer, but that also ensured the Bruce couldnae lash out across the border."

The King nodded slowly in thought. "Aye, if I

could bind the Bruce in a treaty, he would be forced to cease his attacks."

Will swallowed to keep from bellowing to the great hall's rafters in triumph.

In Edward's muddled view, a truce would be a victory for him over the Bruce, yet peace and freedom were all Scotland had ever wanted to begin with. And the King of England would give it to them in his quest to find a man who would not be found—not until Mortimer and the Queen had raised an army powerful enough to challenge Edward for the throne.

"A wise course of action, Highness," Will managed, imbuing his voice with gravity.

The King turned to Despenser. "See what you can coordinate through your channels, Hugh. I'll have one of my scribes draw up an agreement, and we will begin arranging a meeting between our advisors and the Bruce's."

Despenser fixed the King with a concerned look. "Are you sure about this, Edward? To abandon your efforts against Scotland, and at the suggestion of a Scot, no less—"

"I can always break the treaty if need be," the King cut in, waving an airy hand. "The Scots have done so several times. Hell, even my father broke truces when it suited him."

Despenser opened his mouth to voice his disapproval once more, but at Edward's sharp look, he wisely decided to hold his tongue. Aye, the King could be influenced—manipulated even. But just as Eleanor had told Will, when Edward felt he was being betrayed, he could be ruthless—even toward his favorite, and even if the betrayal was no more than a word spoken against him.

The King turned his attention back to the feast laid out on the table. He reached for his eating knife and skewered a hunk of roasted swan. Chewing a bite, he spoke in low tones to Despenser about further arrangements that would need to be made to divert his men from the border to the quest for Mortimer.

Will scooted his chair back beside Eleanor, but instead of settling in for the lavish meal, he leaned toward her.

"Meet me in my chamber. I have a matter to discuss with ye," he said close to her ear.

She looked at him, her brows lifting in a question. But instead of saying more, he rose, giving the Queen and King each a stiff bow and excusing himself.

His heart thundered against his ribs as he stepped from the dais and made his way toward his chamber. Manipulating the King of England into signing a treaty with Scotland was naught compared to what lay ahead of him.

It was foolish, of course, to lose his head so completely at the thought of the conversation he needed to have with Eleanor. The fate of Scotland was secure, as were their lives, at least for the time being.

Yet what was his life worth if he didn't have the one thing he wanted most in this world?

He could only pray she would agree to what he had planned.

Chapter Thirty-Four

✥✥✥

Eleanor pressed a hand over her stomach as she walked down the corridor toward Will's chamber. Inside, a riot of nerves ricocheted off one another.

The last fortnight had been the first taste of true peace and happiness she had known in all her time at court.

On their rides and in the privacy of Isabella's solar, Eleanor had slowly begun to share the truth with the Queen. It wasn't neat and tidy, but life rarely was. Aye, still more remained to be said, yet a quiet understanding had formed between them.

Isabella seemed to accept her, even though it had hurt her to learn that Eleanor wasn't all she'd seemed these last four years. But the Queen understood now that they had always been working toward the same purpose—peace and prosperity on both sides of the border. True to her word, Isabella appeared willing to embrace allies where she could find them—including in Eleanor and Will.

And matters with Will…

They had spent every night since returning to Langley together, finding not only pleasure but safe haven in each other's arms. The complete love and trust Eleanor had so desperately longed for but never allowed herself to hope to possess was finally hers.

Yet they had never spoken of the future. It had felt as though to do so would shatter the delicate, perfect present they had now. But judging from the tension in Will's features when he'd asked her to meet him, mayhap that was about to change.

Her nervousness climbing even higher, Eleanor tapped on Will's chamber door before easing it open. He stood before the hearth, his back to her.

"Come in."

She closed the door behind her but lingered in front of it, uncertain of his mood.

"Your handling of Edward was masterful," she commented. "I feared a time or two that he would reject the idea of a treaty, but you guided him perfectly."

He turned to her then, his shoulders rigid and his brows drawn tight.

"I plan on returning to the Highlands after Edward signs the truce," he said without preamble.

Eleanor's stomach plummeted to the floor. A breath caught in her throat. "Oh."

"There is a keep there, in the northern Highlands, that is my responsibility. Dundale, it is called. Ever since my father died last year, it has been my duty to look after it for the Sinclair clan."

He picked up the poker propped against the hearth and distractedly stirred the fire.

"In truth, it has been my responsibility long before my father died, for he wasnae well for many years. Yet I left the running of it to my chatelaine and seneschal. But after seeing Edward shirk his duty to his people in pursuit of personal indulgence and distraction, I cannae in good conscience ignore my obligation any longer."

"You have been fighting for the Bruce, working in his Bodyguard Corps," Eleanor said faintly. "That is not the same as avoiding your role as a leader the way Edward does."

"Nevertheless." He set the poker down and faced her once more. His blue-green gaze, so like deep water in its clarity and changeability, was troubled as it met hers. "I cannae stay at court—nor in England. I dinnae belong here."

Eleanor felt her heart crumbling to dust inside her chest. He was leaving her. She attempted a weak laugh to chase the sting out of her eyes. "But you make such a fine courtier."

He snorted softly. "Ye are a good liar, Eleanor, but no' that good."

A laden silence fell between them. Light words of well wishes for Will's endeavors in Scotland clogged behind the lump in Eleanor's throat. Her gaze drifted over his features, trying to memorize each hard line when he was gone and she was alone once more.

Will's throat bobbed once, then twice. "I had hoped…" He coughed before going on. "I had hoped that ye might consider coming with me."

Eleanor froze, uncertain if she'd understood him. "Oh?"

"But I ken yer friendship with the Queen means a great deal to ye. I wouldnae presume that ye'd leave her side to join me."

Slow realization began to dawn. "*Oh.*"

Will's gaze flickered over her face, his brows pinched together. "Ye are English, and a noblewoman of the court," he continued, his voice willfully devoid of emotion. "I couldnae offer ye the life ye've grown accustomed to here. It is too much to ask ye to leave yer home, yer closest friend, yer comforts, all for…" He waved vaguely between them.

All for love.
All for him.

"You foolish, rock-headed Highlander."

He blinked at her. Before he could recover, she continued in a soft voice.

"You have it all determined already, don't you? Yet you have not even asked me the question to which you think you know the answer."

He absorbed her words for a moment, then let out a long breath. "The truth is…I am afraid of what ye'll say. I am afraid that no matter how fiercely I love ye, how desperately I want ye to be my own forever, ye'll reject me."

Elated tears blurred her vision. "And why would I do that?" she asked, playing coy.

He flung a frustrated hand in the air. "For all the reasons I just mentioned. Yer whole life is here, Eleanor. The Queen, and yer work, and… And I cannae give ye fine gowns and lavish palaces and an endless stable of horses to ride."

"You think that is what I want, silly man?"

He looked at her with such desolate confusion that she finally took pity on him. In one swift step she was in his arms, her head nestled against his chest.

"I only want *you*, Will Sinclair," she whispered. "I love you, and I will until the day I die."

"I…I dinnae understand."

She looked up at him, smiling gently. "What don't you understand?"

His gaze softened as it traced the tear-tracks down her cheeks. "I am only a man, a warrior—a one-eyed warrior at that. Aye, I have lands and a keep under my care, but…but ye would give up all this?"

Eleanor pulled back slightly so that she could fix him with a serious look. "Do you truly think I care more about gowns and horses than I do about you?"

"Nay, but…"

"The truth is, court life suits me about as well as it suits you." She shook her head slowly. "All the games, the deception, the secrets and gossip…" Eleanor shuddered. "It has been a terrible burden these last four years—one I was willing to bear in the service of the Bruce. But now that Edward will sign a treaty, I want naught more than to be free of this place, this *life*."

Will's lips quirked faintly. "But ye make such a fine spy," he said, echoing her words from a moment before.

She let her head fall onto his chest once more. "What if we could escape those roles—courtier and spy, warrior and lady-in-waiting, Highlander and Englishwoman. What if we could simply be a man and a woman who love each other unconditionally? What if we could simply…*be*. Together."

"Are ye saying…" He swallowed. "Are ye saying that ye would come with me?"

"Wherever you are is where I belong, Will."

"And that ye'll be mine for all our days?"

"Aye. I am already yours."

He wrapped her in a hug so tight that for a long moment she couldn't breathe. But it didn't matter, because she was too busy laughing and crying at the same time against his chest.

"And I am yers, Eleanor de Monteney," he murmured in a tight voice against her hair. "Ye have my heart and ye always will."

At last his grip on her loosened. He ducked his head to catch her gaze. When she looked up, his eye was once again clouded with worry.

"But what of the Queen? I ken ye dinnae take yer friendship lightly, and I wouldnae want to be the cause of yer separation."

Eleanor touched his face gently. "I love that you are taking the matter so seriously. But Isabella is preparing to go to France as soon as the opportunity presents itself—without me. We had always planned that if Roger made it to the royal palace in Paris, she would find the least conspicuous way possible to join him. She cannot take a large entourage, or even her favorite lady-in-waiting, for it will appear as though she means to stay."

A half-smile tugged at her lips. "Besides, after you arrived, she thought she would have to give me up even sooner, given our ruse engagement. We have already planned to correspond by missive, though, and she made me promise to visit her in France, or even England if her plan is successful."

"Speaking of the engagement…" A strange look passed over Will's features—part tentative, part mischievous. "Ye ken things are a wee bit different in Scotland."

"Aye?" she replied cautiously.

"What ye might call an engagement here in England we would call a handfasting. A handfasted couple agrees to pledge themselves to one another for a year and a day. If they both find the match agreeable over that time, then at the end of the year and a day, they wed."

"Are you saying you wish to be handfasted with me?"

"Well, no' exactly," Will hedged. "Ye see, a handfasting is normally performed by a priest. But one cannae always find a man of the cloth when he's needed," Will continued. "So we have learned to make do—as has the church."

"What are you saying?"

Will scrubbed a hand over the back of his neck, his lips twitching. "In Scotland, all it takes to be handfasted is for both parties to declare publicly that it is so. So technically…we are already handfasted."

Now it was Eleanor's turn to blink at Will in stunned confusion. "You mean…you are telling me that we are engaged already—in truth? Not just for show?"

"Ye did agree that ye were my fiancée—in front of the Queen of England—when I declared that we were engaged."

An uncontrollable giggle escaped Eleanor's lips. This was mad and wild—but then again, everything with Will was.

"Of course, if ye dinnae wish to remain hand-fasted, we can break the arrang—"

"Nay." A grin lingered on her lips, but she let the depth of her feelings shine through her eyes as she held his stare. "I do not wish to break the handfasting."

"Then if ye still find me agreeable after a year and a day," he said, his voice a low caress, "ye'll marry me?"

She frowned as if seriously considering the alternative. But when she spoke, she could not keep the joy from her tone. "I think we have already established that we...*please* each other," she teased.

For that, his hands tightened around her and his gaze turned hot with desire. "Aye."

Her eyes drifted to his mouth. How she longed to pull him to the bed and lose herself in his lips, his hands, his hard, strong body.

But she needed the answer to one more question first. She lifted a brow at him. "I do not understand all these Scottish traditions, but mayhap you can clarify something for me. What if I do not wish to wait a year and a day to call you my husband?"

A wide grin split Will's handsome face. "That can be arranged."

Ducking his head, he captured her mouth in a slow, deep kiss that promised a lifetime of breathtaking happiness ahead.

Will backed Eleanor up to the bed, but when the backs of her knees bumped the mattress, she paused.

"You were so prepared for me to reject you. What would you have done if I hadn't wished to go with you to the Highlands as your wife?"

Will shook his head ruefully. "In truth, I dinnae ken. I couldnae think beyond my fear that ye wouldnae want to stay with me, and my hope that ye would. I suppose I might have tried to lure ye to the Lowlands to begin with, ease ye into things. Then once ye had a taste for the joys and freedoms of a life on Scottish soil, I would have coaxed ye farther and farther north until ye were in the Highlands."

"That is a very elaborate—and drawn out—plan," she commented with a chuckle.

"Or mayhap I would have swallowed my distaste for a life in an English palace and remained here with ye," he said, lifting one shoulder. "The fact is, I cannae live without ye, Eleanor. Ye are my home and my heart, my pearl."

"Your pearl?"

"Aye, for the grit at yer core formed the strong, beautiful treasure ye are to me."

After that, Eleanor's throat was too tight for more words, but they were no longer needed, for they tumbled into the bed together and let their bodies continue the conversation.

Chapter Thirty-Five

❧❀❧

November, 1326
Three and a Half Years Later
Dundale Keep, Scottish Highlands

Eleanor groaned at the knock on the bedchamber door. She burrowed deeper into the downy mattress and heavy quilted coverlet. Ever since the new babe in her belly had started kicking a fortnight ago, the little hellion hadn't stopped. She was sure the babe would be another boy, just like the first, for it was clearly as strong-willed and lively as its father.

All the kicking had made sleep difficult. She had just nodded off when the knock had roused her.

When she grumbled into her pillow, a low, rich chuckle rose from beside her.

"Is the wee bairn dancing on yer ribs again, wife?"

She lifted her head to squint at Will. He wore a wide grin that made him devilishly handsome.

"Aye," she grumbled. "I doubt I got more than two winks of sleep last night."

He gave her forehead a swift, gentle kiss. "It will be worth it, my bonny pearl. Once the bairn is done giving ye hell inside yer belly, she can give me hell out of it."

She rubbed her eyes as he slipped from their bed and hastily wrapped a red plaid around his bare hips.

"You think it's a girl?" she asked as he made his way to the door.

"Aye, of course," he said over his shoulder. "I can already tell she'll be as clever and bonny and fierce as her mother."

Will pulled open the chamber door to a servant. The lad held a tray with several missives on it. "These just came, milord."

"Thank ye, Pieter."

Closing the door, Will sauntered back to the bed with the stack of missives in one hand. When Eleanor saw Isabella's distinctive seal—a shield with both an English lion and the French *fleur-de-lis*—she immediately sat up, all traces of exhaustion fleeing.

Will must have sensed her eagerness, for he passed the missive to her before settling into the bed beside her. Eleanor broke the seal and unfolded the missive, hurriedly scanning it.

"Isabella writes from France," she said, her eyes fixed on the elegant script. "She is well, as is Mortimer and Prince Edward."

Nearly a year ago, the Queen had written that she was finally leaving England—and King Edward. Matters had grown worse for Isabella in the time since Eleanor and Will had departed England. Edward had become more dependent on Despenser, and more hostile toward Isabella. They had confiscated all her lands and holdings, refused to let her see her children, and even imprisoned those amongst her staff who were French, accusing them of disloyalty to England.

Despite the fact that the treaty still held between England and Scotland, Edward had no shortage of troubles. Relations had grown tense between Edward and Isabella's brother Charles, the King of France, over a dispute about lands.

The good news was, it had allowed Isabella to concoct a perfect excuse to journey to Paris. She'd proposed that she visit for diplomatic purposes, assuring Edward that she'd work to smooth things between their countries.

The Queen had written an elated missive a few months past to Eleanor that her reunion with Mortimer had brought her true happiness for the first time in years. What was more, she had been able to take her eldest son, Prince Edward, the heir to the English throne, with her to France. They'd carried on under the pretense that it was only a short visit, but once they'd arrived, she'd refused to return to England with her son.

According to the Queen, Edward had apparently sent several notes imploring Isabella to return. When she'd rebuffed him, he'd demanded that Charles send her back. But to Isabella's supreme satisfaction, her brother had told Edward that she'd come of her own will, and therefore could return freely if she wished. But if she preferred to remain in France, he refused to expel his beloved sister.

"She says they have already gathered an army of nearly two thousand men," Eleanor read, darting a wide-eyed glance at Will.

His brows lifted. "Edward's support was built on sandier ground than anyone kenned."

"Indeed. Several more English nobles join Isabella every day, according to the missive. And…"

She scanned ahead quickly. When she read the next few lines, she let out a breath.

"And she says she and Mortimer are finally ready to launch their attack on England. She sounds optimistic for a victory given the support and enthusiasm that has met her, yet also clear-eyed and focused. She writes that if she is successful, she intends to set up her son, Prince Edward, as England's King, and that she and Mortimer will serve as regents until he comes of age."

"Let us hope she is victorious," Will said gravely. "And that when she is, she keeps her promise to make Edward's treaty with Scotland permanent."

It had been an astounding feat three years past when Edward had signed a thirteen-year treaty with the Bruce only a few weeks after Will had planted the idea in the King's head.

The peace had allowed Scotland to flourish. The Borderlands were no longer contested ground, and the tumultuous skirmishes and battles had all but died out. Here in the Highlands, clans were returning to their usual bickering about property lines and grazing rights. Yet from what Will had told her, the whole country was more united than before the long wars with England had begun, for they had their hard-earn freedom at last, thanks to a King who had fought relentlessly for it—for *them*.

Eleanor lowered the missive and placed a hand on her belly, feeling the babe kick.

"For once, I share your enthusiasm, little one," she murmured, smiling.

She glanced over at Will to find him frowning at the unfolded parchment he held.

"The Queen's missive must have been delayed in all the turmoil between France and England," he said.

"The Bruce has written to me as well. There is more news."

Not long after Eleanor and Will had left Langley for Scotland, the Bruce had called the entire Bodyguard Corps together at his palace in Scone. In light of the treaty, the Bruce was hopeful that there would be no more need for the elite group of warriors to protect those most vulnerable in the wars with England.

And things had indeed been calm and peaceful these last three years. The Bruce had given Will and Eleanor his blessing to live quietly at Dundale. He'd even performed their marriage ceremony after the meeting for the Corps members at Scone. As the mysterious Englishwoman spy, Eleanor had been met with much curiosity by the other members and their wives. She'd also received praise from the King himself for her part in securing the peace treaty they now enjoyed.

Since that meeting, the rest of the Corps had settled across Scotland, some staying by the Bruce's side, others returning to castles and keeps in the Highlands. Some preferred to remain close to the political maneuverings at the Bruce's court, while others, like Will, had sought simpler lives.

But though the Bodyguard Corps had been officially retired, the members were still part of the Bruce's most trusted inner circle. He wrote to them often, keeping them abreast of matters between Scotland and England, and sometimes even seeking their council on delicate affairs of governance. And of course they all stood at the ready should the King ever need to call upon them again.

So it was no surprise to Eleanor that the Bruce had written to Will. But she could not stop the wave of trepidation at the prospect of news about Isabella's fledgling rebellion.

Eleanor sat upright, her brows pinching with worry. "Oh? What news?"

"Apparently Isabella's invasion has already happened."

She peered over Will's shoulder to skim the missive herself. It was true. The Bruce wrote that Isabella had landed in England with Mortimer and an army of two thousand men more than a month ago.

Support had flocked to Isabella, for discontent with Edward's rule was stronger than ever before. She was even hailed as a savior the further into England she marched. All those who had attempted to join the Earl of Lancaster's unsuccessful uprising, plus more who had become disaffected with Edward since then, had congregated behind her.

Edward and Despenser, learning of her approach, had apparently fled to Wales, but Isabella and her army had pursued them all the way to the western coast. The King and Despenser had tried to set sail to escape her, but the weather had been against them, and after weeks of evasion, they were finally caught by Isabella's forces.

A gasp escaped Eleanor's lips at the incredible victory. "What do you think will happen to the King and Despenser now?"

Will frowned grimly. "Despenser will likely get a traitor's death. The nobles who have so long resented his abuses of power will demand naught less. As for Edward…" His brows drew together. "He will probably be stowed away in some palace or other—one that is truly a glorified prison. But I wouldnae be surprised if he disappears or dies under mysterious circumstances within the year."

"Truly?"

"He is still technically King, and Isabella's lawful husband, so they cannae strike him out in the open. But no new ruler wants his—or her—predecessor lurking about, plotting his own uprising to reclaim power. Did ye see what they are calling Isabella now?" He held up the parchment. "The She-Wolf of France. Ye were right about her, Eleanor. She proved to be stronger and more fearsome than anyone gave her credit for."

Eleanor leaned back in the bed, marveling at that. It was true, Isabella was unlike any woman she'd ever known. If she could manage to rein in the wild, bucking horse that was England, she just might be able to pass it on to her son in one piece. *other children*

Just then, the door to their bedchamber burst open and a golden-headed arrow wrapped in red plaid shot in.

Cailean, their two-and-a-half-year-old son, flung himself onto the mattress with a wild giggle.

"What are ye doing, ye wee imp?" Will growled, launching a tickle attack against the boy.

"Time to play, dada!" Cailean shrieked, squirming away from Will's fingers. "Wake up, mama. Wake up, wee bairn."

"We are awake!" Eleanor said, grabbing her son's head and giving it a hearty kiss.

"Where on earth is yer long-suffering nursemaid, imp?" Will demanded, tossing Cailean over his shoulder and stomping toward the door. Cailean screamed in delight as Will pretended to heave him out of their chamber.

"Nay, dada!" he cried happily.

"Nay?" Will hoisted the wiggling lad up to the level of his good eye. "Ye wish to stay in bed with us?"

"Aye, dada."

"Verra well, then, imp." With a dramatic heave, Will tossed Cailean onto the soft mattress beside Eleanor, much to the child's delight.

Eleanor fell into a heap with the laughing, shrieking boy. A heartbeat later, Will launched himself beside them, making the bedframe groan. That only made Eleanor and Cailean laugh harder.

"More, dada, more!"

Aye, Eleanor thought. More was what she had—more happiness, more joy, more love than she ever knew her heart could hold. Yet there was always more and more.

Epilogue

March, 1328
One and a Half Years Later
Edinburgh, Scotland

Will clucked his tongue to encourage Fearghus up the steeply inclining road to Edinburgh Castle. Cailean sat in the saddle before him, squirming with excitement.

"Och, da, look at the pennants!" the boy cried, pointing at the colorful banners suspended from the castle's imposing walls. "And the horns!"

As if in response, the trumpeters lining the battlements raised their horns in unison and gave a trilling blast of notes.

The ceremony was about to begin. They were a wee bit late—traveling from the Highlands with a four- and one-year-old had been no small feat—but they hadn't missed it.

Will caught Eleanor's eye. She rode beside him, wee Isabella tucked securely to her chest. Amazingly, the horns hadn't disturbed the normally-rambunc-tious lass.

Without needing to speak, Eleanor gave him a nod and urged her horse into a faster walk. Neither one of them would miss this moment for the world.

They crossed over the drawbridge and through the open portcullis. When they reached the outer yard, they were met with a riot of activity.

Grooms darted hither and thither, leading the latecomers' horses toward the nearby stables. Scots of all kinds—Lowlanders in breeches, Highlanders in plaids, noble men and women in fine silks and velvets, and modest folk in homespun wool—all began herding in the same direction.

Will reined to a halt and handed Cailean down to a waiting groom before swinging from the saddle himself. Then he moved beside Eleanor's horse, lifting both his wife and wee Isabella into his arms and lowering them gently to the ground.

"The ceremony should begin shortly," the groom offered as he took up both sets of reins. "Follow the others toward the inner yard. The King has arranged everything in front of the great hall. He didnae wish to waste such a fine day."

Indeed, the sun shone overhead in a crystalline blue sky. The spring air was crisp yet heavy with the promise of new life about to blossom.

"Thank ye," Will said to the groom. Placing a hand around Eleanor's back, they fell in with the others. They funneled through the gate in the inner wall, which opened onto the smaller of the castle's yards.

The inner yard was crammed with people who were abuzz with excitement. The wait was almost over.

"Lady Eleanor, cousin!" Will and Eleanor both turned at the call. He found Jane Sinclair, the daughter of his eldest cousin, Laird Robert Sinclair, filtering her way through the crowd toward them.

"Why, Jane," Eleanor exclaimed. "You've transformed from a girl to a young woman since last I saw you."

The lass blushed modestly. Eleanor was right—Will's wee cousin was already a beauty like her mother, Alwin, and had the Lady of the Sinclair clan's poise and quiet confidence as well.

"I volunteered to watch all the bairns of the Corps members," Jane said. "So that ye could all stand together beside the Bruce."

"Thank you, Jane. That is very kind." Eleanor eased wee Isabella from the wrapping that kept her strapped to her chest. "But watch out for this one. She's already a walker—and a bit of a hellion."

Jane laughed as she hoisted Isabella into her arms. "She looks too adorable to cause trouble."

Will and Eleanor exchanged a look. "Ye'd think that," Will said dryly.

With another chuckle, Jane shifted Isabella onto one hip, then bent so that she could meet Cailean's gaze. "Would ye like to come with me, cousin? All the other lads and lasses are over there, bobbing for apples and tossing rings."

Cailean's hazel eyes lit up. "Aye!"

"Follow me, then." Jane extended her hand and led Cailean off to one corner of the inner yard, where Will could now see a veritable army of the Corps' offspring.

Though they were all happily married now, a few of the Corps members hadn't been blessed with children. Others, like Niall Beaumore and Mairin Mackenzie Beaumore, had an entire flock of wee warrior lads and lasses in the making.

Will smiled at the throng of bairns. Some were red-headed, others blond, and others dark. The older ones leaned against the inner wall and chatted, their faces tilted up toward the sun, while the younger ones scampered about like wild animals, laughing and shrieking.

His gaze swept over the crowd to the raised dais

positioned in front of the great hall. Atop the dais, Robert the Bruce sat behind a table in a carved wooden chair.

His hair was almost entirely gray now, with only a few russet streaks remaining. He was thinner, too, his face deeply lined yet at ease as he looked out across those gathered.

He had lost some of the vitality and intensity of his younger years, and no wonder. He'd given all his strength, his vigor, his vivacity, to the cause for Scottish freedom. It had been twenty-two years since he'd declared himself King of Scotland—twenty-two years of fighting, of warfare, of being forced to retreat only to steal victory after victory from the jaws of defeat.

And today, at long last, he would see his life's work come to fruition.

Will's gaze shifted to the men and women who stood behind the King's chair on the dais. Recognition warmed his chest. The entire Bodyguard Corps, along with their wives, were gathered together.

Just then, Eleanor slipped her arm through his, lifting a radiant smile to him. "Come on. Let's join them."

They wove their way through the crowd and toward the dais. Will lifted Eleanor onto the platform and stepped up beside her. The first to greet them were the clump of his Sinclair cousins closest to the end of the dais.

Will clasped forearms with Laird Robert, Garrick, and Burke while Eleanor greeted the men's wives, Alwin, Jocelyn, and Meredith. When Will reached Daniel Sinclair, he pulled the man into a bear hug.

"Uncle Danny," Will said, pounding Daniel on the back.

Though they were technically cousins, Will had always looked up to Daniel. After Will's father William had fallen in that terrible horseback riding accident that left him an invalid, Daniel had lived at Dundale, helping to run the keep and teaching Will how to do so himself once he came of age. Daniel had been called from Dundale on a mission for the Bruce when Will had been just fifteen, but Will still treasured all that his cousin had taught him in those early years.

Daniel pulled back, giving Will a hearty thump on the shoulder. "Good to see ye, lad. I still cannae believe my eyes—ye are a man grown now." His gaze shifted to where Eleanor was greeting Daniel's wife Rona. "I still remember ye as the wee lad who found the idea of marriage to a lass repugnant."

Will looked heavenward and shook his head, causing Daniel to bark a laugh.

He continued down the line of Corps members, greeting Ansel and Isolda Sutherland, who stood with Finn and Rosamond Sutherland. Finn and Ansel, who were distant cousins, were discussing Finn's latest news from the Borderlands—which was blessedly quiet and peaceful these days.

Colin and Sabine MacKay were next to greet them. Eleanor lingered with Sabine, discussing those in the King's network of spies and messengers they knew in common. Though the two women hadn't met until after Eleanor's mission was officially over, they shared much in common and had become good friends in the five years since Will and Eleanor had made their home in the Highlands.

Graeme and Anna MacKay stood beside Colin and Sabine. Colin and Graeme, who were also cousins, were debating some MacKay clan matter or other. Will greeted them both warmly, but as he turned to the next in line, the smile on his face slipped slightly.

Kirk MacLeod met his gaze solemnly. He waited for Will to make the first move, as he always did out of deference to the past they shared.

Slowly, Will extended his hand to Kirk. Kirk took it, giving his arm a firm squeeze.

They weren't the closest members in the Corps, but their relationship had improved in leaps and bounds thanks to Eleanor. Because of her, Will had slowly been able to forgive Kirk and let go of his resentment and bitterness over the loss of his eye. Now the two of them could be together without Will boiling over with anger about what had happened so many years ago.

"How are the bairns?" Will asked, withdrawing his hand and turning to Lillian. Lillian beamed at him, pulling both Will and Eleanor into a quick hug.

Kirk lifted his chin toward the roiling mass of children in the corner. "All are well, thank ye. And yers?"

"Raising hell," Will replied with a grin.

Kirk's pale blue eyes warmed with a smile of his own. "I'd expect naught else."

With a nod, Will moved on to the next Corps members. A clump of Mackenzies stood beside Kirk and Lillian, their heads together so that they could chat and laugh happily with one another. Laird Reid Mackenzie and Corinne, Logan and Helena, and Mairin Mackenzie Beaumore all welcomed Will and Eleanor with wide smiles and warm salutations.

Joining their circle were Reid's half-brother Fillan MacVale and his sweet, shy wife Adelaide. Though a clubfoot had kept Fillan from the front lines, he was an honorary member of the Corps for his efforts in bringing the MacVale clan into line behind the Bruce's cause. Will and Eleanor shared forearm shakes and hugs with both of them.

Just behind Mairin stood her husband Niall. As the only Englishman officially in the Corps, Niall seemed content to stand back and let the Scots be the first to enjoy this moment. He spoke quietly with his sister, Elaine Beaumore Munro, and Elaine's husband Jerome Munro. Jerome was a rather reserved man, yet he dipped his dark head and welcomed both Will and Eleanor.

Beside Jerome was the even more taciturn Kieran MacAdams. The contrast between the gruff Highlander and his bonny, charming French wife Vivienne never ceased to amuse Will.

Eleanor exchanged pleasantries in the limited French she'd learned from Queen Isabella with Vivienne. Because both women had served as ladies-in-waiting to French Queens, Eleanor and Vivienne had become fast, close friends. Will was left to share a few grunts and monosyllabic words with Kieran while the two women chatted.

The only remaining person on the dais was the Bruce himself. When Will and Eleanor reached him, he pushed himself out of his chair and extended thin but warm hands to both of them.

"I'm glad ye both made it," the Bruce said, his dark eyes twinkling with pleasure. "This moment wouldnae be complete without ye, given how much ye've done to get us here."

Though Will knew the King didn't require such formalities of those in his inner circle, he bowed deeply to the Bruce nonetheless.

"It has been the honor and privilege of my life to serve ye in this cause, sire."

Eleanor, too, curtsied low. "As it has been mine."

"Rise, both of ye," Robert said with a chuckle. "And join the others. I cannae wait a heartbeat longer."

Will and Eleanor stepped back from the King's chair to stand with the rest of the Corps. As they did, the Bruce motioned to one of his men positioned on the wall. At the King's gesture, the horns blasted again, and all those in the inner yard fell silent. Even the bairns' merrymaking quieted, as if they sensed the gravity of what was about to happen.

The double doors on the great hall behind the dais swung open. A man wearing the official livery of an English messenger processed solemnly from the hall, flanked by four Scottish guards. The royal messenger skirted around the dais, then mounted in front of the Bruce, bowing low as he extended the scrolled parchment he held across the table.

As the messenger stepped down from the dais, the Bruce unfurled the scroll, holding it out in front of him. He cleared his throat as if to speak loudly to all those gathered, but then he squinted at the parchment uncertainly.

The Bruce hesitated then. He glanced over his shoulder at the assembled Corps members. His gaze landed first on Will.

"Will Sinclair," he said, raising his voice as much as he could. "Would ye do the honors of reading out this treaty so that all present will bear witness to its signing?"

Will immediately stepped forward, bowing low to the Bruce.

"Thank ye for saving an old man from the embarrassment of weak eyes and a thin voice," the Bruce whispered, grinning at Will as he passed the parchment to him.

Will straightened, holding the treaty before him in hands that shook slightly. He read, lifting his voice for all to hear.

"In this year of our Lord, thirteen hundred and twenty-eight, let it be known that we, the Dowager Queen Isabella and regent Roger Mortimer, Earl of March, governing on behalf of Edward III, by the grace of God, King of England, Wales and Ireland, do freely enter into a peaceful treaty with all of Scotland and its King, Robert the Bruce."

Will could have heard a pin drop on the other side of the yard as he paused to draw breath.

"Whereas we and some of our predecessors, Kings of England, have endeavored to establish rights of rule, dominion, or superiority over the realm of Scotland, we recognize that dire conflicts and wars waged have afflicted for many years the Kingdoms of both England and Scotland."

He glanced at the sea of faces before him as he went on. "To end the slaughter, disasters, crimes, destruction, and innumerable evils of such a conflict, which have befallen both realms, and in recognition of the wealth, prosperity, and mutual advantage that both realms could enjoy under a perpetual peace between our lands, we do seal this treaty."

The entire crowd seemed to be holding its collective breath as Will continued loud and clear over them.

"We do affirm that our ally and friend, Robert the Bruce, is by God's grace the illustrious King of Scotland, rightful monarch of the realm. His heirs and successors, separate in all ways from the Kingdom of England, shall continue to rule Scotland in perpetuity, without any subjection, service, claim, or demand to the Kingdom or its inhabitants."

Will's gaze flickered to the Bruce. Tears shone in the King's eyes.

"We cancel wholly and utterly all claim to the realm of Scotland," Will continued, "which is defined by the borders and marches as they existed in the time of King Alexander of Scotland, some one hundred years past."

As he reached the final sentence, he had to force the words out through a tight throat. "We hereby pledge ourselves to the full, peaceful, and faithful observance of this treaty, all and singular, for all time."

The yard was dead silent as Will passed the parchment back to the Bruce. Wiping away the moisture from the corners of his eyes, the Bruce rose and looked down at the items the messenger had discreetly placed on the table while Will had read.

The King took up the stick of red sealing wax and held it over the little flame of a lit candle. Then he let several drops of wax land on the strip of parchment that had been affixed to the bottom of the scroll. Setting aside the stick, the Bruce made a fist, pressing his signet ring firmly into the soft wax.

As he lifted his ring away, leaving the indent of his seal, those gathered at last exploded into riotous cheers. The Bruce lifted the sealed treaty high over his head, and impossibly, the crowd roared even louder.

It was done. Scotland was finally free.

The Bruce continued to wave the treaty in the air, urging the crowd on in their celebrations. It was the culmination of his life's work and his final promise kept in the name of Scotland's independence.

As those gathered thundered their approval, the members of the Bodyguard Corps turned to each other. They hugged, pounded each other on the back, whooped, cheered, and heartily kissed their wives. It was what they'd been fighting for all these years. Peace at last.

Will pulled Eleanor into a hard embrace. She laughed and cried against his chest, clinging to him with all her strength. Will kissed her hair, his gaze traveling over her head. It landed on the bairns gathered in the corner.

The peace and freedom Will and the others had fought so hard for was finally won—but ultimately the victory belonged to their children. The younger ones likely didn't understand the enormity of this moment, but that didn't matter. Their future stretched like a brilliant beam of sunlight before them, full of hope and promise.

This was only the beginning for them.

The End

Author's Note

As always, it is one of my great joys in writing historical romance to combine a fictional romantic storyline
with real historical details. Plus, it's such a treat to
share not only a thrilling, passionate, and emotional
love story with you, lovely readers, but to give you a
glimpse at my research into the history surrounding
this book as well. And this story is particularly jam-
packed with real history and juicy tidbits!

Langley Palace is a real place—at least it used to
be. Today, nothing remains of Langley, but it was
once one of the most beloved and significant palaces
in medieval England. Also called Kings Langley
Palace for its importance to England's Kings, it sat
just outside the village of Kings Langley in Hertford-
shire. Situated next to a vast royal forest, the valuable
estate came into the possession of King Edward I's

wife Queen Eleanor of Castile in 1276. She then set about renovating it to her and her family's tastes for the rest of her life.

The Queen built extra chambers for her, the King, and their son, planted a vineyard, dug a new well, expanded the moat, and added an extensive below-ground wine cellar beneath the kitchens, among other additions. The palace also boasted its own bathhouse, bakery, private gardens, and three inner and outer yards.

Edward II spent much of what appears to have been an idyllic childhood at Langley. Young Edward was enthusiastic about horse-and boat-racing, music, tournament events (though jousting wasn't his favorite, for he was never allowed to participate), and the arts, all of which he enjoyed at Langley. He also kept a menagerie there, which included a camel and a lion!

He retreated here more than any of his other residences to escape the troubles of governance and rulership he faced as King. Langley was also a retreat for Edward II's son Edward III, and subsequent Kings Richard II and Henry IV, and Henry VIII. The palace fell into disuse and disrepair in the sixteenth century. Now, nothing remains of the once-lavish palace.

Speaking of Edward II—he is one of the most fascinating and complex historical figures I've ever come across. He was tall, blond, athletic, and considered very handsome, though not a very good ruler. Most historians agree that he was overall an ineffectual King, desperate to live up to his father's larger-than-life legacy as "Hammer of the Scots," but unable to handle both the ongoing war with Scotland and challenges to his leadership from within his own country.

If you've read the other books in the Highland Bodyguards series, especially *His Lass to Protect* (book 9), then you may be familiar with the Earl of Lancaster's rebellion against his first cousin the King. Lancaster and many other nobles were frustrated at Edward's poor handling of Scotland, as well as his preferential treatment toward his favorites, Piers Gaveston, and later, Hugh Despenser. (More on them in a moment.) Edward successfully quashed Lancaster's rebellion in 1322, but discontent with his reign continued to plague him.

Historians also agree that Edward shared some degree of intimacy with Gaveston and Despenser, though how much is unclear. Some think he had an openly sexual relationship with both, others that they were merely close friends and allies. In my story, I have sought to emphasize the way Edward's relationship with Despenser drove him and Queen Isabella apart.

That tension is supported by history. Even before

Edward and Isabella married, he had already become close with Piers Gaveston, a lesser noble. In fact, Edward's father sent Piers into exile, distressed at how close the two were. Once Edward II took the throne, he welcomed Piers back. Though Piers was disliked by other nobles (not so much because of any insinuation of an intimate relationship with the King, but because of Edward's lavish gifts of lands and titles, which they saw as unfair), young Isabella, newly married to Edward, seemed to get along with Piers. The two apparently had an understanding about their roles in Edward's life.

It's worth noting that Edward and Isabella did indeed have four children together, and in the early years of their union, they seemed to have worked together as a medieval power couple of sorts, even while Piers occupied much of Edward's attention. The other nobles' dislike of Piers, however, would spell his demise. Piers was exiled three times in total, in an attempt to limit his influence with the King. When Piers returned after the third exile in 1312, he was hunted down and killed.

The King was devastated. He had Piers's remains, which had been left at the site where he'd been executed, transported to his beloved Langley Palace and laid to rest in a consecrated grave there. Later, he would punish the rebel nobles who'd carried out

Piers's execution with a similarly unceremonious death of beheading.

Hugh Despenser, who became Edward's favorite after gaining the position of royal chamberlain in 1318, was equally hated by Edward's nobles. They viewed him as taking their rightful patronage from the King (lands, titles, and wealth that had been promised to others). He seemed to be a worse, more power-hungry version of Piers.

From the Queen's perspective, he was certainly worse. The two couldn't stand each other. As chamberlain, Despenser controlled access, both in person and in writing, to the King. Hugh began forbidding Isabella from seeing Edward unless he himself was present. Isabella and Edward's children were given to the care of the Despenser family. Hugh refused to allow Isabella to spend time with her own children unless she signed a pledge of loyalty to him, which she refused. Still, Despenser remained Edward's favorite, in part because Despenser stood by the King's side and helped quash the rebellious nobles led by the Earl of Lancaster. After the failed rebellion, Despenser and Edward's misman-agement of England went unchecked.

Until Isabella's stealth rebellion, that is. But before we get to that, let's back up and talk about Isabella herself a bit. As the daughter and sister of the Kings of France, and the wife of the King of England, she was probably one of the most powerful women of the era. She was considered a great beauty of her time, with blonde hair, a fair complexion, blue eyes, and a slender build. But more than her beauty, she was renowned as clever, intelligent, and charming.

Edward and Isabella's relationship began to deteriorate as he became closer to Despenser. But things reached a major breaking point after the Battle of Old Byland in October of 1322. As Edward launched yet another disastrous campaign against Scotland, Isabella accompanied him as far as Tynemouth Priory. But when Edward retreated to York, Isabella was cut off, surrounded on three sides by Scottish forces and on the fourth by waters patrolled by Scottish vessels.

She begged Edward to help her, but all he offered was to send Despenser and a few dozen of his knights to her. She refused Despenser's help, fearing he would relish the opportunity to see her further weakened. Instead, she undertook a daring and deadly escape. Her squires held back the Scottish army while she and her ladies-in-waiting fled to an English ship. Two of her ladies died in the escape. After barely managing to outmaneuver the enemy vessels, she finally landed safely farther south in England. She did not forget Edward's betrayal.

To avoid Edward and Despenser, Isabella spent the next ten months on an extended pilgrimage.

Many historians believe some of this time was spent in clandestine meetings with…you guessed it, Roger Mortimer!

Mortimer was indeed an Earl along the Welsh marches. Like many of Edward's other nobles, he grew disaffected with the King's favoritism toward Despenser (who was granted some holdings after they'd already been given to Mortimer). He joined Lancaster's rebellion, but when the rebels were quashed, Mortimer was taken into custody and sentenced to death. The sentence was commuted to life imprisonment in the Tower of London.

In August 1323 (I moved it up a few months for the purposes of my story), Mortimer broke out of the Tower. One of the Constable's sub-lieutenants drugged the Constable, allowing Mortimer to escape through a window by a rope. Mortimer managed to flee to France despite warrants for his recapture, dead or alive.

It is unclear what role Isabella played in all of this, and exactly when her romantic relationship with Mortimer began. Some historians believe that she met with Mortimer while he was still imprisoned in the Tower. Others surmise that it wasn't until Isabella joined Mortimer in France that their affair truly took off. Either way, they became lovers. They weren't reunited until Christmas, 1325, when Isabella reached France.

As I've alluded to in the story, Isabella went to her family's palace in Paris, presumably on a diplomatic visit to smooth matters between Edward and her brother King Charles, who were in a dispute about the payment of land taxes. Isabella managed to bring Prince Edward, who would become Edward III, with her as well.

But once she was safely in France, she refused to go back to England as long as Despenser remained so powerful. Edward requested and then ordered that she return, but Charles protected her, telling Edward that his sister was welcome as long as she chose, and that he wouldn't force her to return with the heir to the English throne. All the while, Isabella and Mortimer were gathering an army.

In September 1326, they finally attacked. They landed on the eastern coast of England with an army of under two thousand, but rapidly gained support (Edward was very unpopular at this point). Edward and Despenser fled London when the city backed Isabella. They went west into Wales, evading Isabella and her army for a few weeks.

But they were caught all too quickly. Just as Will so presciently predicts in my story, Despenser was dealt with swiftly and mercilessly. With Isabella and Mortimer presiding over his trial, he was sentenced to a long and painful death.

He was dragged through the streets naked,

harangued by the onlookers, and hanged, then released before the hanging could kill him so that he could be tied to a ladder. His genitals were cut off and burned, then his entrails were slowly removed, all while he still lived. Then his heart was cut out and burned before he was beheaded and quartered so that his head could be displayed outside the gates of London and his limbs around the rest of England.

Edward's fate is a bit more complicated. Though he'd been overthrown, he was still technically the King, and Isabella's husband. To solve the first problem, Edward was forced to abdicate his throne to his son, Edward III, yet because the new King hadn't come of age, Isabella and Mortimer ruled as regents.

But that left the problem of his marriage to Isabella. Edward was removed to Berkeley Castle, where he was essentially imprisoned, but rumors continued to arise about plots to break him out and restore him to the throne. In September of 1327, word reached Edward III that his father had died in his confinement, but the circumstances surrounding his death remain hazy. Some claimed he died of an illness, but many others noted the suspicious convenience of his death. Mortimer is often implicated in arranging for the King to meet an untimely end.

True to their word, Isabella and Mortimer undid much of Edward and Despenser's harmful deeds, redistributing Despenser's amassed wealth and lands to other nobles. And with the Scots, they entered into the Treaty of Edinburgh-Northampton in 1328, which established a permanent truce with Scotland. Many of the lines I included in the epilogue as Will reads the treaty are either directly from the document or are only lightly modified.

But the winds of fate are changeable. Just like Edward and Despenser before them, Isabella and Mortimer came to be disliked for their lavish spending and for falling out of touch with the English people. They also faced growing discontent and disputes with their nobles. Many felt that Mortimer in particular was abusing his power as regent. Only a few days before Edward III's eighteenth birthday, Mortimer and Isabella were taken into custody. For assuming too much royal power, Mortimer was hanged in 1330, and Edward III came into his own reign.

For her part, Isabella was permitted to gracefully exit from her role as Dowager Queen and regent. At Mortimer's trial, Isabella was portrayed as innocent, and no mention was made of her intimate (and adulterous) relationship with Mortimer. She retired to the countryside and led a life of luxury and leisure for many long years. She took nun's orders shortly before she died at the ripe old (at least by medieval standards) age of sixty-two or three. She was buried in the mantle she'd married Edward in, and his heart, which had been preserved in a box, was interred with her.

Unfortunately, the "permanent" peace that was supposed to follow the Treaty of Edinburgh-Northampton only lasted about five years before the Second Wars of Independence between Scotland and England flared to life. Still, Robert the Bruce saw his life's work completed with the signing of the treaty. He died only a year later in 1329, having fought for and won peace and freedom, though only temporary, for his beloved Scotland.

A few final smaller notes. Edward really did sign a thirteen-year treaty with Scotland in May of 1323, though an English noblewoman spy and a Highland warrior's role in it is most assuredly fictitious.

The bawdy tavern song that the guard in the Tower of London sings is adapted from the Watkins Ale song, a wild and raunchy medieval drinking ballad.

Also, apologies to Jane Austen, who inspired Will's line "My trust, once lost, is lost forever"—I couldn't resist the reference to Darcy's "My good opinion, once lost, is lost forever" line from *Pride and Prejudice*.

Lastly, I want to extend my deepest thanks to you, lovely readers, for going on this grand journey with me. Whether this is the first Highland Bodyguards series book you've read, or if you've been following them since the beginning, it has been a true honor to get to write and share these epic stories of love, history, and adventure with you. This series and each one of its characters have a special place in my heart.

Thank you for joining me on this amazing journey, and here's to many more stories of love and adventure still to come!

Make sure to sign up for my newsletter to hear about all my sales, giveaways, and new releases. Plus, get exclusive content like stories, excerpts, cover reveals, and more. Sign up at www.EmmaPrinceBooks.com

Thank You!

Thank you for taking the time to read *Deceiving the Highlander* (Highland Bodyguards, Book 10)!

And thank you in advance for sharing your enjoyment of this book (or my other books) with fellow readers by leaving a review on Amazon. Long or short, detailed or to the point, I read all reviews and greatly appreciate you for writing one!

TEASERS FOR EMMA
PRINCE'S BOOKS

Highland Bodyguards Series:

The Lady's Protector, the thrilling start to the Highland Bodyguards series, is available now on Amazon!

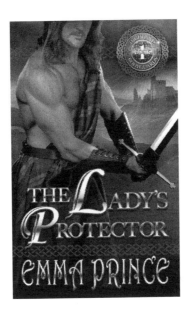

The Battle of Bannockburn may be over, but the war is far from won.

Her Protector...

Ansel Sutherland is charged with a mission from King Robert the Bruce to protect the illegitimate son of a powerful English Earl. Though Ansel bristles at aiding an Englishman, the nature of the war for Scottish independence is changing, and he is honor-bound to serve as a bodyguard. He arrives in England to fulfill his assignment, only to meet the beautiful but secretive Lady Isolda, who refuses to tell him where his ward is. When a mysterious attacker threatens Isolda's life, Ansel realizes he is the only thing standing between her and deadly peril.

His Lady...

Lady Isolda harbors dark secrets—secrets she refuses to reveal to the rugged Highland rogue who arrives at her castle demanding answers. But Ansel's dark eyes cut through all her defenses, threatening to undo her resolve. To protect her past, she cannot submit to the white-hot desire that burns between them. As the threat to her life spirals out of control, she has no choice but to trust Ansel to whisk her to safety deep in the heart of the Highlands...

The Sinclair Brothers Trilogy:

Go back to where it all began—with Robert and Alwin's story in *Highlander's Ransom*, Book One of the Sinclair Brothers Trilogy. Available now on Amazon!

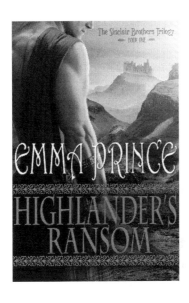

He was out for revenge...

Laird Robert Sinclair will stop at nothing to exact revenge on Lord Raef Warren, the English scoundrel who brought war to his doorstep and razed his lands and people. Leaving his clan in the Highlands to conduct covert attacks in the Borderlands, Robert lives to be a thorn in Warren's side. So when he finds a beautiful English lass on her way to marry Warren, he whisks her away to the Highlands with a plan to ransom her back to her dastardly fiancé.

She would not be controlled...

Lady Alwin Hewett had no idea when she left her father's manor to marry a man she'd never met that she would instead be kidnapped by a Highland rogue out for vengeance. But she refuses to be a pawn in any man's game. So when she learns that Robert has had them secretly wed, she will stop at nothing to regain her freedom. But her heart may have other plans...

Viking Lore Series:

Step into the lush, daring world of the Vikings with *Enthralled* (**Viking Lore, Book 1**)!

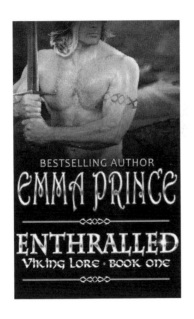

He is bound by honor...

Eirik is eager to plunder the treasures of the fabled lands to the west in order to secure the future of his village. The one thing he swears never to do is claim possession over another human being. But when he journeys across the North Sea to raid the holy houses of Northumbria, he encounters a dark-haired beauty, Laurel, who stirs him like no other. When his cruel cousin tries to take Laurel for himself, Eirik breaks his oath in an attempt to protect her. He claims her as his thrall. But can he claim her heart, or will Laurel fall prey to the devious schemes of his enemies?

She has the heart of a warrior...

Life as an orphan at Whitby Abbey hasn't been easy, but Laurel refuses to be bested by the backbreaking work and lecherous advances she must endure. When Viking raiders storm the abbey and take her captive, her strength may finally fail her—especially when she must face her fear of water at every turn. But under Eirik's gentle protection, she discovers a deeper bravery within herself—and a yearning for her golden-haired captor that she shouldn't harbor. Torn between securing her freedom or giving herself to her Viking master, will fate decide for her—and rip them apart forever?

About the Author

Emma Prince is the Bestselling and Amazon All-Star Author of steamy historical romances jam-packed with adventure, conflict, and of course love!

Emma grew up in drizzly Seattle, but traded her rain boots for sunglasses when she and her husband moved to the eastern slopes of the Sierra Nevada. Emma spent several years in academia, both as a graduate student and an instructor of college-level English and

Humanities courses. She always savored her "fun books"—normally historical romances—on breaks or vacations. But as she began looking for the next chapter in her life, she wondered if perhaps her passion could turn into a career. Ever since then, she's been reading and writing books that celebrate happily ever afters!

Emma loves connecting with readers! Sign up for her newsletter and be the first to hear about the latest book news, flash sales, giveaways, and more—signing up is free and easy at www.EmmaPrinceBooks.com.

You can follow Emma on Twitter at:
@EmmaPrinceBooks
Or join her on Facebook at:
www.facebook.com/EmmaPrinceBooks